FATAL VOLLEY

ROBERT S. ROSS

Library of Congress Catalog Card No.: 94-65013

ISBN 0-9640357-0-7

Printed in the U.S.A.

10 9 8 7 6 5 4 3 2 1

The race is not to the swift
  or the battle to the strong,
  nor does food come to the wise
  or wealth to the brilliant
  or favor to the learned;
  but time and chance happen
   to them all.

Moreover, no man knows
  when his hour will come:

As fish are caught in a cruel net,
  or birds are taken in a snare,
  so men are trapped by evil times
   that fall unexpectedly upon them.

ECCLESIASTES 9:15

ACKNOWLEDGMENTS

Several people must be recognized for their help and support with this book.

I want to thank Lou Weber and Bob Stanik. Without their help this project would forever languish unpublished in an old desk drawer.

Thanks also to Keith Ross, a very busy lawyer, for his excellent ideas and word processing assistance.

Finally, to my wife, Renee, who read the final manuscript in record time and whom I wrongfully accused of immediately skipping to the last chapter to see which characters lived to the end of this book.

To all of you my sincere thanks.

Chicago, Illinois
February, 1951

CHAPTER 1

There is, perhaps, a no more depressing time to be in Chicago, Illinois, than early February. The days are dismally gray, and raw icy winds blow in off a frozen Lake Michigan chilling the bones of the heartiest of its citizens. Darkness comes early this time of year, and the streets are silent as people hibernate waiting for spring. The usually busy downtown is all but abandoned on the weekends.

It was 4:00 PM on a Sunday when the big Greyhound bus from New York City pulled into the station at Randolph and Clark in Chicago's Loop. Aaron Garlovsky stepped off the bus clutching his cardboard suitcase in one hand and a piece of folded notebook paper with his uncle's instructions written in Polish in the other. With his wool cap pulled down over his ears, an old second-hand topcoat buttoned to the neck with the collar up, he left the bus station and entered the dark deserted city streets trying to figure out which way was east. A light snow was falling.

The instructions on the notebook paper said to go east until he was on State Street, then take the subway north to Fullerton, transfer at Fullerton to an elevated train and get off at the end of the line. Then take a CTA bus west on Lawrence Avenue to Avers Street. Walk four blocks north to the big reddish brick building at the southeast corner of Avers and Foster.

This was where he would find Uncle Samuel, his mother's brother. Samuel Polonsky had the good fortune to have left Poland in 1935. It was whispered among the family that Uncle Samuel had killed a man in Warsaw with a butcher knife and left one step ahead of the police, but that was a long time ago in a place far away and a rumor at best.

It took Aaron over three hours to reach his Uncle's building. He had missed the transfer at Fullerton and had to pay the fare to go back to the Loop and start over. He did not have enough money left for the bus fare and walked the mile and a half west down Lawrence Avenue to Avers Street. The pain in his bandaged right knee where the doctors had attempted to repair the shattered kneecap was excruciating, and the bitter cold only added to the pain. By the time he stood under the street lamp in front of the large apartment building, the light snow had turned into a full-fledged snowstorm.

Aaron was thirty years old, and what meager hope he had for his future hinged upon a relative whose face he could not remember. The last time he had seen his Uncle Samuel was in Poland at his Bar Mitzvah. That was seventeen years, a family, a holocaust and two wars ago. Aaron was now alone in a strange new country, chilled to the core, penniless with a crippled right leg. Everything he owned in the world filled less than half of an old cardboard suitcase.

He entered the dimly lit hallway of the building and pushed the button under the mail slot that read "S. POLONSKY, 1C." A loud buzzer sounded by the door leading to the apartments, and Aaron hurriedly limped over to the door and pushed it open. He could see a door open and light from the apartment shining into the dark corridor.

Aaron tentatively entered the small, bright apartment and, to his pleasant surprise, was warmly greeted by his uncle Samuel, who was much shorter than Aaron remembered.

"Welcome, nephew, you look like hell. Take off your coat and stay a while. How about a schnapps to take off the chill," his uncle said with a broad grin. "It looks like you and I, Aaron, are the only ones left," his uncle uttered as he filled small glasses with a fiery reddish liquid. As they lifted the schnapps glasses, they both murmured "L'Chayim, to life."

Samuel Polonsky had been a bachelor all of his life; he was about 65 to 68 years old, no one was sure including him. He was about 5'3" with a tough, wiry build and bald except for a fringe of white hair. He reminded Aaron of a picture of an elf that he had once seen in a children's book of fairy tales. Aaron had not slept more than a few hours in the last two days, but for the next several hours, the two relatives, the last of what had been a large and close family, sat in the parlor of the small warm apartment and spoke about the past. They cried together and spoke of the dead in hushed tones and drank and whispered and cried again. It was an opportunity for both of them after many years of silence to recall family, friends, and events that no one else in this world remembered or would ever speak of again. In those first hours, a bond formed between the men that was not to be broken.

Around midnight the effect of the schnapps and lack of sleep became too much for Aaron and he could not keep his head up. Uncle Samuel finally said, "I have a room for you fixed up in the basement but tonight, nephew, you sleep in my bed; we will have a lot of time to continue with our talk."

The apartment building was owned by Samuel Polonsky. It was a courtyard-type constructed of dark red brick and built around 1920. It contained three walk-up stories with a total of 48 one- and two-bedroom apartments. It was very well maintained by Samuel and almost always fully rented. The quiet residential neighborhood was made up mainly of similar apartment buildings, and it was common for three generations of one family to live in one building. They were first and second generation Americans usually of European descent, who believed in the American dream of a better life for their children. It was predominantly a Jewish neighborhood with a smattering of Italians and Irish. In the early 1950s this was a good place to live and raise children.

Directly across the street from Samuel's building, to the east, was a large park with a fieldhouse, a baseball diamond, two outdoor basketball courts, and four tennis courts with nets made of metal mesh. The park was called Albany Park, although why "Albany" no one knew. From April through October it was the focal point of the neighborhood. From early morning

4

until dark the old men played chess and pinochle on card tables and chairs that they set up in the grass. Young mothers pushed buggies down the tree lined paths. At 3:30 when the schools let out, the softball and basketball games started and continued until 6:00 PM when family dinner temporarily halted the games. During the summer when school was out and it did not get dark until 8:00 or 9:00 PM, the games started up again at 7:00 and many were finished by moonlight. The fieldhouse was utilized by neighbors of all ages for meetings and socializing.

Aaron adapted well to his new home and proved to be an asset to his uncle and the building tenants. He was a tireless worker. He painted the apartments, shampooed carpets, changed lightbulbs, carried out the garbage, shoveled snow and coal, replaced broken windows and screens, and did the hundred odd jobs of a building janitor. At night he read books, studied American history, and prepared for his citizenship exam in his small basement room or listened to music on a small Emerson radio.

By choice, other than Samuel, he made no close friends but had many acquaintances among the neighbors and tenants. He usually ate a simple late evening meal with Samuel, whose life had, now, with Aaron doing the heavy work, become one of relative leisure. It was only with his uncle that Aaron could relax his defenses, and their animated discussions often went on until the late evening hours.

Two years passed uneventfully and their conversations covered all subjects. Usually they spoke in English except when Samuel became excited and lapsed into Polish or Yiddish.

"Aaron, you're young and handsome, do you never

think of women?" his uncle asked with a serious expression one evening. "It would be a shame for our family to end with us. I think the widow, Morelli in 3D, has her eye on you. She is a beauty and I notice that her apartment seems to need more repair than any of the others." Aaron also was aware of this and was, in fact, spending a bit more time fixing minor problems for her than he cared to admit. She was in her late twenties and had told him that her husband had been killed in an automobile accident a year after they were married. She was a legal secretary in a neighborhood law office and led a quiet, reclusive life. She told Aaron that her maiden name was Ryan and laughingly explained that she and her Italian husband had eloped from LaCrosse, Wisconsin, to avoid the wrath of their parents. Her apartment was bright and immaculate, and she seemed genuinely pleased to see him when he came to make repairs. Aaron always refused her offers of coffee and cake, although there were times that he would have liked to stay. She was attractive and pleasant and seemed as lonely as he.

It truly saddened Samuel to think that there were no heirs to their once large family, and he tried to encourage his nephew to seek female companionship. He assumed, correctly, that there had been a lost love somewhere in Aaron's past and he did not push too hard.

Days melded into weeks and weeks into months in a regular, predictable routine. For what seemed the first time in a lifetime, Aaron felt at peace. It is too easy, he would think as he lay in his soft bed at night, like a lull before a storm.

CHAPTER 2

On July 2, 1953, Samuel Polonsky died suddenly in his sleep. He was a lucky man the neighbors said. There was no prolonged illness, no foul play, no indication that he was in anything but good health. He simply went to bed that evening around 11:00 PM and died of a sudden and unexpected heart attack. Aaron found him lying peacefully in bed the next morning when he went to his uncle's apartment to discuss a tenant's request for new screens.

Samuel had never been a religious man and did not belong to a synagogue. At the graveside service presided over by a rabbi, who did not know the deceased, Aaron was surprised at the number of people who came to pay their last respects. At least half of the tenants and a goodly number of neighbors, all uncomfortably dressed in their best clothing, listened to the rabbi chant the ancient prayer for the dead.

"Va yisgadal, va yisgadash, shma rabo...."

Samuel really was a lucky man, Aaron thought to himself. How many of his family and friends had died in agony with no one in attendance and were buried in unmarked mass graves with no rabbi to pray over their last remains.

That evening friends and neighbors came to offer their condolences and Aaron received them in his uncle's small apartment. They brought food and wine, covered the mirrors, removed their leather shoes, and washed their hands at a small bowl placed before the front door. It was a terribly hot night, and even with all the windows open, Aaron was perspiring freely, as much from the unexpected attention paid to him by the mourners as from the heat of the night.

At about 8:00 PM he went out onto the back porch to temporarily escape the heat and commotion of the apartment. He began to think about what he would do now that his uncle was gone. Aaron felt that he could probably find employment as a carpenter or a janitor somewhere in the neighborhood and was additionally saddened at the thought of having to leave the only home he knew in this country. But he had moved many times before. His thoughts were interrupted by Mr. Tilden Reinstein, attorney and counselor at law. Mr. Reinstein had been his uncle's lawyer and had helped Aaron with his citizenship papers. A short plump man of seventy with a shock of white hair, he came out to the back porch to escape the heat.

"Aaron, I have been looking for you. Samuel's estate must be probated, and you will have to come to court with me next week to be appointed executor," he wheezed as he lit his pipe.

"What are you talking about Mr. Reinstein?" Aaron asked, not understanding a word of what the lawyer had said.

"Aaron, didn't Samuel tell you? You are the sole

heir under his will. Even if your uncle had not left a will, as his only living relative, you would have inherited all of his assets. You are quite a rich man. You own this building, and your uncle, at last count, had about $70,000 in cash and savings bonds."

Aaron could not believe what he was hearing. In his wildest dreams he could not imagine himself as wealthy. Wasn't it only a few short years ago that he had stood in front of this very building with his old suitcase in hand and less than five cents in his pockets.

After a few moments of stunned silence Aaron stammered, "Mr. Reinstein if I wanted to give most of the cash and bonds to some people in Israel and not let them know that it came from me, could this be done?"

The old lawyer drew deeply on his pipe and put his hand on his chin thinking for a moment, "I suppose so. Is that what you want to do?"

"Yes," Aaron replied. "I will give you the names of the people and last addresses that I had for them. I want you to send the money, but no one is to know that it came from me. I also want to send some of the money to a priest in Poland. Can this be done?"

"I'm not sure," Mr. Reinstein replied.

"Will you look into it for me?"

"Of course, my boy, we lawyers are good at handling other people's money until it's all gone," and he winked at Aaron. "I think Samuel would be pleased at what you're doing," and he left Aaron to his thoughts.

Early the next morning Aaron Garlovsky, landlord, moved his few belongings into the apartment that his uncle had occupied, and life in the building continued as before.

A month later, Aaron Garlovsky took his oath of citizenship and the same week had Mr. Reinstein file papers to change his name from Garlovsky to Garland. If he was going to live in America and be a citizen, then he wanted a new name that sounded as though he belonged here. The Garlovsky family, for generations of Lodz, Poland, existed no more, he thought, and a final door was closed upon his past.

With his uncle gone, Aaron had no one to really talk to and he began to spend some more time with Mrs. Morelli. He now occasionally accepted some of her offers to have coffee and even went so far as to accept a dinner invitation. They made a strange pair. They had nothing in common other than their mutual feelings of loneliness, and yet both genuinely began to look forward to their meetings.

With his newly inherited property, Aaron began to feel as though he was treated differently by the tenants and neighbors, most of whom envied his good fortune but did not begrudge it of him. Aaron felt a renewed confidence in himself, and began to take some pains with his appearance. He was still ruggedly handsome with his black wavy hair and dark piercing eyes. His physique was still lean and powerful, and his arms and hands exceptionally large and strong. He was flirted with by several of the neighborhood women. Other than his bullet damaged right knee, he was in excellent physical condition, and, for the first time in his adult life, he was secure financially, reasonably content, and marginally happy. Perhaps the dark clouds really were behind him he mused at night as he lay in his uncle's bed waiting for sleep.

Six months to the day after his uncle's death, he

proposed marriage to Theresa Morelli and to his ever-lasting surprise, she gleefully accepted. A few weeks later, on January 16, 1954, they were married by a judge in a civil ceremony in Chicago City Hall. Aaron was resplendent in a new dark blue suit bought for the occasion, with Mr. Reinstein and his wife in attendance as witnesses. The newlyweds took up residence in the apartment formerly occupied alone by Theresa Morelli Garland, née Ryan.

Aaron painted the apartment and Theresa bought new curtains, carpets were shampooed, and the apartment, always bright, took on a new, fresh aura. Theresa at 5'10" was almost as tall as Aaron, and was a classic Irish beauty. Her complexion was ruddy and her hair a reddish auburn color. Her figure was full and her legs long and shapely.

Neither of them was widely experienced in love-making and with each sexual encounter, they experimented and opened new vistas. Aaron never tired of watching her as she slept.

"How little she knows of me," he reflected at night as they lay naked in each other's arms. "Will I ever be able to tell her of the ghosts I see and the things I've done and, if so, how will she handle it?" She never asked and he never mentioned the tattooed numbers on his left forearm or how he had injured his leg.

He will tell me about himself when he is ready, she surmised, and they were both content to let time pass and trust build.

Theresa kept her job in the law office and began to help Aaron with the bookkeeping records for the building in the evenings. They bought a television set and on Tuesday nights chuckled over the antics of Uncle

Milty. On summer nights when it became unbearably hot in the apartment, they took pillows and a blanket and slept in the park across the street, giggling as they listened to the squeals coming from under the blankets of many other couples also escaping from the heat.

They had been married for a little under a year and, for the first time, Theresa was over an hour late coming home from work. Aaron paced the apartment, certain that something had happened to her. He had called her office and was told that she had left early that night because of a doctor's appointment. She had not mentioned anything about a doctor and he was sure she had a terminal disease. By the time he heard her key in the door, he was ready to call the police. She took one look at his face and before he could say a word, she blurted out, "Don't yell at me, it will scare our baby," and she threw her arms around his neck and buried her head in his chest.

Aaron rarely swore. English not being his native tongue, swearing did not come naturally to him, but all he could say, incredulously was "Son of a bitch, you're pregnant?"

"Yes," she replied with mock haughtiness, adding, "and our child will not be a son of a bitch!" and they both danced around the kitchen. Aaron did all he could to keep himself from shouting, "We will live on Uncle Samuel."

Theresa worked until her eighth month of pregnancy. By then she had difficulty going up and down the stairs to their third floor apartment and spent most of her days seated at the kitchen table doing bookwork for Aaron. They had recently purchased the six-flat building next door, and Aaron was spending much of his time refurbishing the apartments that had been allowed to fall into a state of disrepair. At night he would help her down the stairs and they would take a long walk slowly through the park. When her time to deliver was close, they made arrangements with a neighbor to drive them the two miles to the hospital as they did not own a car. On September 1, 1955, her water bag broke while they were eating dinner and four hours later, they were the parents of a 22", 7 lb. 2 oz. screaming infant son. At Theresa's request he was named Kevin after her father, but there was no denying he was Aaron's son. Everyone who saw him exclaimed, "Aaron, he is the spitting image of you," and the new parents would beam.

CHAPTER 3

For the next decade the Garland family prospered and their life fell into a satisfying simple pattern. They wanted another child, but it was not to be. This suited Aaron just as well as he wanted no major changes and relished their quiet, almost monotonous, lifestyle. His real estate holdings expanded to include two more 24-unit apartment buildings in the neighborhood and he hired two part-time janitors to assist him with the work. He called them "foreigners," for they were Russian and had only been in the U.S. for a year, were not yet citizens, and spoke only broken English.

The family moved out of their original apartment into a larger two-bedroom unit that Aaron had completely rehabbed. Theresa now worked full-time as the bookkeeper for the Garland Real Estate Company Inc., and Kevin was about to enter the fifth grade at the Volta Elementary School.

Subtle changes were occurring in the neighborhood as the more affluent residents were moving to the suburbs and into small single-family homes. Their place was being taken by new groups coming to the United

States or from the inner city. What had been a Jewish community was slowly changing to include many diverse ethnic groups. Aaron recognized these changes but felt that the location of his buildings near the park and close to public transportation would always make this a desirable place to live and raise a family. His fully rented buildings appeared to prove him right. Theresa wanted to move into a single-family home but, as was her nature, she did not pressure Aaron, for she knew he felt content and safe in their apartment.

It was difficult for Aaron to communicate with Kevin, and he left most of his upbringing to Theresa who doted on the boy. Kevin was an average student but a gifted athlete. At ten years of age, he was always playing with boys two or three years older. On weekends and after school he spent all of his free time in the park, the sport changing with the seasons. Touch football in the fall, softball in the summer, and basketball all of the time.

With Aaron working in the neighborhood, he could often watch his son from a discreet distance and would marvel at the boy's speed and coordination. At night, after Kevin was asleep, he would boast to Theresa about their son's athletic prowess and she would smile slyly. They agreed that they had truly created a unique individual. His scholarship, she lamented, was another issue.

"Don't worry about his school work," Aaron let slip one evening, "I have done all right without ever graduating from high school." Then, seemingly catching himself, he quickly changed the subject. Even after all these years of marriage, his past remained a closed book.

Theresa usually did the family grocery shopping on Saturday evening after dinner. The grocery store was open until 9:00 PM on Saturday night, and it was never crowded at that time. It was a chore she didn't particularly enjoy, but Kevin would walk with her and help carry the bags home. It gave the two of them a chance to talk, and Kevin knew he could always get her to buy something special that he would pick out.

One Saturday evening in mid-April after dinner Theresa and Kevin were leaving for the store and Aaron was settled in an overstuffed chair in front of the T.V. set.

"Back in an hour Aaron. Do you want anything?" she called.

"No, thank you, be careful. Kevin, take care of your mother," he called back. It was his stock response every Saturday night and kind of a ritual that they played out. Theresa knew what food he enjoyed and she shopped to please him.

They walked the five blocks to the grocery store quickly that evening as it was cool and overcast and the weather forecast had been for rain. This night Theresa bought only those items on her prepared shopping list and within a half hour, each carrying two brown paper grocery bags, they left the store. It was dark and started to drizzle. Theresa decided to take a shortcut through the alley as it would save them about a block's walk. When they were about halfway down the alley, a shudder went through her body and she instinctively felt that she had made a terrible mistake. There were few lights in the alley and in the darkness they had not seen the two men standing under the eave of an open garage door. An empty beer can came out of the air and clattered to a halt in front of Theresa. She and Kevin stopped. This was her second major mistake that night.

"Run," she thought, "drop the damn packages and run," but she and the boy were frozen to the spot. A fear induced nausea welled up from the pit of her stomach to her throat.

"Well, well, well, what have we got here," snarled the larger of the two men who left the shelter of the garage eave and blocked their path. He was in his early twenties, thickset with longish, unkempt blond hair. Theresa could smell the alcohol on his breath. He was wearing a black leather jacket, dungarees, and heavy leather motorcycle boots. Theresa took a step backward, still holding the packages, but the other man had taken a position behind them and blocked any retreat.

"You're getting wet out here, cunt. Why don't you and the brat come into the garage until the rain stops?" the large man said with a leer, and he reached out and grabbed her sleeve. She dropped the packages and yelled, "Run, Kevin!"

Kevin was bewildered for a moment, and before he could move the man behind him grabbed him by his neck and pulled him kicking into the garage. Theresa screamed at the man holding Kevin and tried to attack him but was held firmly by the large blond man who pulled her violently into the garage.

"So, you want to fight, bitch. I didn't think any of you Jew bitches had any stomach for fighting."

A small lightbulb over a tool bench cast a dim light in the garage and the man holding Theresa pulled her head back and put his face up to hers. She could now smell an overwhelming odor of beer and sweat as he whispered, "Do as I say, bitch, or I'll break your kid's arms."

Without warning he hit her full in the face with his fist and she crumpled to the ground. He pulled her up by her hair and again hit her viciously across the face with an open palm. Blood was coming from her nose and lip and she was completely defenseless.

"This cunt's a looker, let's see what she's got under this jacket," the large man grunted and he threw her across the hood of a car parked in the garage and tore open her poplin jacket and blouse. They had gone too far to turn back now, and the large man in a frenzy fueled by alcohol and now lust, ripped at her bra exposing her breasts. He then pulled at her skirt and panties that ripped apart and she felt herself exposed naked on the cold steel hood of the car as the man's hands raked at her breasts.

He viciously impaled her body and her scream was muffled by his hand clamped across her mouth. She had no strength to fight and it seemed like a nightmarish dream. Soon she would wake up in her own bed and this unreal episode would never have happened.

But the nightmare was real and continued unabated as the large man with his pants dropped to his ankles was raping her with his hand still firmly placed across her mouth. For a moment, the second man relaxed his grip on Kevin to get a better view of the scene. Kevin sensing the man loosening his grip on him, swung at the man's testicles and missed, but as the man dodged the blow, he inadvertently let go of Kevin. Kevin knew he could only save his mother by getting help and he turned and literally flew out of the garage screaming, "Help me, they're hurting my mother!"

There was no chance of them catching the fleeing boy and the men started to panic. Now realizing that help might come soon, they quickly dragged Theresa's naked body out of the garage and down the alley. They threw her now limp body into a vacant lot about a block from the scene of the attack and fled.

Minutes after his escape Kevin burst into the apartment startling Aaron who had dozed in front of the television set. He ran trembling to his father and cried, "Poppa, they're beating up Mom!"

Aaron grabbed the boy's shoulders, "Who is beating your mother, where are they?" He tried to be calm as he spoke and not scare his son any more than he already was. "Tell me slowly," he said with clenched teeth trying to control the panic building in him.

"In the alley just north of Lawrence Avenue around the corner from Fine's grocery store, they grabbed us and ripped her clothes and I got away and...."

Aaron needed no more, and as he tore out of the apartment, he yelled, "Kevin, you stay in the house, lock the back door, call the police and tell them what happened." He raced down the stairs and into the street as fast as a man with one good leg could move. It was still drizzling, and the street lamps gave off an eerie reflection. Mixed feelings of rage and panic filled Aaron and adrenaline raced through his body alerting his senses. It had been many years since he felt these emotions, but it was though it had been yesterday. He entered the alley north of Lawrence Avenue screaming her name, "Theresa, can you hear me? Theresa, answer me."

Suddenly a police car with its mars light flashing turned down the alley and he was bathed by a searchlight. The car stopped in front of him, the two policemen got out, one from each side of the car and each with a nightstick in hand. He ran to them yelling, "Help me find my wife. She has been beaten and possibly raped."

One of the policemen said officiously, "Go home and leave this to us."

Aaron collected himself, "I will not go home until I find her," he stopped short of saying, "and those who attacked her." Something in his voice convinced the policemen to back down rather than insist that he leave.

"All right, we'll call for another squad car and canvass the area with you."

It wasn't until several hours later that they found her naked, half frozen, and in shock in the vacant lot huddled under old newspapers where her assailants had dumped her body. She was rushed by ambulance to the hospital where she balanced between life and death for three days and nights. Aaron did not leave her room for the entire time and Kevin stayed with a neighbor.

Finally, the doctors, in hushed tones, advised Aaron that physically she would, probably, recover but no one could be sure of what emotional scars she would suffer.

The police assured Aaron that the perpetrators of the rape and beating of his wife would be caught, but this gave him no solace. He really didn't care whether the police arrested them or not, for Aaron knew that he would not rest until he had extracted his own brand of justice. Ten days after the attack, Aaron took his wife home from the hospital. The bruises on her face and body had begun to heal, and the stitches had been removed from her lip and over her left eye.

"She's suffered a violent physical and mental trauma," the doctors warned. "Now, she needs rest and a lot of care and attention." They gave Aaron a prescription for sleeping pills for Theresa to take.

As days passed Theresa tried to resume her normal life, but it was as though a bright flickering candle had been extinguished. She cooked meals, cleaned the house, and resumed her bookkeeping chores but appeared to move as if in a fog. She did not grocery shop but made up a list on Saturday morning and left it on the kitchen table. Without a word, Aaron would take the list and return with the groceries before dinner time. Any of his attempts at sex or physical contact would evoke a rush of tears and hysteria, and Aaron would not force his attentions upon her. He started to sleep on the couch in the living room so as not to awaken her when he came to bed late.

Kevin felt the change even more keenly than his father. He believed that he had let his mother down, somehow, even though Aaron solemnly assured him that he had done everything that a ten-year-old boy could do.

If only he had dropped the groceries and run when she first told him to everything would be alright today, Kevin thought, and feelings of guilt consumed him.

Over the next few weeks, Theresa's depression worsened. She rarely left the apartment, and every small chore required a major decision. Simple things like getting out of bed and getting dressed required a herculean effort on her part. She would break down and cry several times a day for no apparent reason. Attempts by Aaron and Kevin to comfort her were rebuffed, and they would both stay away from the house to avoid upsetting her. She began to spend most of her time in bed, and the apartment which had always been a cheerful, spotless haven was becoming dreary and unkempt.

"Don't worry, she'll come around. These things take time," the doctors told Aaron, but somehow he felt the ominous black cloud that followed him for most of his life was about to reappear, and he became frightened for his wife and terrified for his son.

It was early morning, about twelve weeks after the attack, when Aaron quietly opened the bedroom door to get some underwear and socks from his dresser. He was momentarily elated to see Theresa, apparently sleeping peacefully, and then a shiver ran through his body as he saw the empty bottle of sleeping pills on the floor beside the bed. He ran to the bed and grabbed her, but she was cold and lifeless. Having witnessed death many times, Aaron knew instinctively that his Theresa was now beyond help.

In that moment a part of him died as well. They had been a couple, a pair. She filled the void in his life and he had been her rock of strength. Now she was gone and Aaron was alone again.

"Not again," he murmured as he held her lifeless body afraid to let go. Images of his father holding his mother's body in that unbearable place flashed before his eyes, and tears flowed down his face into her hair.

CHAPTER 4

In the past when Aaron's life had taken on the challenge of a major disaster he had the luxury of considering only his needs. He reacted more out of a basic survival instinct than a well thought out plan. Now, for the first time, his life was further complicated by Kevin. Aaron had no one to turn to for advice or aid, and although he loved the boy deeply, he knew very little about the needs of a ten-year-old child.

Aaron's very being ached with the loss of Theresa. She was gone as were all the others who had brought light into his life. Those that had taken her must suffer, and his need for revenge gave his life purpose. This feeling he understood.

The police had politely questioned Kevin but seemed to be reluctant to probe too deeply for fear of unduly upsetting what the police psychologists cautioned was the delicate psyche of a young crime victim. Aaron, on the other hand, had no such restrictions, and he interrogated his son over and over, looking for any clue that would possibly lead to an identification of the people responsible for the death of his wife. The proximate cause of Theresa's death was the assault and rape. To Aaron this was cast in granite and he became a man obsessed. He endlessly cross-examined Kevin on each detail of the night of the rape attempting to extract some fact, no matter how minute, that had been previously overlooked.

"Did the blond man have any scars or marks that you could see?"

"No, it was dark and I could tell his hair was kinda long."

"What about the man who held you, any marks or scars?"

"No, I hardly even saw him, but he was not as big as the blond man."

"You heard them speak; did they have any accents?"

"No, I can't remember, I don't think so."

"Kevin, let's go through what they said to you and Mama." For the tenth time Kevin repeated the conversation that he remembered and then almost as an afterthought he said, "The blond man might be named Roy."

Trying not to unnerve the boy after hearing this revelation, Aaron asked in a controlled voice, "Why do you think that?"

"Well, just before I swung at the shorter man I thought I heard him say 'save some for me, Roy, I want a piece of her.'"

Armed with all he could glean from Kevin and now with this new piece of previously undiscovered information, Aaron would nightly comb the bars, poolrooms, and fast food joints of the neighborhood in an ever-widening circle around the scene of the attack.

He reasoned that his prey probably lived in the neighborhood, but only for a short time, and he tried to visualize the type of people and places they would frequent.

"Roy been in lately?" he would ask casually in each dingy place.

"Roy who?" was the typical reply.

"You know Roy, big blond guy, long hair, hangs out with a shorter guy, forget his name," and he would swig his beer, waiting for a reply.

About two weeks after he started searching, he struck gold at a seedy tavern about six blocks from the crime scene.

"Why ya looking for him?" the stocky, red-bearded bartender responded casually.

"The prick owes me a C-note and now I can't find him," Aaron lied.

"Shit, he owes everyone. I hear he and Karl are laying low, some cop trouble," the bartender offered.

"I really need the dough. Any idea where I can find him?" Aaron fought the urge to beat the answer out of the bartender.

"Well, I ain't sure, but LeRoy's brother can probably get word to him, he'll probably be in later tonight. It wouldn't surprise me if they're layin' low at his place." Aaron took his beer and limped to a dark corner table sat down and waited.

At around 11:00 PM a large man in grease-stained coveralls came in, and Aaron could see the bartender whispering to him and nodding in Aaron's direction. Aaron got up and slowly walked toward the bathroom. When he was out of sight of the bar, he ducked out the back door and took a position in the shadows across the street from the tavern. About a half hour later the big man in the coveralls came out of the tavern carrying two sixpacks of beer. It was close to midnight, and Aaron took great pains to follow him at a discreet distance. The man, oblivious to Aaron, stopped to pee against a picket fence, and after a four-block walk, entered a rundown storefront auto body shop. The decrepit frame building had a second story with lights on and shades pulled down, and after a few moments Aaron could see shadows of at least two men outlined against the shades. After watching the building for about an hour, Aaron saw the lights go out and, certain he had found his quarry, reluctantly returned home to gather some items he would need.

LeRoy Raetzman was a bigot; his abusive alcoholic father was a bigot; and his three brothers were bigots. His hate was not limited to the Jews, but extended to Blacks and Hispanics equally. To the Raetzman brothers they were "kikes, niggers and spics" all lumped together. It was just that spics and niggers were historically known to fight back, having nothing to lose, and most carried a blade or gun. At least with the kikes you were almost always sure they were unarmed so they made an easier target. The image of the Jew as a weakling was changed somewhat with the Israeli victories but still, for the most part, they were Raetzman's favorite target. In his wildest dreams he had never contemplated incurring the wrath of any Jew like Aaron.

Two days later there was a murder story on the first page of the Chicago Herald American evening edition under the caption "Two men killed gangland style."

LeRoy Raetzman and Karl Klost, both 24, were found murdered in the alley behind 2525 West Montrose Avenue. The bodies were found early Friday morning by the brother of one of the victims. Police believe Klost died instantly from a blow to the head, probably from a tire iron found near the body. Raetzman was savagely beaten and tortured before he died of strangulation. Both men had long criminal records and had been sought by the police recently as suspects in a series of burglaries and bodily assaults.

What the newspaper article did not say was that LeRoy Raetzman had been mutilated. His penis had been severed from his body and forced down his throat causing the strangulation. No part of his body had escaped his killer's wrath. The police also withheld the fact that they found a small scrap of paper with a hand drawn six-pointed star in the shirt pocket of each of the victims, which was considered odd since both were known members of a neo-Nazi group.

CHAPTER 5

The apartment that had once been a bright and fresh flower-filled home took on a permanent drab dull appearance and feeling. Aaron lacked the ability to overtly show affection toward Kevin and, to alleviate his anger and pain, Aaron worked long hours. The two became as the proverbial ships in the night. They usually ate their evening meal together, generally consisting of heated T.V. dinners. Aaron would then retire to the basement to work on items needing repair or to his bedroom to do the bookkeeping, which he so despised. Kevin would do homework or watch T.V. and by 10:00 PM they were both asleep in their separate rooms.

Two days a week the cleaning woman, whom Kevin only knew as Stella, would tidy up the apartment and prepare a hot supper, which she would leave on the stove. Stella had a key to the apartment and came in after both Kevin and Aaron had left in the morning. She was gone before either of them returned in the late afternoon. Aaron would leave cash for her in a drawer to buy groceries and pay for her services.

For a bachelor it wouldn't be a bad arrangement, but for a forty-two-year-old widower and his ten-year-old son it bordered on the pathetic. Father and son both needed to comfort each other, but neither had the ability to tear down the invisible wall that grew between them.

The dog days of summer in 1966 seemed to slow everyone's pace. July was a scorcher and it became easy to tell the more affluent apartment dwellers from their neighbors. One had only to look at the closed windows of the apartment that signified that the tenant had an air conditioner. Those without this luxury left all the windows open to get some cross ventilation and spent as much time as they could in the shade of the tree-lined park.

During these summer days the baseball diamonds were filled with young and middle-aged men playing a game of softball without gloves, using a ball 16" in diameter. The game, emanating from the cramped schoolgrounds of the inner city in the early 1900s, is played by Chicago natives with a religious fervor, and for anyone to suggest that the ball was too big bordered on blasphemy. At the other end of the park groups of teenagers were playing three-on-three basketball, skins against shirts. Kevin, even at his young age, would have been welcome at either venue as his quickness and natural athletic ability were known and respected by his peers in the neighborhood. But since his mother's death he had lost the desire to play ball, and he carried a heavy weight on his ten-year-old shoulders.

Alone, he quietly sat on a park bench just outside the tennis court area and without much interest watched a tennis doubles match between four men in their twenties. He could not follow the odd way they kept score but was mildly interested in the way the ball seemed to leap off the racquets, and he thought without much enthusiasm that he might like to try it some time. The afternoon waned and dusk began to fall. The games throughout the park ended and the competitors, sweaty and tired, retreated to their homes to eat dinner and prepare for Saturday night events. Kevin knew that his father would not be home much before 8:30 PM. He was not really hungry but with nothing to do he thought he would go home and watch T.V. The park lights were turned on and one of the tennis courts was lit for night play.

As Kevin passed the court he noticed that someone had left a sweater, tennis racket and a can of tennis balls lying on the side of the court near the plywood tennis backboard that was used by the players to practice against and warm up. Kevin casually walked over to the equipment and looked around. Seeing no one in the area, he picked up the wooden racquet. He studied it for a few moments and concluded it belonged to one Jack Kramer as that was the name emblazoned on both sides of the handle near the strings. He grasped the racquet in his left hand and swung it in the same manner as he had seen the players do it that afternoon. The racquet was heavier and longer than he imagined and his hand, although big for his age, covered only about a third of the leather grip. Kevin took one of the fuzz covered white balls out of the open tin can and bounced it gently off the strings a few times, catching the ball in his free hand. He found that when he moved his hand to the top of the leather grip he had more control of the racquet and could continue to bounce the ball a few feet into the air as many times as he wanted to. Now totally engrossed, he bounced the ball on the asphalt surface, and tried to hit it against the plywood backboard. He missed the ball completely the first few times but soon developed a rhythm and was able to hit the backboard several times in a row before losing control. Beads of perspiration started to drip from his face onto the asphalt surface and he could soon hit the ball eight to ten times in a row. He surmised that the yellow horizontal line on the dark green backboard about three feet high represented the net, and he tried to keep his shots from hitting below the line. The way the ball seemed to effortlessly leap off the racquet when he hit it just below the middle of the strings intrigued him.

Kevin had been hitting for about twenty minutes and was bathed in sweat when he heard someone say, "Not bad, kid. Now can I have my racquet back?" Startled for a moment, Kevin spun around and saw a man standing about ten feet behind him. His first instinct was to drop the racquet and run, but he sensed that the man was not angry. Kevin thought he recognized him as one of the men he had seen play that afternoon. They both stood their ground and Kevin in a soft voice volunteered, "I'm sorry, mister, I wasn't going to steal your stuff. I just wanted to try it for a while."

The man looked at him quizzically for a few moments and then asked, "Is this your first time?"

"Yep," the boy replied.

"How do you like it?" the man inquired.

"OK, I guess. I'm not too good yet but I did keep it going for ten times in a row before I missed."

"Yes, I see that you're pretty well coordinated for a kid. Come're, let me show you a few things." The man took the racquet from Kevin and picked up a ball. He bounced the ball and struck it solidly with the racquet. He hit the ball about twenty times in a row with each shot striking the plywood backboard about two to four feet above the yellow line. "Now you try it again. Shake hands with the racquet and don't squeeze it too hard. You're a lefty and that gives you an advantage in this game. Aim about four feet above the yellow line and try to hit the ball right in the middle of the racquet."

They spent about a half hour together that sweltering night, the man patiently teaching the boy some basic techniques and the boy eagerly soaking up each word. The man finally said, "Look, kid, I've got to go. Do you live around here?"

Kevin pointed to his father's building across the street.

"All right, I've got a tennis game here tomorrow morning at 9:00. If you promise to be here then with my racquet, you can keep playing with the balls and racquet, OK?"

Kevin, anxious to practice his newly acquired skills, smiled at the man, "I promise. Thanks a lot, Mr. Kramer."

The man, momentarily perplexed, looked at Kevin and suddenly smiled, "No, I'm not Jack Kramer, son, he was a famous tennis player that this racquet is named for. My name is Mal Grant, but my friends call me Doc. Who are you?"

"I'm Kevin Garland, my friends call me Kevin." They shook hands and the man, fighting to keep a straight face, said, "OK, Kevin, I'll see you tomorrow morning 9 AM sharp. Good night."

Kevin stayed for another hour, hitting forehand shots against the backboard with increasing pace and control.

After leaving the boy, Doc stopped to watch for a few more minutes from the shadows just outside of the lights of the court. "This kid's a natural if I ever saw one," he thought, "I only hope he's honest too, otherwise I've just lost my favorite racquet."

The next day was Sunday and Kevin was up at 6:00 AM. He pulled on his shorts and worn Converse Chuck Taylor gym shoes and quietly made himself some breakfast. He didn't want to wake his father who tried to sleep a little later on Sunday mornings. He wolfed down his food, grabbed the racquet and can of balls and tiptoed to the door, closing it quietly behind him and then raced down the hallway stairs and across the street to the tennis courts. Had he glanced behind he would have seen his father watching him run through the park from their front window.

By the time the first tennis players started to arrive it was 8:00 AM and Kevin had been hitting against the backboard for over an hour. He had a hundred questions to ask Doc about the game but wasn't sure how to go about it. About fifteen minutes later he spotted Doc walking toward the courts carrying a racquet, can of balls, and a small gym bag. Kevin trotted out to him and offered up the racquet and balls.

"Thanks, Doc, I really liked using your stuff."

Doc took the racquet and in a stern voice said, "I can see that. The grip is all sweaty. What'd you do, hit all night?"

"No, I just started around 6:30 until now."

"Well, this racquet is too wet for me to play with today. I guess you'll just have to keep it for another week or so," and he flipped it back to Kevin. Realizing that his new friend had just given him a gift, Kevin didn't know what to say. Instinctively, he reached out and took the man's hand for a moment and, looking at his own feet, mumbled, "Thanks, Doc, I'll, I'll be here next week again, on time." Kevin ran back to the backboard, while a few courts away, Doc and his friends started to play doubles.

Doc couldn't concentrate on the game that morning. He kept looking over at the small figure stroking forehand after forehand against the backboard, and he couldn't believe that the boy had never picked up a racquet before last night. Normally, Doc's group played for about two hours on Sunday mornings, but after about an hour Doc said his ankle was giving him trouble and let one of the waiting players substitute for him.

He limped over to Kevin who, shirtless, was still hitting, "Kevin you can't hit everything with a forehand." For the next hour they worked on some basics. Forehand, backhand, forehand, backhand, Doc was amazed at how quickly the boy grasped the fundamental strokes of the game. Doc had played varsity tennis for two years at the University of Illinois before going to pharmacy school and was a respected local player. He knew that with proper training this boy had the potential of being a real player, with coaching perhaps even at a major college level.

Later that morning they sat in the grass to cool off, and Doc tried to answer the boy's incessant questions about the game.

"Why is the scoring so funny, love 15, 30, 40?" the boy asked.

"I'm really not sure. I think the word "love" came from some French word for egg, which is round like a zero. But you're right, Kevin, the scoring is strange."

"If it hits the line does it still count?"

"Yes, the lines are good." The questions kept coming and Doc could see that he was giving the boy too much too quickly.

"Wait a minute, Kevin, slow down. I'm going to make a deal with you. If your folks say OK, I'll teach you a little of how to play tennis this summer as long as I believe you are interested and show progress. If you do as well as I think you can before school starts again in September, this racquet is yours to keep."

Doc was the first adult, other than his mother, whom Kevin felt he could openly speak to, and he told Doc that his mother had died and he didn't think his father would mind his taking tennis lessons since they lived right across the street. They agreed to meet for a half hour each day. Doc worked in a drug store a few blocks away and got off at 5:00 PM. He wanted to be home by six, so from 5:15 to 5:45 he would teach Kevin fundamental tennis. They agreed to try it for a week to see how it worked out.

For the next week they met promptly at 5:15 each afternoon and they both enjoyed the sessions so much that the lessons usually lasted for at least an hour. During the day Kevin would practice against the backboard. Forehand, backhand, forehand, backhand for hours on end. The lessons would consist of Doc explaining a shot to Kevin and then with a basket of old tennis balls he would drill Kevin on the shot until

35

he was satisfied that Kevin was hitting it properly. Never having played the game before, Kevin had no bad habits to break, and his natural athletic ability and keen hand-eye coordination served him well. They agreed to continue lessons the following week. The lessons served a need for both teacher and student. Doc enjoyed teaching the talented and willing young student, and it brought Kevin out of the shell he had retreated into after his mother's death.

Kevin was further surprised at dinner one night when his father broke the customary silence. "I spoke to your friend Doc today. He says you are a talented athlete. He also says you are a polite young man and I should be proud of you." Not knowing what to say next, they both sat in silence as they ate. As they finished and Aaron got up, he said softly almost to himself, "I am proud of you," and he left the kitchen.

Summer ended and Kevin, now eleven years old, returned to school. The tennis lessons continued through October until the weather started to get too cold and darkness came early. Student and teacher kept in contact that winter as Kevin would find a reason to visit the drug store where Doc worked several times a week. Doc gave Kevin a book on tennis that he virtually memorized.

In the early to mid 1960s tennis was a game played principally by amateurs, and they would talk about Budge, Tilden, Kramer and those incredible Aussies trained by Harry Hopman. Kevin's favorite player was the hard hitting, red-haired, left-handed Rod Laver.

Early the following spring, the lessons started again and Kevin's training moved on to a more sophisticated level. They worked on volley, half volley, overhead, and serve. As a treat for Kevin at the end of each lesson they would play a few games. At first the games were no contest, as Doc was too good a player for the boy to be competitive. By the end of that second summer the only way Doc could win a game was by overpowering his eleven-year-old pupil. Once they would get into a baseline rally, Kevin's stinging deep shots placed side-to-side with pinpoint accuracy, developed from routinely hitting thousands of shots that summer, made it an even match.

They looked for local junior tournaments to enter late that summer and with Aaron's consent would travel to the surrounding suburbs whenever Doc could find a junior tournament in Kevin's age bracket. Kevin had the basics and the natural ability, but he lacked the playing experience and would often lose to less talented, but more tournament-experienced junior players. On the way home in Doc's old Pontiac they would critique each match.

"Why did you lose today?" Doc would start with after every loss. Kevin would not answer as he was usually still brooding as he did after each loss.

"Well, I'll tell you why since you're still sulking," and Kevin knew the lesson was coming. "You let him control the match because you weren't playing his weaknesses. The guy had a great forehand and a so-so backhand. Yet, you hit most of your shots to his forehand. Even when you took control of the net you hit your volleys to his forehand. He was a lefty also so your forehand cross court goes right to his forehand. You should have picked that up early in the match and pounded your groundstrokes and volleys to his weak side. Remember that the next time you play a lefty."

Kevin rarely made the same mistake twice. By the end of the year Kevin received his first local junior ranking in the twelve-year-old-and-under division. When he was notified of the award, winning Wimbledon could not have made him happier.

Age categories in junior tennis are divided every two years. The following year Doc and Kevin decided that even though Kevin was only twelve years old he would compete in the fourteen-year old division to give him the experience of playing against better competition and boys who were physically bigger and stronger. Kevin's speed and groundstroke consistency were his strengths, and by the end of the year his local ranking was among the top ten in the fourteen-year-old division.

It was becoming obvious to Doc that his original assessment of Kevin's potential was greatly underestimated. He started to question his ability to take the boy to the next level, and he decided to meet with Aaron.

The two men met in Aaron's apartment. They had met briefly a few times before and instinctively had felt a certain respect and trust for each other. Neither man wanted anything for himself from this meeting. Aaron knew that Doc was responsible for Kevin's return to enthusiasm about life, and Doc understood the tragic loss that Aaron had suffered by his wife's death and how difficult it was to raise a young boy without a mother. They were both a little uncomfortable, for this was not really a social call.

"Mr. Garland, I want to thank you for seeing me in the middle of the day," Doc said a little too formally. "You know I have spent a lot of time with your son the past few years and, to get right to the point, he's a very talented athlete."

"Yes, I have watched your lessons with Kevin. You taught him well," Aaron offered.

"I'm afraid I have taught him too well and he has advanced to a point where he needs a more advanced teacher."

"Do you know someone?"

"Yes, but it would require some money and, more importantly, it would mean that Kevin would not live at home most of the year, providing we could convince the coach that Kevin is as talented as I think he is."

Aaron did not reply for a long time, and Doc was becoming uncomfortable thinking that he had pushed too hard. Finally, Aaron asked, "Where would he live?"

"There's a training center just outside of Miami where they accept only the most talented young tennis players in the country," Doc explained. "They live there, like a boarding school, and train with the best coaches. But it is fairly expensive, even if Kevin is accepted."

They spoke for about a half hour and Aaron finally said, "We will leave it up to Kevin. Tell him about the school but don't mention anything about money. If he wants to go and is accepted, I'll pay the bills."

The communication ended and they shook hands awkwardly. Both men knew that Kevin would want to go and their lives would be a little emptier. It was at that exact moment that they became friends.

Kevin left for Miami on September 1, his birthday. Aaron and Doc put him on a United Airlines flight nonstop to Miami where he would be met at the Miami airport by his new coach. That night Aaron found sleep impossible. Alone again in the dark apartment, his mind raced and haunting memories filled his bedroom.

Europe: 1900 to 1945
CHAPTER 6

Isadore Garlovsky and Esther Rosenberg met while he was an accounting student studying in Berlin. Esther was the eldest daughter of a well-respected physician and surgeon whose proud and prosperous family had lived in Germany for over two centuries. They were Germans by choice and Jews by accident of birth. When she was first courted by Isadore, her family had deeply ambivalent feelings. They felt this penniless uncouth Pole was clearly not a proper match for their daughter, and yet she was already almost twenty and long past the age when proper girls married. He was a handsome boy and probably, they reasoned, after her money. The alternatives were spinsterhood for their daughter and no grandchildren versus marriage to "that Pole." In the end, consent to the marriage was reluctantly granted when it was agreed that the newlyweds would live in Berlin where Isadore would practice accounting for friends and relatives of his in-laws. The Garlovskys did not move to Lodz, Poland, until 1919. Esther's parents had been killed in a bombing raid shortly before the Great War ended and with Germany a defeated nation, there was little opportunity for a Polish accountant to find work.

Aaron Yale Garlovsky was born in Lodz on July 25, 1920 and he learned to speak German before Polish. His mother, ever the aristocrat, insisted that the family always speak German in the house. Aaron was the third child of Isadore and Esther Garlovsky, and their only son. Aaron, named after his father's father, was doted upon by his parents and two older sisters. By age ten it was obvious that with his large feet and hands, he would be tall. A dark, handsome child, with black curly hair, his sisters would joke that they were going to buy him a big stick for his Bar Mitzvah to beat away all the girls that would be chasing him when he became a man. The family lived in a community of Jews and except for occasional isolated acts of anti-Semitism, life for the family was relatively uneventful.

Isadore's passion was carpentry and working with his hands. After working in an accounting office during the day, he and Aaron would spend hours at night building and repairing furniture and cabinets for friends in the neighborhood. Isadore felt that every boy should be able to work with his hands, and happily his son had inherited his talent for carpentry.

Aaron's sisters' prediction had been right, and by the time he was sixteen Aaron was almost six feet tall with dark curly hair and deep brown brooding eyes. He was the secret heartthrob of most of the young, and a few not so young, girls in the community. Aaron was a well-mannered, quiet boy, liked by his peers and the apple of his father's eye.

The first real harbinger of an impending dark future occurred in April of 1936 when Aaron was sixteen years old. He came home from school mid-week to find his father in the kitchen eating an early dinner. His father never came home from work before 6:00 PM, and from the look on his face Aaron knew something terrible had happened. Before Aaron could ask, his father solemnly said, "Sit down, Aaron, we have to talk." Aaron sat next to his father waiting for what his stomach was already telling him would not be good news.

"I've been dismissed from my position," his father explained pedantically, "Jews can no longer work for the company. After many years it seems I'm no longer qualified for the position I held. Until I can find a new job you will need to help me. I think we can earn enough money doing carpentry work, but it will be difficult as we will need to work cheaper and do better work than any gentile carpenter. I'm sorry Aaron, but you will leave school for a while." Aaron had always enjoyed school, but he accepted his father's edict without question.

"It's going to be all right, Papa, they'll soon find out they can't get along without you or you'll find a better position. Until then we can work together." Brave words said with conviction, but deep down Aaron had the uneasy feeling that his school days had abruptly ended forever.

Local carpentry jobs were scarce. Many of the Jews who would have gladly hired the Garlovskys were out of work also, and the non-Jews were either anti-Semitic or, knowing how difficult work was to obtain for Jews, refused to pay fair wages when they paid at all.

Aaron and his father were now taking manual work of any kind, and his sisters did sewing and laundering for hire. Life became increasingly difficult, but the family was together and for that they were grateful. Many of their friends and neighbors who had relatives in America and elsewhere were hastily making plans to leave Poland. Isadore would have left Europe at once, but Esther refused.

"This madness will end," she would state emphatically, and the subject was closed.

On September 1, 1939, the German Army invaded Poland and twenty-eight days later Poland was conquered. They then commenced a heretofore unprecedented systematic extermination of Polish Jews, who represented around ten percent of Poland's 33 million people. Still the family survived and stayed together, but escape from Poland was now impossible.

In March of 1943 their luck ran out. The Garlovskys were abruptly taken en masse to the train depot and loaded into cattle boxcars overcrowded with bodies for what was to become the final destination for all but a select few. They were packed in so tightly that they could not sit or lie down. The cattle train rumbled on for three days and two nights. In the freezing boxcars, without food, water or toilets, by the second day the weaker ones began to die. Among them was Aaron's mother who had been weakened from pneumonia and who had lost all hope and desire to live. She never understood how her countrymen, for she always considered herself a German, could inflict such indignities and pain on others. Esther Rosenberg Garlovsky was to the end a German first and then a Jew. Aaron felt his mother died as much from a broken heart as from her pneumonia. He watched his exhausted father, spirit broken, holding his mother's lifeless body long after she died. Tears streaming down his face into his black-gray beard, he refused to let her drop to the floor where she could be trampled upon. It was this picture of his father that would remain in Aaron's mind throughout his life, and it was this memory that gave him a purpose to live—revenge!

Sometime during the last night of the terrible trip Aaron sleeping as he stood was startled awake by his father. "Aaron, for me and your sisters this trip has only one destination, but you must do whatever it takes to survive. Forget everything you have learned about fair play and the sanctity of human life. These people are devils, and I command you to be the avenging angel for your mother, your sisters, and me. Do you hear me?" His father's eyes burned into Aaron's face.

"Yes, Papa, whatever it takes."

It was the last time Aaron was ever to speak to his father. An hour later the train stopped, and its human cargo was pushed and prodded out of the cattle cars into a surreal scene of mass confusion with barking dogs, bright lights, and black-booted uniformed soldiers screaming orders and clubbing to death those who did not respond quickly enough.

CHAPTER 7

Because of his physical size and carpentry skills Aaron was temporarily spared from the crematorium. Instead, his oppressors would work him until he no longer could do the tasks they assigned and then they would kill him. There were plenty of bodies to take his place on the work detail, and Aaron quickly realized that his reprieve was only for a limited time. He tried to shut his mind to the fate that had befallen his family and concentrate on his father's last words to him. He must do whatever it took to survive.

His clothing had all been taken from him and he was issued rough-hewn pajama-like trousers, a jacket with wide gray and blue stripes, and wooden clogs.

The Germans, ever so detail oriented, tattooed a number on his left forearm, and it was in this line, waiting naked to be numbered for life and receive prison clothes, that he made a friend. Zalman Zacksman stood next to him and silently nodded to Aaron. They were about the same age, but Aaron was tall and lean, whereas Zalman was shorter and stocky. In a hushed whisper, and at the risk of a beating, Zalman said, "Don't give up hope. I'm going to escape or die trying."

Without even thinking, eyes still looking forward, Aaron whispered back, "If you need a partner, I'm with you."

That night they found each other in the dark, wooden, windowless barracks and managed to squeeze next to each other in the rack that served as a bed for a dozen men. Zalman's story was similar to Aaron's.

He had been raised in Warsaw. His father was a tailor and had taught him the trade. It was this skill that had so far saved his life. His family had been arrested over a year ago and he had no idea where they were taken. Zalman had managed to evade his captors and had joined some partisans. They taught him the rudiments of how to use some captured weapons, and he had participated in a few daring but essentially fruitless actions to dismantle railroad ties and rails and to cut telephone wires. He had shot at the enemy but was certain that he had never hit his target. Most of the time they spent scavenging for food and changing their hideout.

Zalman had been captured while foraging in the woods for food. Luckily he did not have a weapon with him, or he would have been summarily shot. His captors were regular army, not S.S., and upon discovery that he was circumcised he was sent to the deportation area for immediate transportation to this place.

The concentration camp was virtually escape proof, and dotting the perimeter of the camp was the grisly evidence of the hanged bodies of those who had tried to escape and failed. The guards had standing orders to shoot without warning anyone near the fence, which was charged with a high tension current. If a prisoner did make it through the first fence, an outer ring with closely situated watch towers presented an almost impregnable blockage. Vicious dogs, a mine field, and a civilian population close by who would have recognized an escapee by his clean-shaven head and striped clothing were additional barriers to freedom. The civilian populace had no love for the prisoners and additionally had been warned that any aid to an escaped prisoner subjected one to death.

It was late March 1943, and although Aaron and Zalman had only been in the camp for ten days, the pattern was painfully obvious. They would perform backbreaking physical labor all day and subsist on a watery turnip soup and an occasional crust of sawdust laden bread covered with some rancid margarine.

The longer they remained in the camp the weaker they would become as a result of the poor food, the polluted drinking water, dysentery, typhus, and skin disease. The barracks were rat infested, and medicine for the prisoners was nonexistent even though the inmate doctors did their best.

Aaron kept his knowledge of German a secret. There were some German prisoners, who by comparison with the Jews, lived in luxury and were in charge of the labor parties and the barracks.

Aaron and Zalman quickly devised a simple escape plan. The first early morning that it was raining they would overpower and kill the two German prisoners that were in charge of their barracks. The fact that neither of them had ever struck anyone in anger, much less killed anyone, was irrelevant and discounted. They would quickly don the clothing of the German prisoners and leave the barrack for the mess area reserved for the privileged prisoners.

The mess area was near the vehicle depot where the trucks brought supplies to the camp. They would sneak into a truck and wait. They knew that each truck was thoroughly checked before leaving the camp, both visually by guards and by dogs that would tear a man apart if he were found hiding in one. They reasoned that the weather would help them, as the guards would not want to spend too much time out in the cold rain. Zalman had stolen some pepper, which they would sprinkle across the back of the truck in an attempt to irritate the dog's sense of smell. They would look for a truck that had boxes or a tarpaulin that could hide them.

If they were lucky enough to get out of the camp they made no plans other than staying in the forest until they could figure out their next move. They reasoned that their chances of getting out alive were less than one percent, but better than staying in the camp where death was certain. At twenty-three years of age they were both prepared to escape or die trying.

Plans made, they waited for it to rain. Three nights later the rains came in torrents.

It was around 4:00 AM and pitch dark in the barracks when they crept out of their rack, ostensibly to urinate. The area reserved for the German barrack leaders was cordoned off and for a Jew to be caught in that area meant a severe beating.

Between them they had one small kitchen knife, which meant that they would need to kill one German prisoner after the other rather than both at the same time. Aaron was the stronger of the two, and they decided to have Zalman kill one first with the knife while Aaron would attempt to hold the other down until Zalman could stab him also. They decided that the knife stabs should be to the stomach and neck, for they feared that if they hit bone the knife would break before they had finished. Barefoot, sneaking into the privileged prisoner area, there was now no turning back. For a moment Aaron thought, "At least I'm fighting, so this is as good a way as any to die."

The two German prisoners each had his own cot and blanket. Aaron and Zalman sneaked up to the two beds and prepared to attack when Aaron, to his horror, discovered that one of the beds was empty. He turned to motion to Zalman to wait, but it was too late. Like a man possessed Zalman ripped back the flimsy cover on the snoring prisoner and with all the force he could muster plunged the knife deep in the man's neck. Zalman had no particular hate or feeling for the man he was trying to kill. He was an obstacle, someone who had to be killed to implement an escape plan that had little chance of success. The startled victim grabbed his throat as Zalman withdrew and again plunged the knife into his body. This time the knife was aimed at the man's ample belly. Aaron had clasped his hand over the man's mouth to prevent a scream, while Zalman continued to plunge the knife in and out of his body.

They were both covered in blood when they felt the man's body go limp. The entire attack had taken less than a minute. They hastily decided to put the body under a cot and as they were both lifting the corpse off the cot, the second German prisoner suddenly appeared. "What is going on. . . .," he started to shout when suddenly he crumpled to the floor. He was dead before he hit the ground, his skull crushed. Immediately behind him stood one of the gentile Polish prisoners holding an iron bar. Aaron and Zalman dropped the body they were holding and Zalman raised the knife. They had both seen the Pole in the barracks, but he had never spoken to them. Seeing that they misunderstood his intentions he lowered the iron bar, stepped towards them and whispered, "I am going with you. What is your plan?"

They had no choice: to refuse to include this stranger in their escape meant he could claim he saw them kill the Germans and be rewarded. No one would believe a Jew if he implicated them. At best they would all be tortured and hanged. As a Polish prisoner he had boots and did not wear the striped clothing. They nodded at the man and Aaron and Zalman quickly changed clothes with the dead prisoners, pulled on the Germans' worn boots, and put the bodies under their cots. They quickly told the Pole their simple plan and the three of them slipped out of the barracks and heads down started to walk to the mess area.

It was still dark at 4:15 AM and icy cold; torrential rains continued to pelt the grounds. The three men pulled their caps down over their faces and turned up their jacket collars against the cold rain. The boots Aaron and Zalman had taken from the dead Germans were thin and worn and afforded little protection against the large puddles that they walked through on the way to the mess area.

They stopped close to the kitchen building to avoid being seen and as protection against the weather.

They spotted only one small truck in the depot area and carefully looking around and seeing no one scrambled into the empty back of the truck.

At this point the fallacy of their escape plan became painfully obvious. They had no idea of when the truck driver would come back, and as long as it rained he would probably stay indoors. If they waited too much longer the bodies of the dead barrack leaders would surely be found and an all-out search for them would start. Escape would then be impossible. To compound the problem neither Aaron nor Zalman had ever driven a motor vehicle.

Looking at the Pole Aaron asked, "Can you drive this truck?" The Pole nodded affirmatively. "All right, give me the iron bar and wait here," Aaron whispered. For a moment the Pole hesitated and then, reluctantly, relinquished the weapon. Aaron and Zalman jumped off the back of the truck and carefully crept up to the depot supply building. Peering in through a window, they saw one soldier sleeping in a chair covered with his gray greatcoat, his holster and revolver casually placed on a small table next to a half empty vodka bottle. Aaron told Zalman to get the revolver and then to let him do the rest.

Quickly opening the door, they slipped inside the small building. Zalman took the gun out of the holster and stood in front of the sleeping man. Aaron took the coat off the man who awoke irritated. Then in perfect German Aaron said sharply, "Get up! We are all leaving. If you resist, my friend will shoot you. Ask no questions and follow my orders and you may have a chance of living." Aaron spoke in his most authoritative voice and strangely he felt no fear. He was banking on the basic German virtue of being a good order taker. He was in fact betting his life on it. "Make sure you have the keys to the truck," he warned the man.

It was still dark and the rain became more intense. Aaron had put on the soldier's greatcoat and hat. Zalman took the vodka bottle, and the three went out into the rain. Aaron got into the passenger seat and told the now fully awake soldier to drive. Zalman climbed into the back of the truck with the Pole. "If you make a wrong move it will be your last. We have nothing to lose," Aaron warned the driver as Zalman from behind pressed the revolver against the back of the soldier's head. It was no idle threat, for in this evil place there was nothing cheaper than a prisoner's life and the driver knew it.

The truck slowly approached the gate, and the driver smiled weakly and waved at the sleepy guard who obviously knew him. Aaron waved also and smiled lifting the vodka bottle to his lips. Casually the guard waved back raising the cross bar allowing the truck to leave the compound of death.

CHAPTER 8

For an all too brief few moments they felt the euphoria of having escaped. Neither Zalman nor Aaron ever really felt their escape plan had any chance of success. Now that they were actually out of the camp, they had no idea of where they were or what direction to travel.

It would not be long before the patrols would be out looking for them in a systematic search. S.S. police patrols with bloodhounds would scour the countryside looking for them. They knew that to be caught alive meant immediate hanging in the presence of the entire camp. Even if they were killed outside of the camp they would be returned and seated at the entrance gate with a notice placed on their lifeless hands stating: "Here I Am."

Decisions had to be made instantly, and Aaron ordered the driver to pull the truck off the road. Without speaking the three escapees knew that they had to kill the driver. If they let him go he would tell others where they had abandoned him, what weapons they had, and how much gas was left in the truck. If they took him with them there was no telling what he would do to escape. Alive he was too much of a liability.

Aaron ordered the driver out of the truck and to change clothes with the Pole who was about his size. When the clothing exchange was complete, without warning, the Pole struck him on the head and killed him with the iron bar. Looking at Aaron and Zalman he said simply, "It had to be done and there was no reason to waste valuable ammunition." He was right, of course. They covered the body with branches and with the Pole, who told them his name was Alexy Golmanski, driving they sped down the rain soaked road pushing the small truck to its limits.

They drove silently for a while, but the sequence of events in the last hour raced through their minds. It was still raining, but the sky had lightened somewhat. Aaron tried to assess their situation. He felt that a search plane would not take off looking for them as long as the rains continued. They really had only two options. They could look for a town and try to blend in, or they could try to escape into the forest.

Aaron had no idea where any town was, and the chances of the townspeople turning them in to the S.S. was almost a certainty. If they took to the forests, the truck that had taken them to freedom would become their enemy. They would need to abandon the truck and once it was found the Germans would be able to narrow their search area. Then what about the driver, Golmanski? Could they trust him? Would he figure that his chance of escape would now be greater without Aaron and Zalman? He had unemotionally killed two men that morning with an iron bar. Certainly he would have no reservation about killing two Jews if he felt so inclined.

As if reading Aaron's mind the Pole, Golmanski, started to talk as he drove, "I know you have no reason to trust me, but I know this area and I think I know of a place to hide for a while." Zalman peered into the cab area and Aaron turned to listen as the small truck sped along the dirt road in the dark wet early morning.

"I am thirty years old, and I was in the Polish Army for four years. I left the Army six years ago when I came down with an illness that sapped all of my strength. I went to several Polish doctors who were of no help. In desperation, I was referred to a Jewish doctor in Warsaw who was prohibited from practicing medicine. I knew that my going to him was putting his life in jeopardy if he treated me, but he had no choice. I was dying and I forced him to accept me as a patient. I did not care how he would be affected. He took me into his house where he lived with his daughter. After a while the illness passed, and his daughter and I had fallen in love.

She was only nineteen and the most beautiful girl I had ever seen. I know it broke her father's heart when she told him about me, but he accepted our marriage. I think that he knew what was happening to the Jews and felt that his daughter may have a chance to live if she was married to a non-Jew and an Army veteran. He insisted that we leave Warsaw and encouraged me to take his daughter to America. I would have gone anywhere as long as we were together."

Alexy's story continued, and he described how his wife would not leave Poland as long as her father was alive. They moved about thirty miles from Warsaw to a rural community where Alexy found work as a farm laborer and his wife worked as a seamstress. Although they were strangers in the community, they were accepted. They posed no threat to anyone and kept to themselves. Alexy was trying to save enough money to buy his own farm. When the Germans came, life in the community changed little. The conquerors needed the farm produce and never suspected his wife of being Jewish. About a month ago a new area commander appeared in the small town. He had documentation that Alexy's wife was Jewish. When they came to arrest her, Alexy fought with them and was beaten and sent to the camp with his wife. Being a non-Jew he was not marked with tattooed numbers and treated better than the Jewish prisoners but not as well as the German prisoners.

A few weeks after he was in the camp he received word that his wife, because of her beauty, had been spared the ovens and was placed in one of the camp brothels. In desperation one night Alexy tried to sneak over to see her and was caught. He was dragged before guard Captain Otto Hofbauer, a member of the Nazi Waffen S.S. Totenkopf-Sturmbahn, the "Death's Head Battalion," a stocky powerful man who was known as a sadist. Discovering that the prisoner was trying to see his wife, Hofbauer had her summoned to his office.

She was much thinner than before her capture but still very beautiful. They tied Alexy to a chair and stripped his wife. Then naked, in front of him, she was gang raped and sodomized by the guards until she lost consciousness. Not content, Hofbauer had her revived and the ordeal continued for several hours. When his men were finally through with her, Hofbauer snarled, "Now she's yours, Jew lover," and in an orgasmic frenzy he picked her battered, naked body up by the neck and slowly choked her to death while his men cheered. They then beat Alexy with their rifles and threw him in the Jewish barracks with Aaron and Zalman where he would not survive for more than a few months at most.

When the Pole finished his story there was silence in the truck. Each man had suffered a personal hell, and it was this fact that bonded them together. They continued speeding down the road with the only sounds being the tires pounding the wet road and the rain slapping against the dirt crusted windshield.

The first sign they saw indicated that they were on a road leading to Krakow, and with the sky starting to lighten to their right Aaron guessed that they were heading in a northeasterly direction. Prior to being transported to the camp neither Aaron nor Zalman had ever gone further than from Lodz to Warsaw, a distance of less than one hundred miles. They had no idea of where they could hide to make plans in this part of the country. Alexy, however, seemed to know where he was going and after he told them about his background, assuming it was true, they allowed him to drive without questioning his destination.

The rain had subsided into a fine mist, and the dirt road was pocked with deep puddles. They had less than a quarter of a tank of gasoline left when they saw a small farmhouse a short distance off the road. Alexy looked at Aaron, who nodded, and they drove up to the house and placed the truck out of sight of the road.

The occupants were an elderly couple who were totally intimidated by Alexy's uniform and the Army truck. The small wooden house consisted of two rooms, and a quick search produced no one besides the old couple.

"Bring us food," Aaron commanded first in German, which he assumed the couple did not speak, but did solely to establish authority, and then in Polish. The woman gave them bread and cheese, weakly apologizing for the simple fare. Little did she realize that the food represented a feast for the three strangers who wolfed down the meal. On a hunch Alexy said, "We have been told you have guns here. If you surrender your weapons we will leave you alone, otherwise you must come with us." He knew he had hit the right chord when the old woman started to yell at her husband. Silently the old man removed some wooden planks in the floor of the tiny bedroom and from this hiding place produced an old single shot 12-gauge shotgun and a dozen shells. The escapees' weapons arsenal had just doubled.

"You are wise to have surrendered the weapon," Alexy said sternly, "otherwise we would have arrested you. Now bring out all your clothing and boots so we can take what we need for our soldiers." The clothing was sparse but did produce a sturdy pair of old boots, work gloves, and a heavy, ragged coat that fit Zalman. Aaron was tempted to give the old man the half empty bottle of vodka but decided against it.

They ordered the old couple to stay in the bedroom while, just out of earshot, the three men sat by a small blazing fireplace to plan their next move.

It was Alexy, the oldest by several years, who

emerged as the leader of the small group. He was the most experienced soldier of the three and in hushed whispers he assessed their situation.

"By all rights we should be dead by now," he started, "but by strange twists of fate we sit before a warm fire, with full bellies, trying to decide a course of action. My decision was made the night the Nazi butcher killed my wife. I believe that it is only a short time before we are killed or captured. Until that happens, I want only revenge on those bastards. Trying to escape to a safe haven is not an option for me." His statement made, he looked at his two companions. Aaron spoke next.

"You're right, that we are alive is nothing short of a miracle. We know what our fate is, and I say we do as much damage as we can before we are killed. I have been commanded by my father to be an avenging angel for my family." Brave words for a twenty-three-year-old apprentice carpenter who before this day had never lifted a hand in anger against his fellow man. Zalman spoke next, "I agree, there is no safe place for us. The least we can do is exact some measure of revenge for all those who went passively into the flames."

For the next few hours they discussed ways of implementing their goal of doing as much damage as possible until they were captured or killed. Their assets, they decided, were Aaron's command of German and Alexy and Zalman's limited knowledge of weapons. What was unsaid but tacitly acknowledged by all of them to be their greatest asset was the fact that they had accepted that they were fighting a lost battle and thus had nothing to lose. It was not an issue that they would be killed—only when. The trio had another advantage, for when acts of sabotage or the killing of a German soldier or a collaborator were discovered, the Germans' main ploy was to exact expiation for those acts by taking local hostages and shooting them. None of the three conspirators had any feeling for the local populace, who certainly knew of the plight of the inmates in the camps and either were too frightened to object or concurred with what was being done there. In either case they agreed this would have no effect on their plans. This was war and as they knew only too well innocent people are unfortunately victims in a war.

"It would be unfortunate," Zalman said half to himself, "if no one knew who was responsible for the damage we do. I want those bastards to know that someone is standing up and spitting in their faces."

They thought about this and it was Alexy who volunteered, "Since it is the Jew they hate so much, why don't we give them some additional fuel for their fire. We could leave some sign, say a six-pointed Star of David at the scene of what we do. That should really drive them crazy, and we know there is nothing more that they can do to the Jews!"

Plans started to take shape. What they needed immediately was a reasonably safe place to hide, to find and store weapons, and to reconnoiter. It would only be a matter of hours before the S.S. patrols found this place.

Alexy insisted that they remain and do their fighting in the Krakow area and Aaron and Zalman did not object. They both suspected Alexy had an ulterior motive for wanting to stay relatively close to the camp and where they fought the Germans was of little concern to Aaron and Zalman.

They remained in the farmhouse for the rest of the day and left only when it became dark. The old couple had fallen asleep and did not hear them leave. The rains had stopped but clouds covered the moon, and they drove without incident toward the city.

Krakow was an ancient city, in existence for almost 900 years. Before the war it was almost twenty-five percent Jewish but now it was "Judenfrei," a true success in the eyes of Poland's conquerors.

About a mile outside the city limits a rear tire on the small truck hit a pothole and went flat. The road was becoming fairly heavily trafficked and after examining the damaged tire, which was beyond repair, they decided to pull the truck off the road, abandon it, and sneak into the city on foot. Headlights of a German staff car coming from the city caught them momentarily unprepared. The car stopped directly in front of them with its headlights shining on the three.

"What's the problem?" the driver shouted. Aaron, still wearing the hat and gray coat of the Army truck driver they had killed shouted back, "Flat tires from these lousy potholes." Aaron could see the outline of two occupants in the vehicle. On impulse he shouted in German, "Could you help us push this off the road? We'll get killed if we try to fix it in the middle of this road." He could see the two men in the car talking and then, apparently reluctantly, getting out to give them aid.

As they came into view, Aaron could see that one of the men was a black-uniformed S.S. officer and the driver an enlisted regular Army private.

"Make it quick," the officer snapped at Aaron. He ordered his driver to help push as he stood aside to give orders. Zalman had jumped into the truck to steer the vehicle off the road. They pushed, but the truck, with its brake engaged, didn't move. The S.S. officer, now frustrated, yelled at Zalman, "Release the brake, idiot," and he jerked open the truck door. A loud explosion from the barrel of the 12-gauge shotgun blew away what had been a split second earlier the face of the S.S. officer. The faceless body flew backward and landed in the middle of the road. The driver, confused for a moment, stared at Aaron and never saw Alexy point the revolver at his head and pull the trigger.

They quickly pushed both vehicles off the road into the trees where they could not be seen from the road. Stripping the bodies, Aaron put on the S.S. officer's uniform and Zalman the driver's uniform. They next dressed the two dead soldiers in their clothes and placed them in the cab of the truck. Alexy punctured the gas tank of the truck and collected a liter of gasoline, in which they doused the dead bodies, and set them ablaze. Minutes later, Alexy now driving the staff car, Zalman in the front passenger seat with the driver's automatic weapon across his lap, and Aaron dressed in the uniform of an S.S. Captain in the back seat, they proceeded again. The staff car sped towards Krakow as flames engulfed the small truck and its dead passengers in the background. Their first real act of revenge swept through them like an aphrodisiac.

The fire acted as a beacon to the patrols searching for the escapees. Within a half hour three separate search patrols converged on the fire-gutted truck. The two bodies in the cab of the truck were burnt beyond recognition.

S.S. Major Gunther Staub was the highest-ranking officer at the scene. A balding, paunch-bellied little man, he stood only 5'4" tall even with the lifts in his boots. Staub had been a butcher before the Nazi party had recruited him into their ranks. Cruel and basically lazy, he was exhausted from this "Jew chasing" and was anxious to bring the search to an end. A cursory examination of the bodily remains convinced him that his search was over.

"Look at the shape of those skulls," he exclaimed to his equally tired subordinates, "clearly they are the sub-human Jews who committed suicide rather than be captured."

"But what of the third prisoner, the Pole, Golmanski?" one of his lieutenants inquired. "I'm sure we'll find him or his body around this area. Keep a few four-man patrols searching. I will return with these remains and make my report." As far as Staub was concerned the search for the escapees was over. The two Jews were dead, and if the Pole did get away he had no doubt that he would be rounded up in some future arrest. Staub could not wait to get back to his quarters to eat and get out of his damp wool uniform. A visit to the officers brothel would also serve him well this evening. It had been a long, exhausting day, but at least it ended successfully.

The city of Krakow had changed dramatically since the "Blitzkrieg" of September 1939. The Polish Horse Cavalry had been no match for German armor. The Germans and Soviets had divided Poland pursuant to the August 23, 1939, Nazi-Soviet Pact of Non-aggression, leaving Germany in control of the Polish heartland and 22 million of its people.

Krakow was designated as the "capital" as Warsaw was to be destroyed and replaced by a German colony. The appointed Governor General was one Hans Frank, a jaded Nazi jurist. He took up residence in the ancient Warwel Palace in Krakow, and purges of the Polish intelligencia had commenced immediately.

CHAPTER 9

It was a cloud-covered moonless 2:00 AM sky when Alexy drove the black staff car into the city limits. Their immediate goal was to find some place where they could hide and get some sleep. They had no way of knowing that the search for them had terminated upon the discovery of the bodies in the burnt out truck.

"I have a cousin, on my mother's side, who was a priest in this town," Alexy offered, "I haven't seen him for a few years and I don't know if he will help us, but at least I don't think he will turn us in to the Germans...."

"If you know where his church is, let's give it a try," Zalman said. Aaron, dead tired, nodded affirmatively.

An hour later after driving down several wrong streets, they stopped before an old, small, red brick church. Carrying their weapons from the vehicle, Aaron and Zalman followed Alexy into the building. It was the first time either of them had ever been inside a church. They found a tiny rectory in the rear of the church and pounded on the door. A sleepy, thin, balding man opened the door. He was wearing a linen nightshirt, but upon seeing Aaron's uniform he became fully awake, "Can I help you?" he said looking directly at Aaron.

"Who are you?" Aaron snapped at him in Polish.

"I am Father Bruno Block."

"Bruno, do you know me?" Alexy asked.

Shifting his gaze from Aaron to Alexy, the priest could only utter, "Oh my God, Alexy, is it you?"

They all piled in the small room that served as Father Bruno's living quarters. With no real choice, they decided to gamble and talk openly to the priest, who was about the same age as Alexy. When they finished their story there were a few moments of strained silence. Zalman's hand tightened on the shotgun and Aaron had opened the flap on the holster containing his Parabellum. Noticing these reflexes, the priest smiled slightly, "You've put your lives in my hands, not knowing if I'm a collaborator or anti-Semite. Let me try to assure you I'm neither. Alexy, will you and your friends follow me please." Taking them out of the rectory, the priest, still barefoot and in his nightshirt, led them down a narrow wooden stairway to a basement area beneath the main room of the church. In a corner of the basement a large bookcase filled with dust-covered tomes covered a wall area. Pulling a corner of the book case from the wall revealed another damp dust-filled stairwell that led down to a large sub-basement room. Lighting several candles in the room revealed a dozen cots, some food stores, a shortwave radio, and a small cache of weapons.

"Now we are even," the priest said, "If the Germans know about this room I would join the twenty percent of all Polish Catholic priests whom they have already killed."

The priest went on to explain that the room had been used as a sanctuary for many of his parishioners who were hunted by the Germans for any number of reasons. So far, even when captured, they had kept the existence of this room secret. Continued secrecy of the room was the priest's only condition, and the three men readily agreed.

Father Bruno had Alexy hide their purloined staff car behind the church, and they collapsed on the cots sleeping soundly for the next ten hours.

They soon discovered that the sub-basement room had an additional advantage. A second subterranean exit led into the tunnels of the old underground sewer system of Krakow. They could access their hideout from the outside without ever going through the church.

For the next few days the three men rested and made their plans. Occasionally Father Bruno would sit in and lend some piece of information about German positions in the city. Alexy was particularly interested in the taverns frequented by the concentration camp guards on leave. Aaron gave his companions a short course on basic German phrases, and by the fifth night they were ready to put their plan into action.

Dressed in their stolen uniforms, their initial forays of sabotage consisted of setting fire to unattended military vehicles and the cutting of telephone wires. At each place they dropped small pieces of paper with a hand-drawn Star of David, never knowing if it had been found or not but reveling in the feeling of taking affirmative action against the enemy. All their activities took place a few blocks from the church and at night. As they became more familiar with the streets they ventured further from the church, scurrying through the damp underground tunnels like mice. Soon their actions switched from simple property damage to direct attacks on soldiers.

Any German soldier walking alone at night became a potential target. By the end of their first month in hiding they had permanently dispatched seven unsuspecting victims including two officers. Father Bruno advised them that they had attracted the attention of the German police authorities who were randomly picking up any suspected perpetrators and summarily executing them in an attempt to quell the attacks against their military personnel. The partisans were being blamed, but small scraps of paper with a Star of David found beside several of the bodies added a peculiar element to the crimes. Most of the partisans were not particularly fond of Jews, and the German military police surmised that it was simply a partisan ploy to attempt to throw blame elsewhere. After all, the Jews were either dead or in deep hiding and, being cowardly, would never attack a German soldier. Yet it was puzzling. Orders were issued to all military personnel in Krakow not to travel alone at night.

During the second month the acts of violence increased and a dozen German soldiers met their maker. There was no pattern to the killings other than that they all occurred at night. Several were shot at close range, two were stabbed to death, and three were garrotted. The only common thread was the small slip of paper beside several of the bodies with the hand-drawn Star of David.

The trio had established a lifestyle of sleeping during the day and scouring the narrow streets at night looking for potential victims. Dressed in uniforms that they continued to change, with Aaron usually disguised as an officer, they would frequent the soldiers' taverns and select a victim. Aaron did not try to strike up conversations, but his perfect German served him well. He overheard loose talk about a myriad of subjects and was surprised to learn that the activities of a murderer or a group of murderers nicknamed "Der Juden Stern" or simply "the Star" was the most frequently discussed subject. Everyone had a different theory on who it was, except they all agreed that it could not be a Jew.

Aaron would rendezvous with Alexy and Zalman after an hour or so in a bar, and they would wait in the shadows of buildings for the victim to leave the tavern. "Like spiders waiting for a fly," Aaron would think. They tried to strike at officers rather than enlisted men, and an S.S. officer was a prime target.

Alexy would always interrogate Aaron about who was in the bar and particularly whether any camp guards had been present. Aaron knew the general description of the man that had become Alexy's obsession and made a special effort to scan the taverns to see if anyone fit the description. It was like looking for a needle in a haystack but he did it out of respect for his comrade.

By the end of their second month of freedom the German military police had two dozen investigators working full time on finding "the Star." Considerable extra resources were being expended to make sure no soldier traveled alone, and even the rounding up, torture and summary execution of over 200 civilians did not bring them any closer to discovering the identity of "the Star." Rumors of a Jewish avenger spread like wildfire throughout the "general government," and, fearing similar problems in other cities, the orders went out that no soldier traveled alone or unarmed until the cowardly killers were captured. Isolated copy-cat killings occurred in Warsaw and Gdansk where hand-drawn Stars of David were found beside the mutilated bodies of dead Nazi soldiers. Special investigative police teams were created in each of those cities as in Krakow. Two dozen officers and guards were assigned from the concentration camp to assist the investigation units. The Germans reasoned that if on some outside chance it was a Jewish group, who better to deal with the problem then those who specialize in exterminating them. Leading the officers from the camp was Captain Otto Hofbauer, a fact that, if known to Alexy, would have been the source of great satisfaction.

Father Block told them that the police had narrowed the search to an area of about three square miles, and house-to-house searches were being made within the area. The church was on the border of the targeted zone.

Two nights after the priest's warning a troop truck with ten soldiers commanded by Captain Otto Hofbauer screeched to a halt in front of the small church.

CHAPTER 10

Pressed against the rear of the movable basement bookcase, Alexy's entire body shook uncontrollably as he recognized the voice of Captain Otto Hofbauer shouting orders to his soldiers searching the bowels of the old church. It took all of his strength to restrain himself from bursting through the wooden panels of the bookcase and strangling the fiend that had so viciously killed his wife. Aaron and Zalman, standing on either side of Alexy, could feel the emotion raging in their friend and knew that it was only by a super-human effort in self-control that he had not exposed their hiding place by attacking the man who had become his overwhelming obsession.

Frantically, Alexy turned to Aaron, "I can't let him escape, this may be my only chance to kill him," as tears flooded his eyes. "I don't care about myself, but you and Zalman and Bruno . . . ," the rest left unsaid.

"We'll think of something," Aaron whispered. They could hear the soldiers' boots clomping up the wooden stairway to the main floor of the church, and Aaron slipped from behind the bookcase.

"You two stay here." Aaron was afraid to let Alexy see Hofbauer, fearing that he would not be able to control himself. Dressed in his S.S. major's uniform, Aaron slipped out the rear of the church as Captain Hofbauer led his men out the front taking the young priest with them. Aaron could hear him shouting to his men, "Throw him in the truck and we'll see what information this man of God has when we are through with him."

Running around to the front of the church, Aaron confronted Hofbauer, "What is going on here, Captain?" he snarled. Caught by surprise and staring at the death's head insignia on Aaron's cap, Hofbauer snapped to attention.

"We have suspicion that this priest may be a partisan sympathizer, and we are taking him for interrogation."

"Did you search the church?"

"Yes, Major, but we found nothing."

"Step over here, Captain," Aaron motioned as he walked out of earshot of the soldiers who were holding Father Bruno. In his most conspiratorial tone and improvising on the spot, Aaron spoke softly to Hofbauer. "We have been watching this church, and we believe the priest has been hoarding gold and jewels taken from his parishioners. That property now legally belongs to the Reich; however, I'm sure that a few articles could be liberated," and he winked at the very attentive captain. "I think the Reich would be doubly served if we convince the priest that we will protect him if he helps us. Once we have the gold and jewels, he's all yours. I think we will have a better chance with these religious fanatics by first trying a soft approach, and I think he is beginning to trust me."

Aaron could see that Captain Hofbauer was not fully convinced but had listened attentively when he thought he would share in any liberated booty.

"Come back in an hour without your men, or at best bring one to do the dirty work, if necessary. I'll be here with the priest." Hesitating for a few moments and then without another word, Hofbauer turned and ordered his men to release the priest and seconds later they were gone. Aaron was not sure if he would return or report the incident to his superiors, but for the moment Father Bruno was spared and the possibility of Hofbauer returning existed. It was the best Aaron could do under the circumstances. He hoped Alexy would understand and not be too disappointed, but the next hour or so would be difficult.

"Aaron, I owe you my life," Father Bruno said as they reentered the church.

"If that's true it is only a small part of what I owe you for your kindness, my friend," Aaron answered, putting his big arm across the thin priest's shoulders.

It was about an hour and a half later when a military motorcycle with a sidecar slammed to a noisy stop in front of the church. Captain Hofbauer climbed out of the sidecar and the large driver, a private, removed his goggles and followed his commanding officer into the church.

The door leading to the basement stairwell was open and Hofbauer could hear voices from below. The two men, boots noisily echoing in the stairwell, hurried down the stairs. Aaron and Father Bruno were standing in candlelight apparently examining a book taken from the bookcase.

"I have returned, Major," Otto Hofbauer announced as he came to attention. Looking up Aaron smiled, "So you have, Captain, so you have."

Facing the bookcase neither Hofbauer nor his driver saw Alexy and Zalman step from behind the stairwell. A blast from the 12-gauge to the back of the large private's head shattered the silence, and the body of the driver fell forward at the feet of a confused and startled Captain Hofbauer.

Instinctively, he reached for his holster but feeling the barrel of Alexy's revolver against his temple, he immediately raised his hands.

It was the supreme single moment that Alexy had lived for since the brutal murder of his wife, and he fought back the almost overwhelming urge to immediately strangle the "animal" that stood before him.

A quick death is not in your future, Captain Hofbauer, he thought, you must pay in some small measure for your terrible acts, and that will take some time. Alexy had fantasized about what he would do to this man if the opportunity ever arose, and now his dream of vengeance was about to come true.

Both Aaron and Zalman would have preferred a quick bullet to their captive's head, but they both knew that Hofbauer's fate was strictly Alexy's decision.

They stripped Hofbauer of his uniform and tied him naked to a chair in the sub-basement room that served as their living quarters. Aaron and Zalman then silently left the room.

It was cool in the sub-basement, but the burly Captain Hofbauer, naked and tied to the chair in the middle of the room, was bathed in sweat.

"What do you want of me?" he screamed at Alexy

who had not yet uttered a word. "If you are going to kill me, then get it over with," he yelled without much conviction. Hofbauer felt that by not showing fear perhaps he could convince his captor that he was a soldier just doing his job and generate some measure of mercy from this silent man. The Pole stood before his captive.

"Don't you recognize me, Captain?" he asked softly. The naked man squinted at his captor without recognition. "I was a prisoner of yours not too long ago."

"Are you a Jew?" Hofbauer yelled.

Continuing in a strained yet soft unhurried voice, Alexy answered, "No, you Nazi pig, I am not a Jew, but my beautiful fragile wife was and you strangled her to death after your men raped her before my eyes. Do you recognize me now?"

It was obvious that Hofbauer did, for he stared at Alexy for a few moments and his body slumped as he realized that his plan to try to exact some measure of mercy from this man had no chance of success.

Continuing slowly Alexy said, "Nothing that I do to you will bring my wife back, for she is in God's hands now. What I do to you I do solely to satisfy my basic human weakness for revenge. I have dreamed of this moment. Your screams of pain will be like beautiful music to my ears. Your only salvation will be your death, which is inexorable but won't come for quite some time." Any facade of bravado that Hofbauer had intended to maintain evaporated as he started to sob, and the fear he felt raging through his body caused him to lose control of his bowels and kidneys. Continuing to speak softly, intending to add insult to injury Alexy said, "And by the way, Captain, you have found 'Der Juden Stern'."

The torture of the concentration camp officer went on for over six hours. Aaron and Zalman waiting in the church basement above could easily hear the screams emanating from what was supposedly a soundproof room. The screams would stop for a while and then start again. They assumed that the silent periods meant that the prisoner had lost consciousness. Finally, after a silent period of about an hour, they decided to investigate. Upon entering the room they found Alexy sitting on the floor in a corner of the room. He was covered with blood. His head buried in his hands, he sobbed quietly. Hofbauer, or what was left of him, was dead. There was no part of his body that had escaped Alexy's rage. All of his fingers that had strangled Alexy's wife had been amputated. His face had been smashed beyond recognition. Blood and body parts covered the room. Death had come through suffocation. Alexy had cut off Hofbauer's penis and testicles and forced them down his throat, forever cutting off his supply of air.

Aaron and Zalman had seen the worst of man in the camp, where cruelty, suffering, and pain were the norm, but what had taken place in this room shocked even them. The hate that Alexy had been harboring knew no bounds, and Aaron could only wonder if Alexy had mentally gone over the edge.

They tried to clean the room, for they did not want Father Bruno to be a witness to his cousin's horrendous deeds. It was late morning and they could not dispose of the bodies of Hofbauer and his driver until nightfall. Father Bruno had placed the motorcycle with the sidecar behind the church and there was nothing left for them to do except sleep and wait for darkness.

The killing of Otto Hofbauer brought them to a new stage. Their actions up to now had been planned to put fear into their conquerors and to divert as much material and manpower as they could from the German war effort. The simple plan was a good one and so far had succeeded. "The Star" had gained notoriety not only throughout Krakow but, in fact, their exploits had reached the far corners of the General Government and Berlin. Dozens of German police and soldiers who would otherwise be at the front lines were combing the streets and back alleys of the city searching for them. The reprisals against the citizenry only served to fuel the flames of hatred against the Germans as more young Poles, men and women, fled to join the partisans, knowing that to stay in the city meant an uncertain life at best.

CHAPTER 11

Aaron wanted to expand their acts and make a bold statement by trying to free some concentration camp inmates before they were all killed. That night as Alexy fell into a deep sleep, having drunk one of Father Bruno's last bottles of wine, Aaron and Zalman spent several hours formulating their new plan.

To break into the camp to free prisoners was a suicide mission without any chance of success. Neither had any reservations about sacrificing himself, but they wanted their plan to have some reasonable chance of success. They reasoned that they could probably get into the camp with some weapons, but there would be no chance for them or any inmates to escape once the shooting started.

They next thought about making an attack on the local prison, but no Jews would benefit from their actions. It was then that they hit upon the trains. Cattle cars loaded with human cargo arrived at the camp with regularity. If they could intercept and stop the train in an area where "the cargo" could be given weapons, then perhaps, just perhaps, some of them could find their way to the forests or mountains and survive. This would be a plan worth dying for.

Alexy had been the unacknowledged leader of the three, but after the previous night's events, he seemed to have lost the drive that had motivated him. When they explained their plan to him and Father Bruno, he quietly agreed that it made sense but offered no input. Father Bruno, on the other hand, was excited and felt he could get them the information they needed about train routes and schedules from his parishioners' partisan contacts. He knew of a small partisan band that had some Jewish members, and he arranged for a meeting between the partisan leader and Aaron, Zalman, and Alexy. In this land of anti-Semites, Aaron and Zalman were always amazed at the risks the young priest took to help them. Aaron did not plan to ask the partisans to help them stop the train nor to fight the Germans guarding the train. He wanted their help supplying weapons and wanted to make sure that any escapees making it to the forests would not be shot by partisans, who generally hated Nazis only a little more than Jews.

Three nights later in the sub-basement of the old church seven men met by candlelight to discuss a plan to stop a German death train and save some unfortunate victims on their way to the ovens. Joseph Fibek was the leader of a band of about thirty partisans. He was twenty-four years old, 5'4" tall, and weighed no more than 120 pounds. As a child he was always the shortest and skinniest of the group and was always the one the bigger children picked on. When the Germans marched into Poland they considered him too small and weak for factory work and assigned him to their barracks cleaning latrines. He proceeded to blow up the barracks and escape to the forest. He formed a small band of partisans and took in anyone hunted by the Germans including women and Jews. He made no distinction by sex or religion; his band members were judged by their actions and nothing else.

He was only too pleased to meet with "The Star" and took an immediate liking to these men and they to him. Father Bruno was overjoyed, for he could not have made a better match.

Fibek, with blue pipe smoke surrounding his head, explained that most of his men would not get involved in a scheme simply to save Jews on their one-way trip to a concentration camp. They would need a more practical reason. Aaron and Zalman argued that each train generally carried a number of armed guards with modern weapons, ammunition, and foodstuffs, and, if captured, the material could arm and supply his band for months. He relented and agreed to leave the decision to his band. At the very least, he felt, his Jewish partisans would decide to participate in the battle. This was a major concession, and Aaron and Zalman did not push any further. They were prepared to proceed without any outside help and the prospect of additional armed support, however limited, buoyed their spirits. Aaron's main objection was to be assured that any escaping prisoners making it to the forests at least had some chance of survival and he had Fibek's promise on that. The quid pro quo for Fibek's group were the weapons and supplies from the train and the possibility of recruiting some of the escaping prisoners to his partisan army. They spent the balance of the evening planning the time and place for the attack. It had to be far from any German reinforcements yet close enough to the partisan camp to allow them to retreat to safety.

The terrain and the speed of the train at the point of derailment were next considered. It would do no good to derail a speeding train and kill all the passengers. They all knew that a significant number of the prisoners would be killed in the derailing and subsequent fighting, but at least some would have a chance to live. For those that could potentially escape and survive it would be their only chance.

CHAPTER 12

In 1943 the Polish railway system employees in the General Government consisted of about 9,000 Germans and about 140,000 Poles with a few thousand Ukrainians. Between 1942 and 1943 more than two million Polish Jews had ridden these rails to their deaths. There was no way this could have occurred without the knowledge and complicity of the Polish railway workers. Poland was the site of six separate killing centers for Jews that were supplied by trains running typically no more than 200 miles to deliver their human cargo. For the most part the deported Jews offered no resistance and simply appeared as ordered at deportation centers for rail transport to one of the killing centers.

Meyer Bishov was seventeen years old, a Zionist, and a member of the Revisionist Party. He was also a member of the military arm of the party called the Irgun Zwai Leumi, the National Military Organization. Bishov and his friends had held secret talks and distributed pamphlets in the Ghetto advocating resistance but without weapons, there was little more that could be done. On this warm, sunny day in July 1943 he found himself, along with his parents and his fifteen-year-old brother, Jacob, part of the "quota" scheduled for railway transport to what he knew would be a final destination. At the deportation station he could see several members of his party who gave unconvincing feeble signs of encouragement to each other. They had been told the trip would take about fourteen hours and they were allowed to take some luggage and cooking utensils. Meyer Bishov was not fooled and concealed a large kitchen knife in his knapsack. He had decided not to go passively at the end of his journey.

They had been traveling south for several hours and conditions in the cattle car that they had been crammed into were beyond intolerable. Meyer was tired, thirsty, and hungry. He had been able to stand close to his family and was pressed against the wall of the cattle car. He had whittled a small hole in one of the wooden wall planks and peering out he could see that it was dark and the train seemed to be slowing down. He could see the ominous shapes of trees fairly close to the tracks. Suddenly and without warning he felt the train brake screech as it rounded a curve. Had the people in the cars not been so crammed together they would certainly have been thrown into the walls and been killed or injured. Meyer could feel the car tipping and coming to a rest on its side. Parts of the roof of the car had broken open and screaming people were scrambling to get out.

As Meyer and his family crawled out of the cattle car roof he could hear gunshots and automatic weapons fire. It was a scene of mad confusion. People were shouting and screaming, shots were being fired, and guard dogs barked. Meyer could see several small fires illuminating the macabre scene. From both sides of the track small arms fire crackled from the forest and was taking a deadly toll on the German guards, many of whom had been riding on top of some of the cars and were firing back at unseen targets in the forest. Partisans were urging people to get away from the train and run into the woods. Suddenly a tall man dressed in black appeared next to Meyer, holding a submachine pistol in his hands. It was the size of his hands that Meyer noticed first; they were extraordinarily large and powerful.

"Can you shoot a gun?" the man asked looking directly at Meyer who could only nod. "Good, take this pistol and start pushing people into those woods," and the man pointed over his shoulder. "If a German soldier tries to stop you, kill him." The man was deadly serious as handed Meyer a large revolver and moved down the train to help others. Why he had nodded affirmatively Meyer would never know, for not only had he never fired a revolver, he had never held one before. But as he pushed the weapon into his pant waist, helping his brother and parents into the woods, he thought, at least now I'll go down fighting, and he felt a surge of adrenaline flow through his body. He never felt more alive as he gripped the revolver handle and watched the dark form of his benefactor calmly move down the track firing his weapon.

Aaron, dressed in black, fought his way down the tracks. Firing at the guards, pulling the confused and dazed people from the overturned cattle cars, and occasionally dropping a small piece of paper with a hand-drawn Star of David. He had not seen Zalman or Alexy since the fighting began. Callously he did not spend any time helping the very elderly or seriously hurt but rather directed his efforts solely to those who he felt had some chance at survival. Strangely he felt no fear or anxiety but rather moved quickly and effectively without emotion. Almost, he thought, like the hated officer at the camp stoically selecting those who would live or die. It was different, he knew, for these people were all destined to die, but for a fleeting moment the comparison haunted him.

The entire battle lasted less than ten minutes. About ten of the German guards remained alive and surrendered by throwing down their weapons and raising their hands. The partisans took no prisoners and could ill afford to leave behind guards who had seen their faces and knew what weapons they had. The guards were quickly rounded up and summarily executed.

Fibek's men scavenged the area and the cars of the train that housed the guards and officers. Each partisan took as much as he could carry, with weapons and ammunition being a priority followed by boots, first aid medical supplies, and tins of food. The heavier weapons were loaded on a few pack mules, and within forty-five minutes after the first shot was fired, the well-organized partisan band was moving out.

Conversely, many of the prisoners still milled around the train, either too hurt or too confused to move. Aaron spotted Zalman about fifty yards down the track yelling at the prisoners to run to the forest and try to escape.

"If you stay here you will die," he screamed at a group of elderly people who appeared unhurt but dazed.

"Where do we go?" came a reply.

"Anywhere but here," Zalman screamed back, "hide, steal food, kill Germans, don't just stay here like sheep waiting to be slaughtered and slaughtered you will be," his voice, now fever pitched, fell mainly on deaf ears, but a few people did move off into the forest. "Head south," he admonished, "try for the Slovakia border, trust no one."

"Let's go, Zalman," Aaron said quietly as he grabbed his friend's arm, "we can do no more here, and we have to see if we can help those who have fled." Reluctantly Zalman turned to leave.

True to his word, Fibek instructed his men to aid the escaping prisoners where they could and to keep an eye out for potential recruits.

It was Fibek who had watched the seventeen-year-old Meyer Bishov, revolver in hand, lead his younger brother and parents into the forest. Pointing at Meyer he told his aide, "That one with the revolver looks like a fighter. Bring him to camp." The aide ran to Meyer, and after a few moments he breathlessly returned to Fibek.

"He says he wants to kill Germans, but he won't come without his brother and parents."

Fibek grinned, "I pluck him from certain death, give him a chance to fight his enemy and just perhaps survive this war, and he is already negotiating for a better deal. No wonder these Jews have survived for 5,000 years. All right, bring them all. I like the little bastard's style."

It was four hours later when the partisan band returned to their camp hidden deep in the forest. They had brought about twenty "recruits" with them, who would, if they desired, be given a chance to join the group. They were all exhausted but still flushed with their victory. They knew that the Germans would not take this defeat lightly and extra guards were posted to warn of any counterattack. Fibek did not really expect counter actions for at least a day or two, but he preferred to play it safe even though the extra guards he posted were themselves exhausted.

Aaron was anxious to return to Krakow but couldn't find Alexy. Physically drained, he and Zalman decided to spend the night with the partisans and sneak back into town with Alexy as soon as he returned. They were sure Alexy would turn up with the stragglers at some time during the night.

Aaron propped himself beside a tree stump, folded his large hands around his weapon, and within moments was asleep. He could sleep anywhere. He never heard the young Meyer Bishov ask one of the partisans, "Who is that man sleeping by the tree stump?" Nor did he hear the man reply, "That is the Juden Stern. He is the man you owe your life to."

The following morning Alexy had still not returned. One of the partisans had seen him during the fighting and thought he might have been wounded, but things were happening so fast he could not be sure. Aaron and Zalman knew it would have been pointless to return to the battle scene. Anyone who remained there was surely dead by now. The methodical Germans would not want word of this partisan success to reach the camps and would have killed any survivors on the spot. Their general staff would spare no effort in tracking down as many escapees as possible, and as for that very small lucky percentage that would escape, few in the outside world would pay much attention to their plight or their story of how they escaped mass extermination.

It was 1943 and the civilized world was still not ready to accept the horrors that the Jews of Europe knew so well.

By the second day Alexy had still not returned, and Aaron and Zalman, now deeply concerned, decided to return to Father Bruno's church in Krakow. Fibek assured them that he would let them know anything he discovered about Alexy's whereabouts.

It was four days after the attack on the train when Father Bruno raced down to their sub-basement to tell them about Alexy.

"He was wounded in the battle and apparently lost consciousness. The Germans found him and realized he was not a prisoner but a partisan. They have taken him to Stanish prison for interrogation, God help him."

Pensively Aaron added, "I don't think God will have anything to do with it Father, but Zalman and I will."

CHAPTER 13

It was a suicide mission and both Aaron and Zalman knew it, yet nothing could prevent them from going. They waited until shortly after midnight when activity in the small Stanish prison would be slow and, they hoped, security lax. The prison was actually a small converted Polish police station taken over by the Gestapo. Aaron, dressed as a Death's Head S.S. battalion colonel, and Zalman as his aide, using his newly-acquired driving skills, arrived at the prison in a stolen staff car. Striding brazenly through the front door, Aaron demanded to see the officer in charge. As he had expected, a sleepy-eyed young captain was summoned who quickly snapped to attention upon seeing Aaron's uniform.

"What can I do for you, Colonel?" he offered.

"First, you can button the top button of your tunic and tell me your name," Aaron snapped back. Now intimidated and caught off guard, the young officer fumbled with his collar button. "Secondly, you can bring me the file on the partisan prisoner you are holding and then bring me the prisoner for questioning." As the young officer hesitated, Aaron produced a small pen and small notebook. "Spell your name for me, Captain," he snarled.

"Hans Kohl, sir, H-A-N-S K-O-H-L."

Not wishing to get deeper into trouble, he shouted at the desk sergeant, "Sergeant, have the partisan prisoner brought to my office, at once." Then, trying hard to redeem himself, he led Aaron and Zalman to his office and produced Alexy's file. Not wanting the young captain to telephone his superiors, Aaron sat behind his desk.

"Stay here, Captain Kohl, I may need your help," Aaron ordered, as he casually started to peruse Alexy's file. Zalman took a position by the door. Minutes later two stocky guards dragged a shackled body into the office. Alexy was unrecognizable, his face was a mass of blue welts forcing both of his eyes completely shut. All of the fingernails on his right hand had been pulled out. An untreated bullet wound oozed from his right shoulder.

"As you can see from the file, Colonel, he has not spoken."

"Remove his shackles and have the guards wait outside," Aaron ordered.

"But Colonel. . . ."

"You question my orders, Captain Kohl?"

"No, sir, but it is highly unusual."

"It is also unusual that you haven't been able to make this filthy Polish swine talk in four days, Captain."

That was all the young officer needed. "Remove the shackles and wait outside," he shouted at the bewildered guards.

Alexy, more dead than alive, slumped in a chair in front of Aaron. Captain Kohl standing in a corner of the small office watched as Aaron approached the prisoner and bent to whisper in his ear. He could not hear what was said but to his amazement saw the prisoner, through broken teeth, smile weakly, make a sound, and reach for Aaron's hand.

Now looking at the awed captain, Aaron said, "I imagine, Captain, you are wondering what I told him." Without waiting for a response, Aaron continued, "I told him that his friends would not let him die in a Nazi jail." Now completely confused, the young officer stared at Aaron and then at Zalman who had his semi-automatic weapon aimed at his head.

"Call the guards in here," Aaron ordered. When the captain did not respond immediately, he continued, "Captain, either you call the guards in now and help us remove this man from your prison or you will be dead in two seconds, it makes no difference to us." Apparently deciding that Aaron meant what he said, the guards were called in.

"Put this prisoner in my staff car at once," Aaron said. He did not look at the guards but faced Captain Kohl. He saw the captain nod as the guards responded by dragging Alexy from his chair. "Don't kill him, you idiots, he is no good to us dead," Aaron shouted.

Captain Kohl and Aaron, followed by Zalman, watched as the guards deposited Alexy in the back seat of the staff car.

Aaron felt he could almost read the young captain's mind. He would, by now, realize that either Zalman would kill him on the spot or he would be shot by his superiors for allowing the prisoner to escape and he was wrestling with the decision.

Softly Aaron said to him, "Don't even consider it, Captain. With us you will take a short ride and we let you go. Perhaps you will be able to convince your superiors that you were overpowered and they won't kill you. But if you resist now you are a dead man." But it did not work, and the captain screamed at the guard, "Stop them they are. . . ." Zalman ended his shouts with a short burst of gun fire. The two stunned unarmed guards ran back into the jail and Zalman, after firing a short burst of gunfire at them, scrambled into the staff car as Aaron grabbed his automatic weapon and continued to fire at the prison entrance.

Their escape complete, they abandoned the staff car a few blocks from the sewer that they had used so often going in and out of the old church. Carrying and dragging Alexy through the sewers back to their underground room, there was little they could do for him other than clean his wounds and try to make him comfortable.

Two nights later Alexy Golmanski died from his wounds, but the three men in attendance that evening knew that he had really died the night he had completed his act of vengeance on his wife's murderer.

It was a quiet mass for Alexy Golmanski, presided over by Father Bruno and witnessed by Aaron and Zalman. They buried him in an unmarked grave beneath the church with the promise to someday erect a proper marker for both Alexy and his wife.

It became obvious to Aaron and Zalman that they could no longer continue their nocturnal forays into the bars and taverns of Krakow dressed as German soldiers. By using that ploy to free Alexy, the police would be spot-checking all I.D. cards and looking for them dressed as soldiers. Although neither of them had any reasonable expectation of surviving the war, they did not want to throw their lives away frivolously, especially since their descriptions were now known and it was further known that Aaron spoke perfect German.

They remained in hiding in the sub-basement of the church for a full week after Alexy's death, spending their days tediously cleaning their weapons, sleeping, reading, exercising, but mostly waiting as they pondered their next move.

CHAPTER 14

It was 3:00 AM when Father Bruno woke Aaron and Zalman from a restless sleep. He was accompanied by one of Fibek's partisans, who, speaking quickly, advised them that Fibek had been contacted by British agents. It seemed that two of the prisoners who were freed from the ill-fated German death train had actually reached safety in England and told the British about the attack on the train led by someone called "Juden Stern." The practical British reasoned that if, in fact, there was such a person or persons, he could serve as a beacon for others and was more valuable alive than dead or a German prisoner. Reports had been filtering out of Poland to London for several months about this mysterious hero, but this was the first report that could be verified by eyewitnesses.

"They want you to come with them to London. Fibek thinks you may be able to convince them to send supplies, and he said, anyhow, you owe him a favor."

They agreed to leave at once, and Aaron had a strong premonition that he would never see Father Bruno again. So much had happened to Aaron in the last few years that he came to rely heavily on his instincts, which were generally correct. As they prepared to leave the church Aaron and Zalman approached the thin priest who, it seemed, had aged significantly over the last several months since they first met.

"If we never meet again, but I had a chance to do something for you, what would it be?" The priest was not surprised by Aaron's question, for he too felt that the parting this early morning was final. It had been a strong alliance between the Catholic priest and the two young Jews. They came from worlds apart yet could not have been closer if they had been brothers. Each had placed his life in the other's hands, instinctively knowing that their trust was secure.

"You have been true friends and allies," the priest answered, "for me you can spread the word that there are those in the church that would risk their lives to protect good people of any religion," and then as if to break the mood that had grown somber, "and a case of good Polish Slivovitz would not be so bad either," and he clasped the hands of both of his friends.

Zalman answered, "Father Bruno, if we possibly can we shall honor both of your requests." With that Aaron and Zalman left the sub-basement haven that had served them so well.

It was dawn two days later when they arrived at Fibek's camp. They were exhausted, but sleep was out of the question. German patrols had increased since the raid on the train, and Fibek's partisans were preparing to move to a new camp miles away. They were quickly introduced to a very tall, lean British officer.

"Captain Desmond Stein, gentlemen. I have instructions to get you to England. We leave this evening." Captain Stein spoke perfect Polish. It was Aaron who responded.

"I'm not so sure, Captain, who instructed you to deliver us to London and why?" A bit irritated now Stein replied, "I'm not at liberty to reveal that, gentlemen." Stein responded pompously, adding, "I repeat we must leave tonight." Aaron and Zalman looked at each other, and it was Zalman who next spoke.

"Captain, we are through taking orders from anyone without knowing who we go with and why we go. It's a luxury we have risked our lives many times to be able to exercise." Stein had not expected this response. He had assumed, wrongfully, that his charges would be more than anxious to leave this place for the relative safety of England. Several of the partisans gathered around and witnessed the exchange. Among them Aaron recognized young Meyer Bishov, who, with a bandolier over his shoulder and rifle in his hand, looked much different than the boy Aaron had pulled from the train. In his belt he still carried the large revolver Aaron had handed him that night. Meyer nodded at Aaron who nodded back.

Confused and now under extreme pressure Captain Stein relented slightly, "Please, gentlemen, a lot of people have risked their lives to see that you get to England." Seeing that he again had their attention he continued, "My superiors can be of great service if you would allow them to meet with you. A plane will land under tremendous risk this evening, and if you are not on it, a great deal of effort will have been expended for nothing.

It was Fibek who finally convinced them to go.

"You can do more there than here," he reasoned. "Tell the world what is going on here. Take this shopping list of supplies and do what you can to get them to me," and he handed Aaron a piece of paper.

Now addressing an anxious Captain Stein, Aaron asked, "How big is this plane of yours?" Without waiting for an answer he continued, "Is it big enough for a few more people?"

"I suppose so if they don't weigh much. The makeshift runway is short and.... "

Aaron abruptly left the captain in mid sentence and approached Meyer Bishov. "Is your family still here?"

"Yes, but I've been told my parents and brother must leave because the new camp is too hard for them to get to and they will slow us down."

"What will you do?"

"I stay with my family of course. Perhaps I can lead them out."

Without hesitating Aaron blurted out, "Get them ready, you're all coming with us tonight." Maybe this way I can make up for those I couldn't help at the train, Aaron thought.

When Captain Stein heard that the only way he could get Aaron and Zalman was to take four more passengers, he could only shake his head in disbelief. "You'll kill us all," he complained, "the plane will never get off the ground."

"This is not a debate, Captain," Aaron snapped back, "You want us, we will go, but only with them," and the discussion was over.

That evening when Aaron and Zalman saw the small plane descend onto the short grassy torch-lit runway even they questioned the reasonableness of so many people going on so small a plane. They stripped the plane of all excess baggage, including parachutes, and climbed aboard. Other than the pilot, co-pilot and Captain Stein none of them had ever flown before. As the small plane laboriously lifted off the ground, barely clearing the treetops, Zalman whispered to Aaron, "I now know what it is to be truly afraid." Aaron, whose stomach was in a turmoil, could only nod.

The plane flew at treetop height to avoid radar, and the pilot, a veteran Polish airman, seemed to delight in the look of stark fear he elicited from the ever proper Captain Stein seated beside him.

The trip to England took over three days with danger of capture at every turn. Aaron grudgingly had considerably more respect for the pompous Captain Stein who never lost his composure or the press in his pants during the tortuous route. It was his demeanor not his courage that irritated Aaron and Zalman. The Bishov family stoically accepted the rigors of the trip, knowing that this was their one chance at survival. Meyer Bishov treated Aaron and Zalman with reverence and never questioned their decisions.

The last day of travel was via a small fishing vessel sneaking into the English coast under heavy fog cover.

That evening in a posh London hotel, for the first night since he was taken from his home and shipped to the concentration camp, Aaron slept alone in a bed with clean sheets in a room with a window, toilet facilities, running water and a telephone. Aaron would have liked to use the telephone but, of course, knew of no one to call. He knew that in this crowded city the luxury of being housed alone in a room in a quality hotel with all these amenities meant that someone was paying a lot of money for his comfort, or some agency or group felt he and Zalman were more important than they really were.

Totally exhausted, both physically and mentally, Aaron didn't care who was paying for his comfort this night or why. Stripping off his dirt-encrusted clothing, he luxuriated in a hot soapy shower, and after washing his clothes he collapsed into the bed where he slept without moving for ten hours. Aaron was awakened by a sharp knock on the door and instinctively reached for his pistol before he realized where he was. Stumbling out of bed, still half asleep, he opened the door to a waiter who rolled in a small table covered with a full English breakfast. Speaking no English, Aaron could only smile at the waiter, who quickly realized that he was not going to get a tip and exited without a word.

Aaron stared at the table in front of him, which was laden with tea, sugar, milk, biscuits, marmalade, a small pat of real butter, soft-boiled eggs, fruit, and a salty fish, which he later discovered to be kippers. For a few moments Aaron thought others were coming to join him before he realized it was all for him. He ate slowly, savoring every taste, and forced himself to finish everything not knowing when he would be this fortunate again.

He had just finished eating when Captain Stein knocked briefly on the door and let himself in.

Staring at the empty plates in front of Aaron he snidely commented, "Hungry, aren't we?"

Aaron was about to respond but then thought better of it. What an ass, he thought as he smiled at the impeccably uniformed officer.

"Debriefing for you and Zalman Zacksman will commence at 0900 hours. You are to be ready and waiting in the lobby at 0830 hours where you will be collected and taken to M15 headquarters." Getting no response from Aaron, who simply stared blankly at him, Stein seemed to let his guard down slightly.

"Listen, Garlovsky, I know you don't like me and that we have little in common, but I've been given a job to do and I'm doing it. You've been through hell for the last few years and I know it, but you can sit out the rest of this war now if you want to. My orders are to act as your mother-hen until the debriefing is over. A few weeks I should guess, and then we deliver you to a Zionist group with whom I'm sure you will be more comfortable. Meanwhile, I suggest you start to study this," and he flipped Aaron a Polish/English dictionary. He had a second dictionary in his hand and left as abruptly as he came. Aaron assumed he was on his way to Zalman's room to deliver the same message.

For the next several weeks Aaron and Zalman were interrogated by Polish speaking British officers for several hours each morning. The questions centered on their lives and activities over the past few years. The questioning stopped abruptly each day at noon, and English classes for an additional two hours a day from 2:00 PM to 4:00 PM filled their afternoons. They were issued "temporary" commissions as captains in the British Army and after two days were moved from their luxurious hotel room to an officers' barracks just outside of London.

Aaron had a natural ability with foreign languages and enjoyed the challenge of learning English. He would study for several hours each night and made rapid progress. For Zalman, learning English was a chore, and he became frustrated with his lack of linguistic ability. It irritated him to see Aaron comfortably chatting in English with the locals after only a few weeks.

The daily morning debriefings elicited two major intelligence factors. The British intelligence officers were not overly interested in the plight of the Jews being slaughtered in the camps and tended to gloss over the extent of the atrocities that Aaron and Zalman would describe as having witnessed. They tended to cross-examine on those issues with questions like, "Well, gentlemen, did you actually see people being forced into the gas chambers?" Aaron and Zalman would answer that they had not because the only witnesses to those events were either German guards or ashes. The next question would be along the lines of, "Then you only assumed that those things were happening, isn't that correct?" Aaron could almost rationalize the thought process of the intelligence officers, most of whom did not look kindly upon Polish Semites, even if they were "temporary" English officers. The carnage described was so heinous that it almost defied comprehension. Therefore, granting that there were some acts of cruelty, the extent and nature surely must be exaggerated by these witnesses.

Aaron and Zalman, rather than encourage the enmity of their hosts, and early on realizing that this was not the proper forum to dwell on the barbarism of the death camp, tended to move on to the phase of their life after their escape. On this subject the British had a keen interest and encouraged them to minutely describe their activities. Aaron and Zalman had "accidentally" become experts in German small arms having "liberated" or "stolen" and then used almost every small arms automatic weapon issued by the German army.

The interrogators spent two entire mornings questioning them about the effectiveness of the new German Model Sturmgewehr assault rifle that had been Zalman's favorite weapon. It was the best light arms weapon the Nazis produced and Zalman, in Polish, preened a bit as he described how easily it handled and how mechanically perfect it was during fire. With a 30-round double-column removable magazine, the weapon fired at 500 RPM, using a short 7.92-mm caliber intermediate cartridge. The gun weighed about 11.5 pounds and Zalman detailed how he had used the three-foot-long rifle in a series of hit-and-run attacks that he, Alexy, and Aaron staged. They even had him draw a freehand sketch of the parts of the rifle, which Zalman had often broken down and cleaned.

They also showed great interest in Aaron's favorite, which was the lighter weight submachine pistol. It had a new light alloy frame and folding shoulder stock. Aaron would describe how the weapon with the butt folded was only two feet long and could easily be concealed under his overcoat as he walked with his victims. With a 32-round double-column removable magazine using a 9-mm Parabellum cartridge, the eight-pound machine pistol created a shower of death from Aaron's hand on numerous occasions. It was this weapon that he had used during the attack on the train. At final count they calculated that Alexy, Aaron, and Zalman had accounted for over ninety-five known kills of enemy military personnel. The man hours and military material used by the Nazis to attempt to capture them were incalculable, and when one of the interrogators speculated that they were probably the most hunted men in the German-occupied territories, he was not far from the truth.

Unknown to Aaron and Zalman, the British intelligence secretly implemented a plan to continue the charade that the "Juden Stern" was still in Poland and had two of their deep cover agents leaving small hand-drawn Stars of David on paper scraps dropped by an occasionally assassinated enemy soldier. They reasoned that even though the German reprisals would be swift and brutal, the perpetuated myth that this hunted hero was still in Poland served to continue to divert the efforts of scores of soldiers from the battlefield.

By the time the debriefings ended Aaron and Zalman had gained the grudging respect of their interrogators.

"Other than their obvious attempts to exaggerate the atrocities heaped upon the Jewish prisoners in the camp," the questioning officers reported, "we believe they have been relatively truthful, extremely resourceful, and extraordinarily lucky. They have done more to damage the enemy and confuse the German authorities than any known allied espionage organization currently operating in the German-occupied territories," read the final paragraph of the British Intelligence report on Zalman Zacksman and Aaron Garlovsky.

CHAPTER 15

After four weeks the morning debriefings were abruptly canceled, and Aaron and Zalman were assigned to train with a special "enemy infiltration" unit at an English countryside estate where they acted as "advisors" to a select group of men and women who were preparing to be sent behind enemy lines. Neither Aaron nor Zalman had any desire to return to Poland but felt that as soon as the English had no further use for them they would be returned to Fibek's partisans. At least, they reasoned, they should be able to bring some needed supplies from Fibek's shopping list when they went back.

Upon returning to their barracks one evening they were unpleasantly surprised to find Captain Desmond Stein surveying their quarters with obvious disdain.

"A bit messy, aren't we?" he offered and eliciting no response from Aaron or Zalman and knowing that they would refuse any direct command he gave them, he continued in Polish, "Would you, gentlemen, please accompany me. There is someone who would like to meet you." Both Aaron and Zalman took a perverse pleasure in antagonizing the arrogant Captain, and it was Aaron who replied in proper English, "Who wants to see us, and why?"

Now, taken aback by Aaron's obvious, newly acquired, excellent command of English, Stein responded, in English, "I'm not at liberty to say, but if you will trust me just this once I believe the meeting will be to your benefit." Aaron looked at Zalman and after a few moments of silence, Stein continued, "I believe these people will treat for a meal as the meeting is to take place at a small but excellent Middle Eastern-type restaurant."

An hour later, dressed in civilian clothes, they entered a tiny dimly lit restaurant in London's east end. The aroma was intoxicating as they passed diners noisily slurping hot golden liquid from large bowls of chicken soup filled with noodles and matzo balls and soaking up the last drops with pieces of freshly baked braided challah. These were the smells that Aaron and Zalman had known as children, and a wave of nostalgia engulfed them both. They were led by the proprietor to a table at the rear of the restaurant where a late middle-aged man and woman sat at a table filled with the foodstuffs of a bygone era. It had been years since Aaron and Zalman had seen gefilte fish or chopped chicken livers in schmaltz. Zalman could only utter, "I didn't know places like this still existed."

The couple smiled at them, and the man said "Somehow, gentlemen, we survive. Hopefully places like this will be here long after you and I are gone." The man stood and offered his hand, "I'm Wolf Posner, and this is my wife, Elisa." He could not have been more than 5'5" tall, but there was an aura of power that surrounded him. Then looking at Captain Stein, Posner continued, "You will, of course, join us, Desmond." It was an order, not an invitation, and Stein quickly mumbled an acceptance and sat down. "Enjoy yourselves, please, gentlemen. We can talk after you eat."

Bowls of chicken soup filled with noodles and large matzo balls were brought piping hot. Thereafter, plates of kishke, tsimas, and broiled chicken filled the table. As he finished eating Aaron looked around and quickly observed that theirs was the only table in the restaurant with these delicacies. Wolf Posner noticed Aaron's quizzical look and, as if reading his mind, said, "We thought you boys had earned something special. Anyway, to paraphrase an old saying, beware of Jews bearing gifts," and he laughed heartily at his own play on words.

Over glasses of tea and honey cake Wolf Posner got directly to the point. "Gentlemen, we know all about you. We know where you come from and what you have been through. The European world that you came from before this damned war started lives only in our memories and will not rise again in our lifetime." He paused to sip some tea and take a bite of cake. Wolf Posner had been trained as a lawyer, and was a persuasive speaker who was just getting started on his audience who were too stuffed with food to move. "But," he continued, "there is a new world that needs you and wants you desperately. We want you to come to Palestine." His voice rose a bit as if it was an effort to control his emotions as he spoke. "On the holiest days I'm sure you heard your parents and grandparents say, 'Next year in Jerusalem.' Gentlemen, next year is here." Again he sipped tea from his glass. "When this monster Hitler is finally dead and buried we will have one more war to win, a war for independence in our own country, a place where you are not a visitor, a second class citizen, or an outsider, but a place where you are truly home." Now there was a fire in his voice and his face was turning red with emotion. His wife put her hand on his own, "Wolf, you're scaring the boys."

"Not these boys, Elisa, these boys don't scare."

Neither Aaron nor Zalman could answer. Thoughts raced through their minds and both concluded that they would probably prefer going anywhere other than back to German-occupied Poland. Neither of them could have found Palestine on a map. "Of course when you get there," Wolf continued, "you'll have to learn to speak Hebrew," and Zalman groaned.

USA/Israel: 1968

CHAPTER 16

The National Junior Tennis School was based in Miami. The school, actually a dormitory located in the middle of a dozen tennis courts, became Kevin's home for the next five years. His days consisted of attending school classes from 9:00 AM to 2:00 PM each weekday and tennis instruction from 2:30 PM to 5:30 PM. On weekends tennis started at 9:00 AM until noon and again from 2:00 PM until 5:00 PM. There were exactly one hundred students aged thirteen to seventeen and they came from all over the U.S. and a dozen foreign countries, although it seemed as though most were from Florida and California. There were seventy boys and thirty girls, with one professional tennis instructor for every four students. The school director was Steve Wild, a pudgy taskmaster in his mid-fifties whose claim to fame was that he had been a Wimbledon quarter finalist in the mid-1930s. His students revered him. He was tough but fair and pushed each student to their limits. They knew it was a privilege to be in the school, and he gave each student their money's worth. Anyone not working, either on the court or academically, to his or her potential got a public tongue lashing. If it continued, without cause, they were summarily sent home and replaced by the next applicant on a long waiting list. There were very few dropouts; Uncle Steveo, as he was called by the students, ran a tight ship and insisted that each student write postcards home at least once a week. He insisted on postcards so he could read them before they were mailed and nip any potential problem before it got out of hand. Kevin dutifully wrote one card to Doc and one to Aaron each week. They always said the same thing, "Feel fine, doing well. Kevin." In mid-summer for six weeks and at Christmas for one week they closed the school, and everyone would go home with instructions not to pick up a tennis racquet until they returned from their vacation. This eliminated the possibility of picking up any injuries or bad habits that couldn't be immediately corrected. It also served to make them anxious to return to school to start playing again. Kevin acclimated quickly to the school and enjoyed the training and competition.

By the time he graduated high school, Kevin had received offers of a full athletic scholarship from every major university that had a quality tennis program. He was sixteen years old and had grown to 6'1" and weighed 160 pounds. He knew his father wanted him to go to college, although Kevin had reservations. Doc sided with his father and suggested that he take one of the scholarships and give college a try for at least a year or two. But Kevin was anxious to compete with the best in his sport. He was ranked in the top five nationally in the eighteen-year-old division, and several of his contemporaries were considering turning professional. Kevin reasoned that in the past few years tennis had changed from a sport for amateurs to one where a professional player could earn a decent livelihood. It was popularized by television, and most of the current great players were now on the professional circuit. Even the grand Wimbledon tournament was now open to amateurs and professionals alike.

"I've spent the last five years training for a tennis career," he would say. "I have to find out if I have what it takes to make a living at it. If I fall on my face I can always say at least I tried." In the end there was no arguing with him. Aaron called Steve Wild to get his opinion and was told that Kevin had the ability to make it big in the professional ranks with a few years of intense tournament seasoning. Aaron offered to give him enough money for a year on the road as a high school graduation gift. Kevin insisted the funds be a loan and not a gift. With the decision to delay college made, Kevin and Doc meticulously planned his schedule of tournaments for the coming year.

He would play the professional tournaments on the Midwest circuit for the next few months and have the opportunity to come home to Chicago often between tournaments to rest instead of being on the road for prolonged periods of time. If he did well, he would move on to the tough southern United States circuit in the late fall and winter, and then, if his record warranted, try the European circuit next year. Heady stuff for an almost seventeen-year-old just out of high school.

CHAPTER 17

The main draws of the various midwestern professional tennis tournaments usually started on a Wednesday with thirty-two singles players and sixteen doubles teams. Finals were on Sunday with the winner usually pocketing about $300 in prize money. If the match was exceptionally well-played spectators would pass the hat among themselves, and the finalists could pick up an extra $50 to $100 a piece. No one got rich this way, but if you did well you made enough for meals, a motel room, and bus fare or gas to get you to the next tournament. Competition was fierce and more often than not the players called their own lines until the semi-finals when there was usually a chair umpire. Each town seemed to have its local star who would redefine the concept of fair play when it came to calling lines. If the local players got to the semis or finals it was not uncommon for a close relative to be the chair umpire or linesman. After six tournaments in Wisconsin and Illinois, Kevin, who was the youngest player on the circuit, had won two events and gotten to the finals in two more. His reputation as a tough competitor was growing, and he now typically found himself seeded in the top four.

The circuit's next stop was Indianapolis, Indiana, where first prize was a whopping $1,000, enough money to support a "circuit rat," as they were called, for a few months on the road. Kevin breezed easily into the quarter finals where the next day he was slated to play the local favorite, Eric Fox, a former All-American from Purdue. Kevin was showering in the locker room after his morning match when it happened.

Three men grabbed him as he left the shower and dragged him struggling and kicking to a corner of the deserted locker room. The blows seemed to rain from all sides and stopped only when he lost consciousness. When he awoke he was in a stark white hospital room with his father dozing in a chair at the side of the bed. Kevin's groan woke Aaron who got up and leaned over the bed.

"Kevin, can you hear me?" he asked.

"Yeah, but everything hurts."

"Well, they did a good job on you. You've got some broken ribs and a fractured right wrist. They must have thought you were right-handed."

"How long have I been here?"

"Two days. It's Saturday, Kevin. What happened?"

Kevin described how the three men beat him until he lost consciousness.

"Would you recognize them?"

"I think so. They were all kinda young guys. I just have the feeling it had something to do with the match I was scheduled to play in the quarters."

He left the hospital the next day with Aaron and against the advice of his hospital physician.

"If you leave I will not be responsible for anything that happens to you. You have had some severe internal injuries and should stay here at least for a few more days," the Doctor warned. But Aaron had a mission. He helped Kevin dress and told him, "Mr. Fox made it to the finals, and we are going to see who is in his cheering section this afternoon."

They got to the tennis stadium at the start of the second set, and they stood at the fringe of the crowd. Kevin was wearing sunglasses and a jacket draped over his casted wrist. He felt weak and light-headed, and Aaron held his arm to steady him.

Kevin scanned the crowd but wasn't able to see his assailants and started to feel that he may have been mistaken about them being tied to Eric Fox. Abruptly the match ended and the crowd cheered lustily, as their favorite had won. As the winner raised his arms in victory he looked over a section of the crowd where three young men were standing and cheering.

"There, those three guys in the second row. I'm sure it's them. Let's get the cops," Kevin was dizzy with pain and the excitement of seeing his attackers.

"No, no police," Aaron said, never taking his eyes off the men who had left their seats and were now crowded around the winner laughing and slapping him on the back. "For all we know, they are the police. I'll take care of this. Wait here." Aaron limped over to the winner and the three men and with a big smile said, "Congratulations, you're a wonderful player. Are these your coaches?"

"Thanks, no, just friends," Fox said as he packed his gear.

"It's a shame you didn't get to play the Garland boy.

I would have liked to have seen that match." He watched their faces as he spoke, and read guilt on all four as they turned now ignoring him.

Aaron next limped over to the chair umpire who was talking to a linesman.

"That was a fine match, you did a good job," he said in his most patronizing whine.

"Thanks."

"By the way, do you know who those men are with Mr. Fox?"

The umpire looked over to where Aaron was pointing. "Oh, those four are inseparable, we call them the four musketeers. The largest two are the Steiner brothers, Tom and Bob, and the dark-haired one is Mike Smith. They all went to Purdue. Kind of a rough bunch, but really just good old boys."

CHAPTER 18

That evening Aaron and Kevin took the bus back to Chicago. Kevin, on pain medication and weak, slept all the way home.

They arrived home at midnight and both went right to sleep. The next morning Aaron called Doc to tell him what happened and asked Doc to check on Kevin for the next few days as Aaron said he had some business out of town. Doc thought it was strange for Aaron, who rarely left the neighborhood to be leaving the city, but assured Aaron he would take care of Kevin.

That afternoon Aaron, carrying a small duffel bag, took the bus back to Indianapolis.

At the bus station in Indianapolis he located a public telephone directory and looked up "Steiner, Thomas and Robert," both lived at the same address. He then looked up the address of Michael Smith and Eric Fox. We'll start with the brothers, he thought. He rented a car, purposely not asking directions from the rental agent. He drove to a gas station and got directions to the Steiner brothers' address, which turned out to be a small rented townhouse in the better part of town, and then worked his way to Fox and Smith's apartment. For two days and nights Aaron did a thorough reconnaissance on his quarry. On the third night he made his move. It was about 7:00 PM and still light out. He parked about 100 yards from the Steiner townhouse and waited. About an hour later the Steiner brothers came out and both got into a red Pontiac convertible that was parked in front of the house. Aaron waited for another half hour until it was dark and then, carrying the small duffel bag, limped slowly to the rear of the townhouse where he proceeded to quickly break a window and slip into the dark house. Once inside he opened the bag and removed a small flashlight and an iron truncheon about two feet long wrapped with black electrical tape. He used the flashlight sparingly to get his bearings and removed the light bulb from the front hall where someone coming into the dark house would first turn on the light. He sat in a stiff wooden chair looking out the front window hoping that the brothers would return alone. It could be complicated if they came home with other men or dates. Aaron's actions were calm and methodical, and he was in complete control of his emotions. Around 10:00 PM the red Pontiac with the top now up screeched into the parking spot in front of the house and the two brothers got out. He heard one say, "Hurry up, I forgot my key and I've gotta take a leak." He heard the key in the lock and the door open. "Shit, the light's out, I can't see a fucking thing." Aaron had been waiting in the dark room and could see them quite clearly when he struck. He hit the first brother to come in across the left knee and he could feel bone and cartilage shatter. The man collapsed to the floor grabbing his knee, screaming in agony. The second brother, not being able to see, yelled, "Tom, what...." when Aaron's truncheon struck him across the face, breaking his jaw. As the man reached to his jaw, Aaron struck him on the left side across the ribs, and he crumpled to the floor next to his brother. Aaron then brought the heavy club down on the ribs of the first victim who again screamed in pain. "Scream again and you're both dead," he whispered and he snapped on the flashlight into their faces. They were both groaning in pain and he whispered again, "Whose idea was it to attack the Garland boy?" Neither answered, and the truncheon came down again breaking the right wrist of the brother whose broken jaw was probably preventing him from speaking even if he had wanted to. Aaron shined the flashlight on the broken wrist and whispered to the other brother, "If you don't tell me now, I will break your arm within two seconds."

"It was Eric." He couldn't get the words out fast enough. "It was Eric. He knew he couldn't win. He told us to break the kid's wrist, he said 'break the kike's wrist,'" he fairly screamed the indictment against his lifelong friend.

"Who broke his wrist?" Aaron whispered.

"Mike, Mike did it."

"If you're lying to me I'm going to come back and I will cut out your tongue. Believe me," he whispered, and the two men on the floor bleeding and broken did believe. "If you or your brother call your friends or the police I will break your other wrist."

"My other wrist?" And the truncheon flashed across

his right wrist smashing bones and tendons. Without another word Aaron snapped off the flashlight, picked up the small duffel bag, and limped out the front door, quietly closing the door behind him on the broken bodies of his sobbing victims.

Mike Smith and Eric Fox had been tennis teammates at Purdue and shared a two-bedroom apartment near the local indoor tennis club owned by Smith's family. While Fox was attempting to make a name on the professional circuit, Smith was teaching tennis at the club. Most evenings they ended their days drilling and practicing against each other. Usually being the last ones there, they would lock up the club. This evening they finished drilling at about 11:30 PM and were in the shower room alone.

"Did you talk to Tom or Bob today?" Eric asked as they were drying off.

"No, but those bastards could be hung over for two days the way they've been drinking." Suddenly the lights in the locker room went out.

"Damn, I'll bet we blew a fuse," Smith muttered. "I'll go check." He wrapped a towel around his waist and stumbled to the room where the electrical box was located. He had been gone for about five minutes when Fox called out, "Hey, Mike, what's taking so long?" There was no answer. "Hey, Mike, you O.K.?" He found his shorts, pulled them on and went looking for his friend. "Mike, you asshole, quit screwing around!" he shouted. Fox saw what looked like a light from a flashlight from a small room at the far end of the darkened indoor courts and he trotted over to the room. He pushed the half-opened door and saw Smith lying face down on the floor with a flashlight lying next to him. "Mike, what the hell happened?" and he knelt and quickly turned his friend over and gasped as he saw his bloodied and broken face and jaw. He felt rather than heard a presence behind him and turned just in time to raise his arm to block the blow from an iron bar. The bar caught him on the right elbow, and he felt no pain for a moment but could feel his arm dangling straight down. The shock then hit his brain. He tried to scream but the sound never came as the iron bar caught him across the mouth knocking out all of his front teeth and breaking his lower jaw. As he slumped to the floor he heard a whispering voice say, "You made a bad mistake, young man, and your tennis career just ended." The iron bar next cracked against his left knee, shattering bone and cartilage and forever ending what had been a short but promising tennis career.

The police in Indianapolis received four different stories from the four victims. Two said that there were two assailants that beat them. Two said there was only one, but he was a large man who could have been a Negro or Indian. The only things they all agreed upon was that they never clearly saw his face, their assailant seemed to limp, and whispered with some sort of an accent.

CHAPTER 19

It was six weeks before Kevin was able to resume playing tennis, and he returned to the practice courts with a renewed vigor. In the past seven years he had never been off the tennis court for that long a period of time. He started slowly, rallying with Doc for a few hours a day. After a week of moderate practice he was able to run again with limited pain in his ribs. He next moved his practices up to two hours, twice a day, drilling against the best of the local Midwest talent. After a month of practice, he felt strong enough physically and his game was again sharp enough to resume his tournament play, and he scheduled four Florida Circuit events over the next eight weeks. He called Steve Wild in Miami and made arrangements to use the National Junior Tennis School as his home base. Steveo was more than happy to accommodate what he called his "soon to be famous alumnus."

By the time the final Florida tournament was over Kevin had won $1,500. More importantly, he had reached the semifinals in two events and won the last event in Miami with Steve and most of the students of the school in attendance. The consistent good showings boosted his world ranking to the high 100s.

He celebrated his eighteenth birthday that September in Florida at Steve's home and made plans to travel to Europe to play the fast grass courts of England and then the slow red clay of the rest of the continent.

For the next eighteen months Kevin lived the life of a tennis vagabond. He played red clay in Hango and Ekenes in Finland, grass courts at Roehampton and Tunbridge Wells and the Edgebaston Priory Club outside of Birmingham, England. Clay again in Bostaad and Lycornas in Sweden. He went to tournaments in Thessaloniki and Corfu in Greece. Spain was a favorite; he played Tarragona south of Barcelona on the Mediterranean, and then won at Granada. He moved on to Istanbul and then to Ankara where he won again.

He traveled by himself and found that his dollars went further in Europe than in the States. Travel by train was easy, and bed and board accommodations were good and cheap. He had a natural penchant for languages and enjoyed trying to speak to people in their native tongue. Many of the small tournaments, hungry for good talent, gave the players housing and food during the event. His only restriction was a request from his father not to play in Germany. Since he had taken money as a loan from his father, he felt morally obligated to honor the request.

By the end of a year in Europe he was ranked among the top 100 players in the world and after paying Aaron back the loan, had even put a few dollars in the bank.

It was during this period that Kevin began to question and reflect deeply upon his relationship with his father. Sure, his father had provided food, clothing and shelter, but he had always envied the easy way his contemporaries related to their parents. Aaron never pushed him nor did he appear to share in Kevin's success. He had given financial support, but Kevin rationalized that this was his father's way of compensating for his lack of affection or real interest in his son. Kevin could not remember his father ever putting his arm around him or telling him that he had done well. They had simply existed in the same house after his mother died.

He never questioned his father in depth about his past, although he knew that the numbered tattoo on his father's left forearm had left deep emotional scars and that his father's limp had been the result of a wound received during a war in Israel. He knew also that his father had been born in Poland, but other than his Uncle Samuel, who died before he was born, his father never mentioned any member of his family. Kevin never knew a family of aunts, uncles, and cousins. In the time that he traveled alone in Europe he corresponded regularly with Doc and Steve, but only infrequently did he send a short post card to his father, never getting a card in return. Feeling isolated and rejected, Kevin became increasingly bitter toward Aaron.

"If my father wants it this way, so be it," he thought, "it's time to cut the cord anyway, and we'll both probably be happier." Near the end of his time abroad he wrote a short letter to Aaron saying that he would be returning to the States in about a month and would be moving permanently to the Miami area where the weather conditions would allow him to train all year. He enclosed a check for $500 with a notation that it was an interest payment on the loan his father had given him to start his professional career. He knew that his father had never expected nor wanted to be repaid. The "interest" was purely a vindictive act on Kevin's part. The check was sent as a message that Kevin was now totally independent and did not need nor want Aaron's help anymore.

If only he had cared, Kevin reflected on the flight back from Europe, we could possibly have been friends. God, we look so much alike.

Kevin found a small apartment near Steve Wild's school in Miami, where he was able to use the practice facilities in exchange for some minimal teaching duties. With his ranking in the top 100, he was now eligible to play the larger prize money tournaments and could get directly into the main draw of the prestigious grand slam events including Wimbledon and the U.S. Open. It was early 1975 and the golden age of professional tennis was dawning. Two years earlier the world's best tennis players had boycotted Wimbledon and forever changed the face of the sport. A Yugoslavian player had refused to play for his native country in the Davis Cup Tournament and as a result was banned from playing at Wimbledon by the International Lawn Tennis Federation. The professional players, tired of amateur officials controlling their destiny, successfully banded together and seventy-nine of eighty-one Association of Tennis Professionals members who were scheduled to play Wimbledon that year withdrew, and ultimately took control of the game by forcing rule changes favoring player's rights and having players' representatives active in decision making roles.

Prize money, fueled by television, was escalating at a record pace. Where only a few years earlier the winner of the prestigious U.S. Pro Indoor Championship in Philadelphia had won a tape recorder as first prize, it was now possible for a top fifty ranked player to win $100,000 and more in prize money on the professional circuit.

Confident of his talent and at nineteen years of age certain that he was immortal, Kevin had a disastrous year. He took it upon himself to schedule his tournament play, make his own travel plans, and arrange his own practice schedule. As any professional will tell a potential client if you represent yourself you have a fool for a client. Similarly, a professional athlete who takes it upon himself to handle all aspects of his career will quickly find his performance suffering. Kevin's world ranking dropped to below 200 that year, and he was forced to again play qualifying events to get into the main draws of the big money tournaments. He had to win three rounds of a qualifying tournament over a three-day period, and when he did get into a main draw he was already physically exhausted and usually had to play a seeded player in the first round. He was barely able to earn enough money to sustain himself and had to supplement his prize money earnings with teaching and exhibition events. Kevin started to believe that he would never get over the hump and began to think that he had made a serious mistake by not taking one of the numerous college scholarships that had been available. At least he would have gotten a free education and some preparation for a career in later life other than just hitting a ball over a net more times than the other guy. His letters to Doc, once so full of optimism, now were dull and smacked of despair.

Doc felt the defeat in Kevin's correspondence and decided to meet and discuss the problem with Aaron. He was surprised when he discovered that Kevin had stopped writing to his father altogether.

"You mean he hasn't written to you in six months?" he asked incredulously.

"No, we seem to have lost touch," Aaron said with a shake of his head. "It happens in the best of families," and he smiled sadly at Doc. "All right, Doc, let's put my wounded feelings aside. What do we do to help Kevin?"

"I've been thinking about it. Aaron, I think what he needs is a good coach and someone who can handle his travel and scheduling so that he can concentrate on playing and not be exhausted before a tournament starts." Aaron thought the idea made sense.

"How do we get him such a coach? It's got to be someone who know's what he's doing and someone Kevin will respect."

"Aaron, I think I know the right guy, but he's expensive and Kevin probably can't afford him." They sat for a while discussing a plan. Then, Aaron stood up and looked directly at Doc.

"You just get the best. I'll pay the fees, but Kevin's not to know, OK?" Doc nodded.

"Aaron, you're a better father than he deserves."

"No, that's not true. Doc, you just make sure that he won't find out about our secret, or he'll probably not accept the coach."

CHAPTER 20

They started to put their plan into effect with an evening call to Kevin from Doc. After opening pleasantries and inquiries into Kevin's nonexistent love life, which was an inside joke between them, Doc opened the door.

"Kevin, I need a favor from you. A friend of mine wants to spend a few months in Florida. He's just gone through a tough divorce and hasn't got much dough.... "

Kevin listened as Doc told him that his friend was a talented tennis coach and manager and would trade his services for room and board and spending money for a few months. It was almost too good to be true. Kevin knew he was ruining his career by doing everything himself, and because his career was failing, he could not afford a coach and manager. If Doc's friend knew what he was doing, it would be great. If he didn't, Kevin could always call it off and he'd be no worse for wear.

A week later Seymour "Sy" Rosen appeared at Kevin's front door. He was a nondescript looking man in his mid-thirties. A little overweight, thinning brown hair, glasses, and standing about 5'8" tall, Sy was the type of person who could rob a bank in front of a dozen witnesses and no one would quite remember what he looked like. Kevin soon found out, however, that he had the personality of a Marine drill sergeant. That first night they laid out ground rules and agreed that until one or the other decided to call it quits, they would each give 100 percent. The minimum time would be thirty days, and neither would quit the arrangement before then. Kevin would supply room and board and $50.00 per week, and Sy would be coach, travel agent, and manager. Kevin's only job would be to train, practice, and play tournaments; Sy would do the rest. Kevin didn't ask for any references because he knew Doc would not have set this up if he didn't feel Sy could do the job. They started early the next morning with Sy, a man of few words, announcing his program.

"Kevin, I've seen you play several times. Your groundstrokes are sound and need no change, but I believe in four things: serve and volley, heavy topspin, complete concentration, and conditioning. If you work with me for a month, I truly believe you'll be back on the road to success."

"OK," Kevin answered, "you've got my undivided attention, for at least a month."

Their days started at 6:30 AM with stretching exercises and a brisk three-mile run. They then ate a large breakfast, showered, and moved to the court where serve and volley became the "password." Kevin had always primarily been a baseliner, relying on his steady powerful groundstrokes to keep his opponent pinned back and on the defensive. Sy's philosophy was to get to the net as quickly as possible.

"He who controls the net controls the match," he would say over and over. They worked on concentration, focusing not on the match or set but each stroke of each point. Outside distractions were to be shut out. Sy would purposely schedule practice on courts next to a beginner whose play would be a distraction to other players, or on public courts where the noise would normally be upsetting. In the evening they would work with light free weights and do sit-ups and push-ups until Kevin would be completely exhausted. Sy was always pushing, "Five more Kevin, c'mon five more, what are you a pussy, c'mon five more." Kevin never made it to watch the 11:00 news, as he would fall into bed totally wiped out by 9:00 PM. At 6:00 AM he awoke and they started again.

During the next thirty days they spent almost every waking hour together. At night after Kevin would fall into bed, Sy would prepare a handwritten outline of their activities and progress for that day, copies of which he would then secretly mail weekly to Aaron with a personal letter. Aaron would then call Doc to review the letter with him, and they agreed that it appeared as though their plan was working. Each week Aaron would deposit $500 into Sy's local Chicago savings account.

Intensely competitive by nature, Kevin rarely displayed emotion on the court, and to watch his demeanor, it was difficult to tell whether he was winning or losing a match.

"We've got to change your image," Sy would say. "You're in a spectator sport and people will pay not only for your talent, but they want to see some emotion as well. No more Mr. Nice Guy; if you're pissed off over a bad line call, let them know about it. The chair umpire and linespeople may not like you, but you can be damn sure they'll think twice before giving you a bad call if they think you may embarrass them on national television."

At the end of the thirty days Kevin felt strong and in the best physical condition of his life. He was still wary of his ability to transform his game from a baseliner to a serve and volley player, and he and Sy agreed that it was time to return to the tournaments to give it the acid test.

They selected a few hard court tournaments for small prize money. This would allow Kevin to get directly into the main draw even though his tennis ranking had dropped to around 250. The hard court surface was best suited for his new aggressive style of play. They agreed that Sy would travel with Kevin for two weeks, handle the arrangements, and they would split any prize money that Kevin won.

The trip was a smashing success with Kevin winning both tournaments in straight sets even after being penalized a game in the finals of the second tournament for throwing his racquet and verbally abusing a linesman after a questionable line call. The small crowd booed his antics and cheered his talent. After expenses they split $2,000 and agreed to the same formula for the next month.

Sy made all the travel and tournament arrangements in addition to training and practicing with Kevin every day. Kevin's job was to win matches, which he now did with regularity. His world ranking began to climb, even though he was now regarded as an "oddball" on the court and subject to flying off the handle on any close call. The crowds started to flock to his matches, for they knew that in addition to exciting tennis, there was always the chance of some on court fireworks when that Garland kid was playing.

Now, regarded as an emerging star with crowd appeal, he was solicited by representatives of tennis apparel and equipment manufacturers, all of whom he directed to Sy, who would carefully screen each offer before making any recommendation to Kevin. Soon he found himself making more money off the court than on it, but he knew that this would last only as long as he continued to win and the crowds kept coming. By Kevin's twenty-first birthday his world ranking had climbed to 50. He was 6'2" tall and weighed 180 pounds. His dark curly hair and handsome features were starting to make him an idol of the teenage set, and it was impossible to pick up a tennis magazine and not see his picture hawking some product for which he had been well compensated.

"What a stroke of luck, us finding each other," Kevin toasted to Sy at his small birthday party. "If we're not careful, we might end up rich." All at the table, which included his newly retained personal attorney, Al Patzik, and two of Kevin's apparel sponsors, laughed politely.

The party had been held at the Doral Country Club in Miami, where Kevin was invited to play an exhibition match. The party ended at 11:00 PM and Kevin, who was unaccustomed to drinking, had consumed three beers and two glasses of champagne. He unsteadily made it back to his complimentary suite in the penthouse. He fumbled for his room key and thought he heard giggling behind the door but figured it was coming from an adjoining suite. He entered the suite and headed straight for the bathroom to relieve his bladder, which was ready to burst. Then he heard the giggling again and flipped on the bedroom light.

"What the hell is going on. . . . ?"

They couldn't have been more than eighteen, sitting stark naked on the bed, two of them with pillows at their backs. "C'mon birthday boy," one purred, "We're your present for the night, compliments of Goldfine Apparel," and they both jumped out of the bed and grabbed for him. Without the alcohol he probably would have asked them to leave or left himself, but tonight the world was his oyster.

What the hell, he thought, I'm entitled to a break. I just hope they're not minors, and he let himself be taken to the bed where for the next three hours they did amazing things to him and to each other.

The next few years flew by and Kevin Garland's world ranking climbed steadily. He was a promoter's dream and drew large crowds whenever he stepped on the court. Even his detractors had to concede that the kid had great talent. On a given day there was no one he couldn't beat. His first Grand Slam title came on the red clay of Stade Roland Garros, and the win catapulted him to "superstar" status. But true to his "bad boy" image, he infuriated the French crowd when he told a T.V. interviewer that the French knew even less about tennis than the Italians, who knew nothing. The comment cost him a $5,000 fine, and he was almost refused entry into the Italian Open. The following year he rubbed their noses in it by winning both the Italian and French Open titles and refusing to grant any interviews for which he was again fined. Sy felt they were lucky to get out of Italy alive, as the fans threw coins on the court at Kevin throughout the final match. On two occasions Kevin picked them up and threw them back at the crowd, requiring police protection around the court. T.V. ratings worldwide for the Italian final that year were the highest of all time, and sponsors were lined up for the next year prepared to pay premium advertising rates on the express condition that Kevin Garland returned.

That year Kevin was constantly pressured and pursued by the super-agents who promised him untold millions if he would sign with their agency. He was tempted on several occasions but he was just superstitious enough to stick with Sy Rosen. Like many gifted athletes, Kevin did not want to change his luck. He was confident of his abilities but realized that an injury as insignificant as a minor ankle or wrist sprain could cost him a fortune. He had been lucky with Sy and although he felt Sy was now grossly overpaid he did not want to change his luck.

CHAPTER 21

Kevin was now a bona fide star with an ego to match his star status. Several well-paid employees depended upon his ability to hit a tennis ball for their livelihood. His accountant, lawyer, and financial planner all met weekly to chart an investment strategy for K.G., Inc. An office staff of three created and typed his fan letters, mailed out publicity photos, arranged travel schedules, and paid bills. A full-time publicist kept his name in print with exclusive leaks to gossip and sports columnists. Kevin Garland was a world class personality, not just an athlete. He traveled with a personal trainer who doubled as a bodyguard, and an ever changing girlfriend, usually a model or rising starlet. Heading the entire staff was Sy Rosen, whose official title was Executive Vice President of K.G., Inc. and whose real strength lay in the fact that he was the only one who took no crap from Kevin.

At twenty-four years of age, Kevin was ranked fourth in the world, but in the hearts and minds of tennis fans worldwide there was no denying that he was number one. His matches always drew standing room only crowds who were assured of seeing great tennis and usually an emotional explosion. He rarely disappointed them. Generally despised by his confreres, they nonetheless unanimously admired his talent. "If he'd only keep his mouth shut," they muttered when he was out of earshot, but they all knew that he generated the big bucks off the court as much for his mouth as his racquet.

"Stay focused for at least five more years," his financial advisors told him, "by then your investments will have made you rich beyond your wildest dreams." What was left unsaid was they also would be rich and for that they could put up with this young, handsome, arrogant ass whom they felt believed his own press releases.

He would still occasionally call Doc, usually from some exotic port of call. The conversations were short, and Doc got the feeling that the calls were made as a way for Kevin to say to Doc "Look how well I've done, and I've done it all by myself." The calls always left Doc feeling empty afterwards. Kevin would never ask about his father, and Doc knew the two had not communicated for years. A line from Kipling always ran through Doc's mind after talking to Kevin, "If you can walk with the kings and yet not lose the common touch. . . . you'll be a man my son." Too bad, kid, you're a long way from manhood.

Aaron's life had changed little over the past few years. He had no desire to add to his real estate holdings and filled his days doing menial janitorial duties that he could well afford to delegate to someone else. The makeup of the neighborhood changed, and his tenants were now new first generation Americans with last names of Patel, Lee, and Kwan rather than Cohen and Greenberg. The park across the street still rang with laughter and shouts of the competitors, and the old men now played dominos and mah jong rather then pinochle, but other than that things in the neighborhood remained pretty much the same.

"I saw your son on the Johnny Carson show last night, Mr. Garland," one of his tenants said as he passed him in the hallway. "You must be very proud of him. He's so handsome."

"Yes," he answered, "I'm very proud of him."

"Have you ever seen him compete?" Doc asked Aaron one night as they were taking a walk.

"Have I ever seen who compete?" Aaron asked.

"Don't be a jerk, Aaron, you know exactly who I mean."

"Oh, you mean Boy Wonder, the star of T.V. and the Johnny Carson show? No, I've never seen him compete in person, but I've watched him play on television."

"Why don't we jump on a plane and fly over to Europe to watch him play in person at the French Open?"

"Doc, I was born in Europe and I left it for good many years ago. Wild horses couldn't drag me back there. Besides I've got buildings that need attention."

"Bullshit, Aaron, you can well afford to leave for a few days. If you won't go to Europe, let's watch him at the U.S. Open at the end of August. I'll have Sy Rosen get us tickets and Kevin won't have to know we're there. They play it in a huge new stadium at Flushing Meadows, New York. He'll never see us."

Aaron didn't answer, but Doc knew his statement

about Kevin not knowing they were there piqued Aaron's innate sense of mystery.

"All right, let's go but only for a few days. I don't trust these foreigners who'll be watching my buildings while I'm gone," Aaron said half in jest, but not fully.

"Spoken like a true American bigot," Doc retorted as they continued to stroll leisurely through the park.

CHAPTER 22

In 1978 the U.S. Open Tennis Championships had moved its site from the sedate, old, established West Side Club in Forest Hills, New York, to a huge, tacky, new complex at Flushing Meadows right next door to Shea Stadium. The courts' new surface was Decoturf II, a form of acrylic cement, well suited for American players who were at a disadvantage on clay and grass. Planes flying into and from LaGuardia Airport every few minutes screamed overhead often drowning out the cheers and groans of the spectators.

The new National Tennis Center in Flushing Meadows was, like everything else in and around New York City, bigger than life; crowded with strangers, the great majority of whom spoke English as a second language; and constructed of cement and steel. Yet it was like an oasis in a sea of asphalt highways, graffiti and industrial waste. The National Tennis Center had a certain charm, and if one could stretch his imagination a bit once inside the gates, the parklike interior was alive and vibrant for two weeks in late August and early September where the world's best vied for the elusive Grand Slam title of United States Open champion. The inviting smells from the food vendors that dotted the grounds, and the hawking of goods by vendors of all types of tennis paraphernalia gave the event an international carnival atmosphere. Twenty-seven tennis courts were strategically located throughout the grounds capped by the premier stadium court with seating for over 20,000 fans. This tournament is the final and most grueling of all the four grand slam tennis events, consisting of the Australian, the French, Wimbledon, and the U.S. Open. Play goes on for fourteen days and nights, starting at 10:00 AM and often going on past midnight if a player is unlucky enough to draw an evening match. The players all seem to hate the event, but not one wouldn't sell his birthright to be the champion at the end.

Kevin had never done well at the U.S. Open, but the surface was well suited for his game and he had worked hard to prepare for this year's tourney. The New Yorkers had a love/hate relationship with him, and his matches were always scheduled on the Stadium or the Grandstand Court where they could accommodate the largest crowds. He decided not to play doubles or mixed doubles this year so he could conserve all his energy for singles, and when the draw sheets were posted he was seeded third among the 128 male contestants, with a first round match against an unknown qualifier.

In the restricted confines of the players' lounge, where no one could enter without a special pass, sponsors, coaches, agents, and lawyers made endorsement deals while the players either mingled among themselves or sat alone contemplating the impending battle.

This year Kevin was the undisputed "hot" player, and Sy was bombarded each time he entered the lounge. He methodically set up his office in a corner of the room and listened to a stream of offers seeking Kevin's endorsements. With each win the ante would be increased and Sy calmly analyzed offers that would make Kevin and himself millions over the next few years. Kevin had nothing to do with this end of the business. He knew that Sy, having a vested interest, would cut the best deal possible, and Kevin focused only on his game. Never particularly liked by the other players, who abhorred his on court antics, Kevin had no trouble being alone and somewhat isolated.

This year he even ignored the tennis groupies who somehow always wrangled a pass to enter the players' lounge. In the past he had not been above "honoring" a particularly attractive tennis fan who was only too happy to spread her legs for a growing legend of the game, but this year he had a mission and would not be distracted.

Sy Rosen had sent Doc and Aaron tickets respecting Doc's request that Kevin not be told. Box seat passes were available for special friends and relatives of the highly ranked players, but Doc insisted on general admission tickets where they would be high in the stands and far enough from the court surface so Kevin could not recognize them.

The opening stadium court match of the day was a first round women's singles duel and the large stadium court was less than one quarter filled. The match ended at noon, and Doc and Aaron could start to feel the excitement build. By 12:20 the stadium was completely packed with spectators, and Aaron could see the contestants entering the court area. The chair umpire was saying something over the loudspeaker, but the noise of the planes overhead completely drowned out any chance of hearing him. The contestants started to warm up, and Kevin's opponent appeared overwhelmed and somewhat terrified. He had trouble keeping the ball in play during the warm-up and appeared to be concerned only about not being humiliated. Winning was not even a consideration. The match was little more than a tune-up for Kevin, who won handily. The crowd was disappointed because there was no emotional outbursts, but with scores of 6-0, 6-1, and 6-2 there was little reason for Kevin to exhibit his famous temper. He treated the fans to a few trick shots, ending the match by returning a volley behind his back. His opponent, a young German who spoke almost no English, could not leave the court fast enough. As was his style after a win, Kevin took a few balls and hit them high into the stands as souvenirs. This showboating generally infuriated his opponents, but the fans loved it. For a moment Aaron thought Kevin had seen them in the high cheap seats, but he had been mistaken. Anyway Kevin would think his father wouldn't be caught dead in a place like this, and if Doc came, he was sure he would have called Kevin for tickets. For a few moments Aaron debated with himself about going down to talk to Kevin, but he resisted the urge.

Two evenings later Doc and Aaron were in their same seats for Kevin's second round. It was an evening match under the bright stadium floodlights. The evening was warm and balmy, and the New York crowd was especially noisy. Kevin's opponent was

Jeff Bernard, a blond, muscular twenty-two-year-old from California who, like Kevin, had a powerful serve and volley game, and unlike Kevin's first opponent, Bernard came to win. Everything bothered Kevin this evening. The lights were not to his liking, bugs hovered over the court like a cloud, and his opponent, who grew up on hard courts in Southern California, felt he had nothing to lose and was playing the match of his life. The first outburst came in the middle of the first set when Bernard served an ace on the line down the middle of the court to go up five games to three.

"Are you blind?" Kevin screamed at the chair umpire. "That ball was out by a foot!"

"I'm sorry, Mr. Garland, it was good," the chair umpire replied politely. He knew he was in for a long, difficult night.

Kevin broke his opponent's service game, and the first set went into a tie breaker. At set point against Kevin another close call against him, giving the first set to his opponent, induced another tirade.

"For Christ's sake that shot was out by a mile, are you asleep?" This time Kevin was yelling at an unfortunate linesman. "Has someone paid you to have me lose, you dumb shit?" he screamed. The linesman, knowing he was in a no-win situation, remained silent hoping that eventually common sense would prevail. But Kevin, seemingly out of control, demanded that the linesman be removed before he would continue play and he sat down and refused to continue until the chief referee was summoned and acceded to his demand.

The match continued, and with each close call Kevin stomped and swore and stalled. Anything to throw his opponent off balance. Even the crowd, who at first egged him on was now tiring of his histrionics and booed him for his tactics. Each time Bernard won a point the big crowd cheered in delight. In the end Kevin won in four sets, and his opponent, thoroughly frustrated by his gamesmanship antics, refused to shake his hand at the end of the match, for which he was again lustily cheered by the crowd. Kevin answered their cheers for his opponent by sticking up the middle finger of his left hand at the crowd of 20,000 fans. Millions watching the event on T.V. were shocked and titillated by his actions.

"He's really turned into a schmuck," Aaron said as they left the stadium.

"Yeah, but he won and this will only increase his box office appeal," Doc answered. "Remember, he's the one who filled this stadium tonight and the promoters know it. He's a prima donna, but I think it's mostly an act and he knows exactly what he's doing. He's tough and not afraid of making enemies as long as the dollars roll in and people flock to see him play."

The next morning's sports section of almost every major newspaper in the United States and Europe had a picture of Kevin "giving the crowd the bird" as it was delicately described. He was fined $5,000 by the tournament committee and one of his equipment sponsors sent him a letter reprimanding him for his unsportsmanlike conduct. The letter was careful, however, not to threaten any withdrawal of sponsorship. That afternoon Sy received three telephone calls at his hotel from the major television stations requesting Kevin's appearance for interviews on talk shows that would generate over $75,000 for him in T.V. guest appearance fees.

Millions of sports fans worldwide read the articles under his picture, and ticket scalpers doubled the prices of their U.S. Open tickets. The tournament sponsors publicly deplored his behavior and privately were elated over the free worldwide publicity.

"Doc, I've seen enough. He's acting like a jerk, but he's still my son and I hate the thought of the crowd booing him," Aaron said the next morning at breakfast. "I'll watch him on T.V. That way I can turn the set off if I don't like what he does." Aaron looked tired, and Doc had to get back to work anyway.

They took the late morning flight back to O'Hare and rehashed the two matches on the flight back. Doc was genuinely surprised at Aaron's depth of knowledge about the game and realized that he must have learned a lot about tennis over the past few years. When he questioned Aaron about it, Aaron sarcastically replied, "When you're the father of the most famous tennis player in the world you have to know a little about the game."

By the middle of the second week of the tournament, Kevin had reached the quarter finals without losing another set and played to a packed stadium or grandstand court during each match. His tantrums on court had earned him $7,500 in fines and the outright contempt of every chair umpire unlucky enough to officiate his matches. While the print media sports headlines cried, "Shame and disgrace" the United State Tennis Association, as sponsor of the U.S. Open was already contemplating an increase in ticket prices for the following year as giant corporations sought more and better seats for Kevin's matches. No athlete in the history of the game had gained more press than

Kevin Garland at the U.S. Open. Only Kevin and Sy knew for sure that Kevin's on court antics were a well rehearsed act and each played their role to perfection.

"I can't control him," Sy would tell sponsors and interviewers, "no one can. Kevin is the most talented and yet potentially self-destructive player the game has ever had," knowing that the operative word was "self-destructive," for that is what the fan came to see along with great tennis. They were rarely disappointed on either count.

The men's singles finals of the U.S. Open was a major T.V. network event, and everyone in the Chicago neighborhood around Albany Park knew that Kevin Garland had learned to play the game on their courts. His opponent this Sunday was the number-one ranked player in the world and an opponent who had beaten Kevin in each of the three occasions that they had previously met in tournaments. Erwin "Duke" Steuben was 6'4", 190 pounds, twenty-seven years old, and at the pinnacle of his game. The big-shouldered Steuben had been ranked number one for the last six months and seemed to be getting better with age. He had lost only three sets during the entire tournament on his route to the finals. Kevin's antics would have no effect on him. He was tournament tough and could play mind games as well as Kevin. What he didn't know was that the night before the finals Kevin and Sy had decided that win or lose Kevin would play this match without antics. If he lost, the crowd would laud him for controlling his heretofore uncontrollable emotions, and if he won on sheer talent he would undeniably be ranked number one in the world and the darling of the fickle tennis community.

The match was one that was to go down as a tennis classic. Like two prize fighters they attacked and counterattacked. The tide seemed to shift with each game, and the huge New York crowd loved it. It was sport at its finest, and after four and a half grueling hours Kevin won in a close fifth set with a final bulletlike down-the-line backhand winner. They both received a standing ovation from the 20,000 fans that lasted unabated for over five minutes. The fans, emotionally drained, refused to leave the stadium, realizing that they would probably never again witness a match to equal this one. The same newspapers that only a few days before had vilified Kevin and demanded that he be banned from the game, now proclaimed him to arguably be the best tennis player in the world.

CHAPTER 23

After Kevin's victory at the U.S. Open, the staff at K.G., Inc. had to hire two additional part-time clerks to answer all the requests for publicity photos of Kevin, and his fees for exhibition and personal appearances rose by fifty percent. His guaranteed fee for simply showing up at a regular tournament was now more than the first place prize money, which he usually won as well. But he was worth it, for his presence guaranteed the tournament's success.

Kevin's reign as the top player in the world lasted without interruption for over twenty-two months. During that time he won six Grand Slam events, including Wimbledon and a second U.S. Open title. His major antagonist during the next two years continued to be "Duke" Steuben, who was never again able to raise his game against Kevin to the level of their first U.S. Open title match.

Kevin's financial empire continued to mushroom, and he instructed his financial advisors to buy millions of dollars of highly leveraged quality real estate in the southwest United States. After all, he reasoned, no one ever lost money by buying quality real estate. *Forbes* magazine estimated his fortune at over fifty million dollars by the end of 1986.

Sy Rosen, the architect of the Kevin Garland mystique, had decided to call it quits. He met with his pupil at Kevin's Florida estate and resigned.

"Kevin, I've had it. My job is boring me to death. I'm as rich as I ever wanted to be, and you don't need me anymore." Kevin also was convinced that he really didn't need Sy anymore but was genuinely sorry to see him go.

"We've been through a lot together, Sy. I can still remember the first time we met and all I could pay you was $50.00 a week and room and board. I was glad to be able to do Doc a favor. I really should call him, it's been months."

Sy wavered for a few moments torn between his original promise to Doc and Aaron not to disclose their secret and his compelling desire to tell this talented ass that he never would have reached these heights without the intervention of people who loved and cared for him without any ulterior motives.

"Ah well," Sy thought to himself, "maybe some day when I'm feeling especially depressed and vindictive I'll call him up and burst his bubble."

CHAPTER 24

Kevin had heard it said many times that what goes up must come down. However, until recently, he never thought that a cliche like that applied to him. He was becoming ancient as far as the tour was concerned. At thirty-eight years of age when doctors, lawyers, and corporate executives are still considered young, professional tennis players seriously examine other options for earning a livelihood.

Although he was still ranked among the top twenty players in the world, he had cut down on the number of tournaments he played, and it had been several years since he won a major event. The crowds still came to watch him play, but new, much younger heroes now dominated the tennis scene. Minor injuries that had healed in days now lingered for weeks, and he started to consider retirement. After Sy Rosen left his organization, Kevin had retained a series of coaches, but the chemistry was lacking and none lasted more than a few months.

He now called Boca Raton, Florida, his home. A real estate developer had given him the deed to a luxurious condominium in exchange for two weeks per year of his time for exhibitions on site and the use of his name as the "touring pro" for the complex. Life was still sweet, but Kevin felt the changes. His staff was reduced to three people. A secretary, a coach whose duties included scheduling his travel, and an accountant who also managed his assets. If he required legal services he retained a lawyer on an "as needed" basis. His foray into leveraged real estate had almost ruined him financially. Tax reform laws and changes in property values in the "oil patch" states had reduced his financial empire dramatically. He was still wealthy by any standard but had nowhere near the net worth he had reached at his peak.

He never considered marriage and rationalized that it wouldn't have worked anyway. He was on the road most of the year and still liked variety in his women, who were becoming younger as he aged.

It had been a few years since his last contact with Doc and much longer since he had any communication with his father. Strangely, after so many years this started to bother him, and he entertained thoughts of calling Aaron. But what would he say, "Hi Dad, it's me, your son Kevin, what have you been doing for the past seven or eight years? How about coming to Florida for a week so we can catch up on old times?"

No, he reasoned, it is probably best to let the past lie. After all the old man had never called me and the phones work both ways, and I'm sure he prefers it this way. But still the thought persisted.

Kevin bumped into Sy occasionally at tournaments. A few years after leaving Kevin, Sy had been bored with retirement and took on coaching a series of young "up and comers." He had great credibility in the coaching arena. Thanks to his long association with Kevin, Sy had his pick of the new crop of future stars. Anyone who could handle a schmuck like Kevin Garland for so many years had to be a great coach.

Kevin had conquered all there was in the tennis world and fantasized about going out in a final blaze of glory. A promoter was putting together a world championship tennis event in Las Vegas for next year that boasted a first place prize money of ten million dollars and the title of world champion. It was going to be limited to the top thirty-two ranked players in the world so Kevin would need to enter and do well in a few more events to keep his ranking in the top thirty-two to qualify for the event. The more he thought about it the more excited he became. It would be a perfect end to his illustrious career. The prize money alone would be enough, even after taking off a few million for taxes, to live on comfortably for the rest of his life without ever touching his other assets.

He still felt that on a given day he could beat any player in the world. His real problem would be winning five matches over ten days in the desert heat against much younger players who were seemingly unaffected by the elements and whose bodies were impervious to nagging injuries. If he were to do it he would need to get back into top physical and playing condition and to Kevin that meant only one man, Sy Rosen.

He was able to track Sy down in Chicago where he had returned to live after leaving Kevin. Swallowing his pride one evening he called his former employee, "Sy, it's Kevin Garland. How the hell are you?" Sy knew Kevin as well as anyone and could feel that this was not a social call. Kevin Garland did not make social calls.

"I'm fine, Kevin, what can I do for you?" he answered a bit too sharply.

"Jesus Christ, Sy, what makes you think I want anything?'

"Kevin, I know you like the back of my hand. You want something."

Kevin forced a short laugh, "Well, as a matter of fact I do. Sy, I've been thinking of retiring and thought I'd like to try to go out in a blaze of glory and get in top shape for the big event in Las Vegas next year."

"What's that got to do with me? You know I'm coaching Bobby Stanik and the kid will probably be in the same tournament." For a few moments there was silence on the phone. "Kevin, are you still there?"

"Yeah, I'm here, Sy." Kevin had originally thought he would offer Sy ten percent of his winnings. "Sy, I really need you for this one. It's worth fifteen percent of the prize money. That's a cool million and a half if I win it all."

"Kevin, I'm really flattered. I figured the most you would have offered would be ten percent. But I can't leave the Stanik kid at this stage of his career, even though I still think you can kick his ass to hell and back," and there was silence again on the phone line. "Call Lou Weber, he's a great coach and lives in Miami," Sy suggested.

"Sy, I really need you on this one," and then pulling out all the stops he added, "I think you owe me. . . . " Sy could feel the plea in Kevin's voice and he knew how much it took for him to admit that he needed any-one, but he was unmoved.

"No, as I remember, Kevin, you always said you made it all on your own, and as I see it, it's the other way around, you owe me... So long, Kevin," and the phone in Kevin's hand went dead.

"What a prick," Kevin thought, "after all I did for him he's got the balls to turn me down when I need him, screw him." But Kevin knew that without Sy he had no chance of winning and he felt himself grow-ing hostile towards Sy and curiously towards himself as well. He knew that his relationship with Sy had been strained during their last few years together and that perhaps, just perhaps, he had not treated Sy with the respect he deserved. Suddenly, for the first time since he was a small child, Kevin was afraid. It was an irra-tional fear and he understood that but it was fear just the same. My career really is over now. Maybe I can do well in a few more tournaments but the real glory days are gone. It was time to think the unthinkable. What does a retired professional athlete, trained for nothing but his sport, do with the rest of his life.

"Damn you Sy, damn you to hell, I don't want it to be over," he murmured half aloud staring at the tele-phone.

CHAPTER 25

Sy sat by the telephone for a good half hour mulling over the conversation with Kevin. He then called Doc and asked to meet with him and Aaron as soon as they were available.

"My treat for dinner wherever you and Aaron want to eat."

The next evening the three men met for dinner in a small deli on Lawrence Avenue where Aaron regularly ate a few nights a week.

"Aaron, thanks to you and your son, I'm a rich man. You could have picked a real restaurant instead of this dump since I'm buying dinner."

"Well, Sy, the owner here is a friend of mine and I know they'll serve anyone that walks in, so I figured it was safe to bring you here." Aaron had developed a dry sense of humor, and they all had a good laugh at Sy's expense.

There was a bond between these three. They admired and respected each other, and it was easy for them to talk without pulling any punches. They ate leisurely and talked about everything except Kevin.

Finally, over brewed decaffeinated coffee and mandel bread compliments of the owner who, it turned out, was one of Aaron's tenants, Sy told them about his telephone conversation with Kevin.

"Aaron, because of you and Doc and your son, to my everlasting surprise, I have enough money to allow me to live comfortably the rest of my life. I am well respected in the tennis world and have my pick of the best young players to coach if I choose to do so." He swallowed some coffee and cleared his throat, "Your son is selfish, very stubborn, and self-centered, but he is the best tennis player I have ever seen and quite possibly in his prime the best of the best." He stopped again to sip his coffee and then continued, "Kevin called me yesterday to ask me to come back to train him for one last major tournament in Las Vegas next year. I feel a debt to you and Doc, and even with my help, he probably won't win this Las Vegas thing, but without me he hasn't a chance. What do you want me to do?"

Doc looked at Aaron, who was staring as his coffee cup. He was aching to tell his old friend not to ask Sy to go to Kevin's aid, but all he could say was, "Aaron, he's your son and it's your decision. Just remember he hasn't called or seen fit to visit you in many years. Maybe he deserves a little of his own medicine."

Softly Aaron spoke, still staring at the coffee cup.

"You're both right, he is stubborn and selfish and probably deserves not to have this last opportunity. But, he is my son and I want him to have his chance. Sy, I'm asking you to go to him, do it for me. How much money will you need?"

"From you, Aaron, nothing, from your son I will graciously reconsider my position for twenty percent of his winnings against a fixed guarantee of $250,000."

"Waiter," Aaron called out, "more decaf and mandel bread and make sure you give the check to my wealthy friend," he said pointing at Sy.

CHAPTER 26

Ten days after the dinner with Doc and Aaron, Sy Rosen took up residence in the guest bedroom in Kevin's home in Boca Raton, Florida. The old training regimen started again, this time with a greater emphasis on stretching and aerobics. It was just the two of them, and other than both being older by close to two decades, they were back to where it all began. Sy had decided that if Kevin pulled rank on him or made life uncomfortable he would leave, but he needn't have worried. Kevin knew Sy did not need to be with him, and he was genuinely grateful that he had changed his mind after all. He chalked it up to Sy feeling that they were friends and the chance to make up to two million bucks and gave it no more thought.

Together they carefully charted a series of tournaments that Kevin would enter over the next eleven months, concentrating on hard courts and staying mainly in the U.S. to avoid the rigors of too much traveling. Kevin would play only the U.S. Open as far as the Grand Slam events. After the Open a final tune-up tournament in Tel Aviv would be his only trip out of the country. Israel's desertlike conditions would be almost like Las Vegas.

Additionally, they figured that since many of the top players were avoiding the Middle East because of the constant danger, Kevin would have a good chance of doing well at that event, which would help keep his ranking high and boost his confidence going into the big tournament.

In the past few years Kevin had let his physical conditioning lapse and had relied more on guile than speed and power.

"Guile is fine, but you don't beat the world's best with it," Sy counseled. He changed Kevin's eating habits, cut out the late hours and worked him unmercifully on speed drills, aerobics and Sy's newest instrument of torture which was a six pound rubber medicine ball which Kevin threw repeatedly against a wall for upper body strength. At the end of each day it was massage and ice to soothe the aging, aching muscles. Six weeks after Sy arrived, they hit the tournament trail. They were back to the beginning and it felt great!

Tel Aviv

CHAPTER 27

Zalman Zacksman had little interest in games and could not recall ever having read the sports section of a newspaper. He knew that athletes, like movie stars, were paid fortunes for their one-dimensional talents and after they reached an elevated plateau of having their names recognized by a substantial percentage of the civilized world, they were mysteriously perceived to be endowed with a higher intellect on subjects ranging from politics to high finance. It always disturbed him to see a public figure flanked by an actor or athlete, as though their mere presence lent credibility to what was being stated.

But this lazy afternoon in late September he had time to relax over tea and sponge cake at his favorite Tel Aviv outdoor cafe on Dizengoff Street. The waiters all knew him as a regular customer and former high-ranking government official and left him alone. It would be at least an hour before his daughter would be back from shopping, and they would walk the half mile to the large apartment building in which they owned and occupied separate small residences.

He had finished reading the Hebrew newspaper *Ma'Ariv* and was about halfway through the English language *Jerusalem Post*, which he read primarily to practice his English. English was his fourth language after Polish, Yiddish, and Hebrew and was still the one that gave him the most difficulty. Probably, he mused, because he didn't start to really learn it until later in life. He started to flip past the section on sports when a picture caught his eye. The caption over the picture stated, "Garland slated to play for last time in Tel Aviv Tourney." For a moment Zalman was inclined to go to the next page but there was something about that face that intrigued him and he decided to read the article under the photo:

> Veteran American tennis star Kevin Garland has entered the Israel Open Tennis Championships for what may be his last time. Mr. Garland, originally from Chicago, Illinois, U.S.A., won this event in 1982 and 1984. The former champion is currently ranked twenty-fourth in the world but has not won a tour championship in the last two years. Mr. Garland stated that he has always enjoyed playing here and is saddened to think that this will probably be the last time that he competes in Israel.

Zalman reread the article several times to make sure he understood every word and continued to dissect the face in the picture. Impossible, he thought, it cannot be. And yet he could not stop thinking that this was a land of miracles and strange twists of fate. Oblivious to everything else, he continued to stare at the picture and he allowed his thoughts to return to the past.

"Dad, are you all right? Your hands are shaking and you're pale." He must have been sitting there for an hour reading and rereading that same article and analyzing the face in the newspaper picture with his mind.

"No, Hannah, I'm fine. It's just that this picture of this tennis player reminds me of someone I knew many years ago." Hannah knew that probably meant in Poland during those horrible years, for her father could not bring himself to speak of that time without great anguish.

Normally as they slowly walked home together Hannah and her father traded gossip as it was their special time together, but today was different and she knew her father's quiet mood indicated some inner crisis. As they reached the apartment building and started to go in, Zalman smiled and faced her, "You know, I'm an old man and I've never seen a tennis match. You and I should go and watch this American champion Garland, and we should get seats as close to the players as possible."

"OK, Papa, I'll call Ari Much this evening. He can get tickets to anything." Both of them knew that tennis had nothing to do with her father's request, but for now it seemed best to leave it lie and play out the charade.

CHAPTER 28

In Israel, next to soccer, tennis is a sports mania. The several national tennis centers are free to all children who want to play the game, which is ideally suited to a tough, wiry desert people not genetically gifted with great height, speed, or leaping abilities. Principally located in disadvantaged areas of the larger cities, the centers do much to help integrate Israel's diverse young population.

Sunday afternoon's tennis matches in the stadium court in Ramat Hasharon were sold out, but Ari Much, who had a yen for Hannah, had come through as expected with two courtside tickets. The crowd passing through the turnstyles were mostly young or early middle aged men and women, and Zalman dressed in a white shirt and black slacks felt ancient. Hannah wore a faded khaki army blouse with two top buttons undone and sleeves rolled up, powder blue shorts, and sandals. Her long tan legs attracted stares from many of the young men in the crowd to which she seemed oblivious. She had a natural beauty that make-up did little to enhance. Tall, slim, dark hair in a pony tail, olive-skinned with straight regular features, she looked more like twenty-five than her thirty-two years. Although she had several male friends and a few who became lovers, there had been no great romance in her life.

It was noon on a perfect day. A little breeze from the Mediterranean kept the heat from being oppressive. Small patches of puffy white clouds periodically blocked the sun, and the crowd was in a festive mood anticipating the oncoming contest. Zalman and Hannah were seated in the first row about two feet above the court surface adjacent to the baseline of the north end of the court.

After they were seated for a few minutes, the players entered the stadium carrying their racquets and large equipment bags and the crowd clapped politely. Kevin Garland was dressed in a white warm-up suit and navy blue baseball cap. The players dropped their bags near the chair umpire's area and started to warm up against each other. Kevin's opponent was on the north side of the court closest to Zalman and Hannah. Zalman leaned forward to look at Kevin, but the cap was pulled down over Kevin's face. He was far away, and Zalman's eyes were not what they once had been. The chair umpire, first in Hebrew and then in English announced, "Ladies and gentlemen, this will be a best two-out-of-three set tiebreak match. To my left from Toronto, Canada, the 1987 United States NCAA champion currently ranked eighty-second in the world, Mr. Jack Michaelson. To my right, originally from Chicago, Illinois, U.S.A., the winner of six Grand Slam events and a two-time champion of this tournament currently ranked twenty-fourth in the world, Mr.

Kevin Garland. Mr. Garland has won the coin toss and elected to serve. One minute, gentlemen."

Both players came to the sideline, stripped off their warm-ups and play began. Zalman knew nothing of the scoring or rules of tennis but was impressed with quickness of the players and the controlled speed of the fuzz-covered yellow ball. Kevin won the first game and the players sat down.

"Papa, they now switch sides so you will get a good look at this mysterious stranger," Hannah whispered to him.

The players stood and Kevin removed his hat and started towards the north baseline. The old man's hands started to tremble and he half rose from his chair as if lifted by some unseen force. This man was taller and heavier, but the face and distinct walk left no doubt in Zalman's mind. As Kevin passed in front of them he winked at Hannah who smiled and winked back.

"Well, Papa, is he who you. . . ." But Hannah never finished the question for as she looked at her father, she saw his face and she realized that what had started as a lark to satisfy an old man's curiosity was now evolving into something far more serious, and she became genuinely concerned about her father. He had been experiencing some irregular heartbeats for the past few months and Hannah now worried that the shock of seeing this strange American would have an adverse effect on him.

"I must talk to him, Hannah, when is this over?" he said in a voice that was almost pleading.

Hannah put her arm on her father's shoulder, "Papa, don't worry I'll arrange it," she assured him.

Hannah thought that if she couldn't set up the meeting herself, her resourceful friend Ari Much would certainly know where the tennis players were staying. Her only concern now was that Garland would lose the match and leave Israel that day.

Jack Michaelson was going to be a good tennis player, maybe even crack the top twenty some day, but at this point in his career he was still a plateau behind Kevin and both players knew it.

Kevin rolled through the first set winning 6-2, delighting the crowd with his solid shot making. Jews cheer for their own, and even though Kevin was only half Jewish, that was half more than his opponent and the crowd was solidly in his corner. The dark-haired girl in the front row with the blue shorts and great legs interested him and he played to her along with the rest of the crowd. She continued to smile each time he passed her, and he had already decided to talk to her when the match ended. The old man sitting next to her was a strange one. Kevin felt that he never took his eyes off him and he was sure the man knew nothing about tennis for his expression never changed throughout the match.

Mercifully for Jack Michaelson the match ended quickly with Kevin winning the second set 6-1. The players shook hands at the net, and Kevin sat in his chair, changed his sweat soaked shirt, and pulled on his warm-up jacket. He started to put his racquets in his bag when a woman's voice purred, "A fine match, Mr. Garland."

"Thanks," and as he looked up he first saw those long, tan legs and blue shorts. "Oh, it's you," he smiled, "I'm glad you liked it. Did your older friend like it too?"

"This was his first tennis match, Mr. Garland."

"Please call me Kevin."

"I'm Hannah, and Kevin I tell you in all honesty you fascinated him." Hannah knew that her father could not bear to wait to speak to him so she went right for the jugular. "Kevin, I know this is bold and you probably have plans, but would it be possible for you to join my father and me for dinner this evening? He would really like to meet you."

There was no resisting this girl. Kevin had no firm plans for the evening and they agreed to meet for dinner at her apartment at 7:00 PM. Kevin had assumed he would eat with Sy, but it was no big deal, and he knew Sy would understand. She wrote out her address and told him that any taxi driver would have no trouble finding the building.

"See you tonight, Kevin," and she reached out to shake his hand. Kevin held on to her hand a little too long as he stared at her face.

God, she is pretty he thought as he reluctantly released her hand. "See you at seven, Hannah," he said softly watching her as she walked away.

CHAPTER 29

Kevin arrived promptly at 7:00 PM, and entered the bright, tiny apartment. Hannah graciously accepted the flowers and wine he brought and took his hand as she welcomed him.

"Kevin Garland, may I introduce my father, Zalman Zacksman."

"Pleased to meet you, Mr. Zacksman," Kevin said with a smile. As the two men shook hands Kevin saw the tattooed numbers on the old man's left forearm and the smile faded from his face.

Noticing Kevin's reaction to his arm Zalman asked, "Have you never seen concentration camp numbers on anyone's arm before?" instinctively knowing the answer to come.

"Yes, as a matter of fact I have," Kevin replied, "my father has a similar tattoo."

"I know, young man, he has the numbers 746216 tattooed on his left forearm and he walks with a limp from an old wound to his knee, doesn't he?" Now it was Kevin's turn for shock. He had never met anyone who had known his father before he had come to the United States.

"Yes, yes, you are absolutely right. My father doesn't speak about his past. Did you know him well?"

"Many years ago we were very close friends," he sighed, and then looking into Kevin's eyes he added, "Do you have any brothers or sisters?"

"No, I'm an only child. My mother died when I was ten."

The old man had so much he wanted to ask this boy but he said, "Would you indulge an old man's whim?"

"What do you mean?" Kevin asked.

"I knew your father very well, and I will tell you about him if you want me to, but tonight I want you to be the storyteller. Then if you would come back to dinner here again tomorrow night I will tell you what I know about Aaron Garlovsky, and I may have a surprise or two for you. Do you agree?"

Kevin looked at the old man and then at Hannah. He was hooked. He needed no excuse to eat dinner with her for a second evening and would have jumped at the chance even without the promise of learning about his father's past.

"Absolutely, whether I win or lose tomorrow, put on an extra plate for dinner."

For the next two hours Kevin told them about his life. Occasionally the old man asked a question, but for the most part he let Kevin tell his story. The old man was not really interested in Kevin's tennis career but asked him to tell as much about his childhood and about Aaron as he could remember.

"How did your father get to buy so much property?" Zalman asked.

"Well, I think it started around 1954, before I was born. I was told his uncle died and left my father some money and a building where my mother was a tenant.

"Did he leave him a lot of money?" Zalman asked.

"I really don't know how much money he left, but I think it was around $50,000 or $60,000. Somehow I remember my mother telling me that she thought my father gave the money away and just kept the building."

It was around 9:00 PM when they finished their coffee and Kevin ended the story of his life. He could not remember ever talking so much, and he had to get up early to meet Sy Rosen for a short practice session before his afternoon match. He assured Zalman that he would be back at 7:00 PM the next night, and as he was preparing to leave Hannah said she would like to walk him back to his hotel. It was dark out and he asked her how she would get back to her apartment.

"I will walk of course. This is not America, our streets are safe after dark," her dark eyes flashed. "I'm a sabra, no one will attack me in my country." Kevin was about to say something clever about sabras being hard on the outside but soft and sweet when opened up, but he thought better of it. He did not want to appear flip in front of the old man and he especially did not want to alienate this exotic, beautiful creature who was going to walk alone with him for the next twenty minutes.

When they left the apartment and started walking she said, "I want to thank you for indulging my father. You know he is very well respected here. He was a famous soldier and a member of the Knesset in the 1970s." She told him about her mother who had died a few years ago. "They had a wonderful relationship for over thirty years. I guess I am looking for a man like my father, but they are too few and far between."

"Do you have any brothers or sisters?"

"Not really, but my parents raised a boy who is like my older brother, and I couldn't love him more if we were actually brother and sister. His mother was killed when he was very young. She was my parents' friend, and they took him and raised him after she died. He's a colonel in the army and lives in Haifa with his wife and two sons. I'd love to have you meet them someday."

It was a warm night and they walked slowly the rest of the way to Kevin's hotel making small talk, neither wanting to push the relationship too fast. About a block from the hotel he took her hand and they walked in silence. At the lobby in the Tel Aviv Hilton they lingered awkwardly, "Listen, Hannah, come to the match tomorrow. I'll have a few tickets left for you at the box office. Please, I really want you there and bring your father."

She kissed him quickly and said with a smile, "OK, until tomorrow," and she was gone.

CHAPTER 30

Kevin rarely had trouble sleeping. He had spent so much of his life in strange hotel beds all over the world that he never acquired the habit of becoming comfortable in one bed. This night, however, was different. He could still taste her fleeting lips and smell her perfume and sleep came only intermittently.

He had been infatuated with several women but always felt he was in control. He knew that to them he was a celebrity, a sports hero, a larger than life personality, and he pulled the strings. This was an exciting and frightening new experience for Kevin. This woman, this Hannah, in one night had him spinning around in circles. He was like a schoolboy with a crush on the prettiest girl in class. It was also dangerous, for he was supposed to be entirely focused on this tournament and the big event next month, but all he could think about was Hannah Zacksman.

It was 4:30 AM and still finding sleep impossible he got out of bed and did some stretching exercises. He dressed in sweats and in the still darkness of the early Tel Aviv morning he went for a half hour slow jog on the beach across the street from his hotel. His match was scheduled for 2:00 PM and he would practice with Sy for no more than forty minutes at 9:00 AM. He had a few hours to kill before leaving for practice and as he sat alone in the coffee shop eating breakfast, odd thoughts filled his mind. This girl who had captivated him, he knew nothing about. What did she do, did she have a boyfriend, had she ever been married? He decided that whatever he discovered about her could not change the way he felt.

What about her father, now what a piece of work he was. He knew my father, that's for sure. These survivors of the death camps lived in a world apart. What surprise is he going to spring tonight and what am I going to finally discover about my father's past? Deep in thought, Kevin hadn't seen Sy approach.

"Up early this morning aren't you, champ?" Sy's smiling face appeared at the table both hands filled with breakfast buffet plates.

"Yeah, I couldn't sleep so I went for a jog along the beach."

"Couldn't have been that looker with the blue shorts that kept you up could it?" Sy saw everything.

"Sy, I can't stop thinking about her. I've never felt this way before. And her old man knew my father." As they ate Kevin related the events of the previous evening to Sy. When he was through he thought Sy would give him a pep talk about getting focused of the match and the tournament, but he was wrong.

"You know, Kevin, this may sound offbeat coming from your coach, but there is more to life than hitting tennis balls. It sounds as though you've got a chance at finding out about your dad and maybe you'll get the girl to boot. Go for it, you're not a kid anymore."

"You know coach, that may be the best advice you ever gave me. Now let's finish eating and go hit tennis balls. That still pays the bills, and I've got a tournament to win."

As he entered the sun-drenched stadium for his afternoon match his mood was solemn. Hannah wasn't in the front row seat, so she probably hadn't picked up the tickets he left for her at the box office. Today the crowd would not be pulling for him, for his opponent was a young Israeli Maccabi champion who would be playing the biggest match of his life. A win against Kevin Garland would go far in enhancing his career. Kevin's opponent had nothing to lose, and with the crowd support behind him, this match had all the elements needed for an upset. They started their five minute warm-up and Kevin could not concentrate on his opponent. Usually in the warm-up against someone he had never played he tried to pick up little points of weakness in his game, but today he was more interested in looking over at the two empty seats in the front row. The players started practicing serves and the chair umpire announced, "One minute, gentlemen."

The match started and as expected the noisy crowd was enthusiastically behind their local hero. They cheered every time he won a point and each time Kevin missed. As the set progressed his opponent's confidence grew as he realized that he was keeping pace with a legend who was still one of the world's top players. Kevin was down four games to three, and they changed sides with Kevin preparing to serve. He again glanced over to the seats and his heart seemed to skip a beat as Hannah smiled and waved.

Seated next to her was a large suntanned man who looked to be about forty. Buoyed by her presence, Kevin's game took on a new dimension. If the man seated next to Hannah was a rival suitor scouting his competition, then he was about to see the best Kevin had to offer. Kevin served four successive aces tying the set at four all. His opponent could feel the change in Kevin's game and demeanor, and the match was all but over. Kevin broke his opponent's next serve and won the first set 6-4. Now down a set his young opponent started to try low percentage shots to get back in the match and Kevin won the second set 6-love. He quickly shook hands with his opponent who was still in shock at how quickly the match had turned and ended. Kevin looked and saw her standing and talking to her companion who was grinning at her, damn him. They looked too comfortable with each other, and now the man put his arm around Hannah and was hugging her.

"Shit, now she's bringing him down to meet me. If he wasn't so big I'd like to punch his lights out," Kevin thought. Before he could say anything she ran up to Kevin and kissed him on the cheek. "That was pure poetry, Kevin, you are marvelous."

All he could mutter was, "Thanks."

"Kevin, I'd like you to meet Barak Friedlander. He drove in from Haifa this morning to see you play, that's why we were late." Kevin seemed confused as he shook hands with the large man, and Hannah continued, "Kevin, Barak is the big brother I told you about last night."

Smiling the big man said, "I had to see for myself

this larger than life figure that my little sister seems to have fallen for," and they both looked at Hannah who was blushing, for the first time in many years.

Suddenly realizing that the stranger was not to be his rival Kevin found his voice, "I'm pleased to meet you, Barak. Hannah speaks very highly of you."

"Well, I should hope so, I'm the one that protected her from all the horny boys that hung around our apartment."

A nice guy, Kevin thought. From the size of him I'd hate to get him pissed off; he looks like he could tear telephone books.

"Kevin, I've got to go to work. Barak and his wife and sons will be joining us for dinner. My father has insisted that this be a total family affair tonight, is that OK?"

"Great," he responded, "I'm looking forward to it."

"Until seven," she said.

"Right, so long, Barak, see you later," and they left with Hannah holding Barak's arm. But this time Kevin was pleased to see it. Christ, I'm hooked, he thought, this is nuts but I'm not going home without her.

"What was that all about?" it was Sy with an Israeli sportscaster and T.V. cameraman in tow.

"I'll tell you all about it later after the interview, but Sy, it's crazy, you're looking at a grown man who is rapidly falling for a girl he met only yesterday and now can't imagine living without."

175

CHAPTER 31

For the second night at 7:00 PM on the dot, this time with flowers, candy, and wine in hand, Kevin rang the Zacksman apartment bell. The small apartment seemed overflowing with people, and Kevin was introduced to Barak's wife Danielle and two boys—Ram, 15, and Max, who was 12. They had all seen his T.V. interview and highlights of his match on the early evening news and even Zalman seemed mildly impressed. The family sat around the table in the dining area passing dishes of humus, tahini, schwarma, and falafel stuffed in pita bread. When Kevin felt he could eat no more, Hannah brought out platters of sliced oranges, watermelon, cantaloupes, and pomegranate. It was at some point in mid-meal that Kevin felt a stab of emotion. He realized that in his entire life he had never sat at a family dinner surrounded by relatives. It was all right, he reasoned, if you never had experienced a family you didn't miss it. Then strangely he thought how hard it must have been for his father, who had a large family as a young man, only

176

to have it all taken away from him by the doctrine of a madman.

Zalman tapped his tea glass with his spoon to get attention, and the room became quiet as everyone turned to their host. Speaking slowly in English, which all in the room spoke and understood, he rose from his chair.

"I am not a good speaker," he started, "but what I have to say tonight will affect all of you, so please give an old man your attention." It was very unlike Zalman to make a speech, and they all waited quietly for him to continue.

"Kevin, last night I promised to tell you about your father, and I said I would have a surprise for you. Barak, what I am about to say will have as much meaning for you and your family as it will for Kevin." He was breathing heavily now and obviously in a state of high emotion.

"Sit down, Papa, you're making me nervous," Hannah said. Zalman sat down and grasped the side of the dining table.

"Barak, may your mother, Abigail Friedlander, rest in peace, you know you are the son I never had and you will always be my son, but I have recently discovered that your real father is still alive. He lives in the United States, and I believe he never knew that he had a son born in Israel. He also has another son, a world champion tennis player." There was an eerie silence in the small room and all there felt a strange emotion. "Kevin, Barak, you are both the sons of Aaron Garlovsky."

Beads of perspiration were now dripping from Zalman's forehead, and he continued to hold on to the side of the table for he felt he would faint if he let go.

Suddenly, they all started talking at once. Hannah was openly crying as Kevin and Barak rose and stared at each other.

"I don't know what to say," Kevin exclaimed, then to Zalman, "Are you certain?" and the old man nodded affirmatively. "My God, I've got a brother, a sister-in-law, and nephews?"

"Yes, and Aaron has two sons, a daughter-in-law, and grandchildren. God moves in mysterious ways," Zalman murmured. It was the first time he had uttered the word "God" in over fifty years.

CHAPTER 32

The evening emotionally exhausted them all and Zalman retired at 10:00 PM, "Tomorrow night I will tell you boys more about your father," and he allowed Hannah to help him to his bedroom.

The family stayed awake talking until midnight then agreed that Kevin and Barak would return the next night and learn more about what Zalman would reveal about their father. Hannah took Danielle aside and Kevin saw her giving some keys to Danielle.

It was an exhilarating feeling for Kevin to say goodbye to his newfound family that night. Hannah was again walking him back to his hotel, and they spoke little as they were both deep in thought. He held her hand as they walked under the bright moonlight reflecting off the Mediterranean. They sat for a while on a bench staring at the water, and Kevin said, "Stay with me tonight."

She smiled back and responded, "I have to, I gave my apartment keys to Danielle, Barak, and the boys. It was much too late for them to drive back to Haifa tonight." They both started to laugh and Hannah started running across the sand toward the water. "C'mon, last one in is a rotten egg," and she quickly stepped out of her skirt and blouse and dove into the warm, inky-black Mediterranean water.

He would have followed her anywhere, and as he pulled off his shirt and slacks he could envision the bold headlines in tomorrow morning's *U.S.A. Today* newspaper, "Tennis player arrested for public indecency on Tel Aviv Beach."

They made love that night, albeit hurriedly on the sandy beach across the street from the Tel Aviv Hilton. Hannah was totally uninhibited, while Kevin, certain they were being watched, fumbled nervously.

"Relax," she counseled as they lay naked on the beach and teasingly as if reading his mind said, "The worst thing would be your bare ass plastered on the front page of the Jerusalem Post. After all, inquiring minds would want to know," and she rolled on top of him.

He had never met anyone like her and had to fight back an overwhelming urge to ask her to marry him on the spot. He assumed she would think he was crazy. They knew so little about each other. Would she like it in the States and if not could he live here? She would certainly not be a camp follower traveling from tournament to tournament beside him as so many of the players' wives did, but that part of his life was coming to an end anyway. What about her family, could she leave them?

"I can hear your mind working," she whispered in his ear, "let's enjoy the moment and let nature take its course." She was right, of course. They dressed quickly and made an odd pair walking through the late evening deserted hotel lobby to the elevator, disheveled and barefoot with sand in their hair. Once in his room they showered and made love again. This time he was the aggressor as he was sure they were alone and unwatched.

He awoke at 6:30 AM and Hannah was still asleep. He had the finals of the tournament in six hours and normally the adrenaline would already be racing through his body as he mentally would prepare for a championship match. But today not even the thought of the $75,000 first place prize money could command his attention. At 7:00 AM the telephone rang and he grabbed it on the first ring, not wanting her to wake up. It was Sy.

"Kevin, meet you for breakfast in five minutes."

"OK," Kevin whispered.

"Why are you whispering?" then a pause and Sy continued, "Do you want to make it thirty minutes and bring a friend?"

"You're too fucking smart for me. Yes, I want you to meet her, and I have a real story to tell you. Give us thirty minutes."

She was stirring, and it was all he could do to keep from ripping the covers off her.

"C'mon, sleepyhead, I want you to meet a friend."

Thirty minutes later they joined Sy in the coffee shop of the Hilton. Kevin and Hannah were ravenous, while Sy had only fruit and coffee. Kevin relayed the events of their previous night's dinner and the amazing resurrection of a family. When he finished Sy, who had asked no questions, pensively said, "When are you going to tell your father?"

"I don't know. I can't just call him up and lay this

on him. I was thinking of going home to Chicago after the Vegas event and maybe trying to mend fences."

"Would you want me to talk to Aaron?" Sy queried. "I was going to stop in Chicago before I left for Vegas."

Kevin thought for a moment, "No, you've never met my father and this really shouldn't come from a stranger." Sy was about to reply but decided not to. "Well, I just think you ought to tell him as soon as possible; after all he's getting up in years." Hannah sat silently during the men's conversation and sensed that Sy knew more about Kevin's father than he admitted, but this was not the time or place for her to interject herself.

Then Sy said in a lighter vein, "You know, champ, you do have a match to play today, and if you win I make twenty percent of $75,000, so say good-bye to this beautiful lady and let's get your ass moving." The spell was broken and they all got up from the table.

"Will you be there today?" he asked.

"Do you want me to?"

"You know the answer to that one."

"OK, leave six tickets at the box office. I'll bring my father, your brother, your sister-in-law and your two nephews, and they better be good seats or your name will be mud in the family. 'Bye, Sy."

When she had gone Kevin looked at Sy with a schoolboy's grin. Sy put his arm around his student, "You better marry this one fast, Kevin. She's pretty, smart, independent, and when she finds out what a philandering schmuck you are she'll drop you like a hot potato. Now let's go practice, I need the dough if

I'm going to buy you an expensive wedding gift."

It wasn't easy even for Kevin to get six front row tickets, so he insisted that extra chairs be placed in the V.I.P. box. "For my family," he explained to the tournament umpire, who had read Kevin's biography which made no mention of any family other than his father. But he accommodated Kevin, whose reputation as a troublemaker was legendary, and the tournament umpire wanted no additional problems.

For the first time in his long professional career he had fans in the stadium that would cheer for him whether he won or lost, played well or poorly. It was an odd, comforting feeling, and he understood how his opponents had felt throughout the years when they had family in the V.I.P. boxes.

His opponent this day was John Haas, a seasoned twenty-eight-year-old veteran whom he had played many times. Haas was ranked number ten in the world and, like Kevin, was using this tournament as a tune-up for the Las Vegas event. Their record against each other was fairly even, with Kevin having won most of their early matches and Haas winning the last three times they played. There would be no surprises in this match as they knew each other's strengths and weaknesses.

The bright September sun beat down upon the hard court surface and Kevin, who was almost ten years older than his opponent, felt that if he was to win, he would need to do it in two sets. The longer the match progressed the more it favored the younger man. But after two long, hard-fought sets they were even at one set apiece. Midway through the third set Kevin could feel the momentum of the match shifting to his younger opponent. At three games each in the third and deciding set Haas was preparing to serve when from the V.I.P. box Kevin heard a cry of encouragement, "C'mon, Uncle Kevin, you can do it!" He glanced over at his two nephews who were giving him a thumbs up sign. Smiling, Kevin raised his right thumb in a salute to the boys. He thought to himself that he would not lose in front of his family. Now, game face on, he put two decades of professional tournament experience to work and broke his opponent's serve at love, and then went on to win the match 6-4 in the third set.

With the Israeli T.V. cameras and microphones in front of him recording the check and trophy presentation, a gracious champion proclaimed, "I want to thank the fans for supporting me and especially my family sitting there in the V.I.P. box. I feel that this will be my final tennis tournament in Israel, but I will be back many times to your country where I feel welcome and comfortable and where most of my relatives live. In honor of my family I want to donate my entire first place prize money of $75,000 to the Israel Tennis Centers to be used for development of their junior tennis program. Shalom."

This was a Kevin Garland that few people knew, and the 10,000 fans in the Ramat Hasharon stadium stood and gave him a rousing ovation. The match and award ceremony was being taped by U.S. cable television and the producer, knowing he had captured something special immediately made arrangements for sale of the tape of the match and award highlights to the major U.S. networks for showing in their evening sports segments.

CHAPTER 33

In his drab Chicago apartment, a tired Aaron Garland was eating a tasteless T.V. dinner in front of his television set. He knew his son was playing in the finals of the Tel Aviv tournament, having followed the match results each day in the local newspapers. He hoped the sportscaster would at least report the results. After the baseball scores the sportscaster did far more than report the match results.

"Chicago-born Kevin Garland, in a brilliant display of tennis, upset favored John Haas to capture his third and probably his final Israel Open championship. Here is tape of match point."

Now glued to the television set, Aaron saw Kevin hit a running backhand down the line to win the match and then he watched the award presentation. As Kevin referred to his family in the V.I.P. box the camera panned those seats, and Aaron felt a shock run through his body as the camera, now in close-up, focused in on several people including an aged Zalman Zacksman. It was over forty years since Aaron had seen that face, but there was no mistaking the man.

As he listened to his son's brief speech his eyes filled with tears and he felt his pulse racing.

I was right not to give up on him, he thought. As he turned off his T.V. the telephone rang.

"Aaron, did you see Kevin on the news?" An obviously excited Doc blurted out, "he was terrific both on and off the court. I think he's growing up, Aaron. Say, I didn't know you had family in Israel."

"Neither did I, Doc. I'm not quite sure what that was all about."

In Tel Aviv they all celebrated that evening at a local restaurant owned by an old army comrade of Barak's who refused to accept any money for the food and drink.

"I saw on T.V. what you did, Mr. Garland, and this is my way of saying thank you. Besides Barak knows about a little nurse in Eilat that he threatened to tell my wife about if I gave you a bill, so your money's no good here. Besides you gave it all away anyhow," and the proprietor chuckled at his own joke.

All evening patrons of the restaurant stopped by their table to congratulate Kevin and he accepted their accolades graciously. He was on an emotional high, and Kevin did not want the evening to end. Sy said his good-byes at 9:00 PM to catch a flight back to the States. Kevin walked him to the street. He felt closer to Sy than ever before as the two had become real friends during the last few weeks and not just business associates.

"Even though you cost me twenty percent of 75 grand by giving away the prize money, I forgive you," Sy said in jest. Then in a serious vein he added, "Something's happened to you Kevin, you've changed. I think you grew up a bit. This girl is good for you; don't let her get away." Then he added what Kevin thought was a strange comment, "I think you're in for some big surprises in the near future, champ. Your whole outlook on life may change, but I think you can handle it. You're not the same jerk I used to know." With an uncharacteristic act of affection he clasped Kevin in both arms, "I'll see you in Vegas. So long, Kevin."

Kevin went back into the restaurant feeling a little melancholy and tired. It had been a long day and he was starting to feel the effects of the last few days. Barak, Danielle, and the boys were the next to leave as Barak had to report for duty the next morning. They planned to keep in touch and agreed to schedule a trip to Chicago after the Las Vegas Tournament. These people, who had not even existed for Kevin a few short days ago, now would be a part of his life for as long as he lived, and he was sorry to see them leave.

Kevin, Hannah, and Zalman lingered over coffee and the restaurant was now nearly empty. "Hannah tells me she's going to show you our country for the next few days. When you come back we'll spend a few hours together before you leave, OK?"

"That's fine," Kevin replied. He knew that Zalman was aware of the fact that he and Hannah were lovers and he felt that the old man had just given his tacit approval.

The next few days were glorious. They drove the country in Hannah's vintage Mercedes, and she took obvious pride and delight in pointing out the biblical points of interest. They visited the Sea of Galilee and the Dead Sea, covering each other in mud baths and then soaking in the warm sulphur pools. They climbed Masada at dawn and spent some time with her friends at a kibbutz in the Golan Heights. At night they slept under the stars and made passionate love. Kevin was surprised at how many people recognized him and congratulated him on his victory. The whole country felt like one large family.

On the third day of their trip Hannah insisted that they stop at a small hospital in Haifa. Kevin felt that she had some ulterior motive for wanting him to visit this particular hospital, but he would have followed her to the moon if he thought that would make her happy.

The hospital specialized in caring for sick children, and Kevin stood by a glass window watching children in a play area while Hannah went to meet a staff doctor who she said would probably want to meet him if the doctor could find a few moments of spare time.

After waiting about ten minutes Kevin saw Hannah briskly returning with a short woman who was dressed in a white lab coat with a stethoscope around her neck. The olive-skinned woman had gray hair that framed a perfect oval face. She looked to be in her early fifties.

As she approached Kevin and could see him clearly, she instinctively hesitated and reached for Hannah's arm as if to steady herself. She had a peculiar expression of wonderment, and tears flowed freely down her face.

"Kevin, I'd like to introduce you to Dr. Schwab. She is one of our foremost pediatric surgeons." Hannah took a step back as Kevin reached out to shake the doctor's hand. Instead of shaking Kevin's hand, the tiny woman took his outstretched hand in both of her hands and for a few moments studied his fingers. Under her breath she uttered, "Such a big hand, I'd know it anywhere."

"I'm pleased to meet you, Dr. Schwab," Kevin said as she shifted her gaze from his hand to his face.

"Please, call me Anisa," she replied. Kevin thought she had a strange accent, but it was more of a minor speech impediment than an accent. "Hannah tells me you are a very famous athlete and the son of a man I once knew."

"I don't know how famous I am anymore but I am the son of Aaron Garland, I believe you may have known him as Aaron Garlovsky." For a few moments Kevin thought the doctor had not heard him for she seemed deep in thought. Finally she responded.

"Yes, that was the name I knew him by. How is he?"

"Well, it's been a long time since I've seen my father, but I intend to remedy that soon after I return to the States. I imagine he's OK."

Looking up into his eyes, the small woman could not stop the flow of tears. "You look so much like him, you should not delay in seeing him. I must tell you that to me your father is a hero. I owe my life and everything I have accomplished to him. Not a day goes by that I do not say a prayer for his well-being. Now that I see you I know that my prayers have been answered. I would like to write to him, would you give me his address?"

"Of course, but don't be surprised if Aaron doesn't write back. He never was much for writing, and he never speaks of his past."

"That's all right. I live, I speak, and I am in some

small way able to help sick children because of what your father has done for me. I won't be upset if he doesn't write a letter back to me." She then took Kevin's hand and started to walk with him down the hospital corridor. They made strange sight, this tall powerful man being led by the tiny white-coated woman. "Let me tell you a little about your father, Kevin, he was so much a major part of my life. He even taught me my first surgery lesson when I watched him slice the throat of a man who raped me. . . ."

They arrived back at her apartment in the late afternoon, and Hannah immediately went to check on Zalman. He assured her that he was fine and was well able to care for himself. The following early morning Zalman and Kevin walked together along the Mediterranean shore. "It's time you learned a bit more about your father, Kevin. You may be surprised and even shocked at what I am about to tell you, but it's a story you should hear, and I am the right person to tell it to you."

Europe/Middle East: 1945

CHAPTER 34

The respect and admiration that Aaron and Zalman had for the English during their brief time in London dissipated shortly after their arrival in Palestine. Here the English were the caretaker authority, and their disdain and dislike for the Arab populace was only exceeded by their feelings for "those bloody Jews."

Their temporary commissions as officers in the British Army had been canceled at the war's end, and Aaron and Zalman had been assigned to work at a farming kibbutz not far from Tel Aviv.

It was November 1945, the war with Germany had ended, but for Aaron and Zalman little changed as they went from one war to preparations for the next.

Immigrants from Europe were flooding Palestine, some legal, most not. The Arabs, deeply resenting the influx of Jews into what had been their homeland for so many centuries, did all they could to stem the flow of refugees. The British authorities, in an effort to appease the Arabs, did what they could to stop the tide of human cargo, but the rickety ships, filled beyond capacity with refugees, kept coming. Some made it to land; most were intercepted and the passengers interred in camps in Cypress or turned back to the open seas in vessels that were often less than seaworthy to make the voyage to displaced person camps in Europe.

Other than the cities of Jerusalem, Tel Aviv, and Haifa the land was primarily sandy desert and rocks, all bug-infested. Roads were poor, irrigation nonexistent, and yet these "bloody Jews" kept talking about it being "a land of milk and honey." The words "fanatic" and "Zionist" became synonymous, and neither the British nor the Arabs understood these driven people whose entire raison d'etre revolved around a reborn homeland in what they called "Eretz Israel."

A Jewish underground army, the Haganah, was a well-known secret and everyone was a soldier without a uniform. Aaron and Zalman's kibbutz was named "Kibbutz Rachel" after a martyred sabra killed by Arab marauders, and it was built over an elaborate underground network of rooms and tunnels that had been painstakingly constructed to hide an entire factory for the making of small arms and bullets. Many kibbutz workers would spend days at a time underground and then sit before sunlamps for a few hours to perpetuate the myth of their doing farm work.

Aaron and Zalman's skills with weapons were invaluable to the tiny underground army. Aaron's ability to speak German, Polish, Yiddish, English, and now Hebrew further enhanced his position, and the Haganah leaders saw him as a future general. The heroic feats of the "Juden Stern" grew with time, and Aaron and Zalman would marvel over the reverence heaped upon them by many of the newly arriving Polish refugees.

When they had an occasional day off they would try to visit Jerusalem and wander through the teeming open fronted markets and winding side streets. Zalman felt an immediate kinship with the land and the people. Even learning Hebrew was not the tortuous chore he had envisioned it to be. Aaron, on the other hand, reserved judgment. He vehemently abhorred the British authorities and their attitude of superiority, and he could not abide most of the Arabs whom he could not forgive for embracing the Germans both during and after the war. He felt this was a place where he probably belonged, and perhaps because there were so many Jews in this place, he was relatively comfortable.

Aaron would idly stand for hours watching the children race and play between century old olive trees and through the new fields of the kibbutz. They exuded a spirit never found in Jews who had lived in the towns of Europe where even after centuries of residence they were only visitors and had to measure every movement, fearing to upset or antagonize the "real" citizens of the country.

Neither Aaron or Zalman had much experience with women their age and felt awkward around them. When Aaron had frequented the taverns of Krakow dressed as an S.S. officer he had been approached many times by prostitutes and always quickly rebuffed their advances. Should someone have discovered his circumcised penis, his life would have ended abruptly with a firing squad. He could not deny, however, that he had often been aroused by them.

In Kibbutz Rachel the young women had far fewer inhibitions than their European counterparts, and they flirted unmercilessly with the young men. Aaron, with his dark, brooding good looks and powerful physique, was a special target. The mystique about his exploits as a resistance fighter during the war served as an additional aphrodisiac.

It was impossible for a healthy young man in his mid-twenties not to be attracted to the girls, especially in the close quarters of the hot underground factory or in the fields where they wore shorts, halters, and little else. Aaron first succumbed to a twenty-year old sabra whose parents had immigrated to Palestine in 1920 from France. After his first encounter, he was certain he was in love until he discovered that her goal was to sleep with every man under fifty living on the kibbutz, and her conquest of Aaron, and soon after Zalman, gave her tremendous status among her peers. She genuinely liked, not loved, Aaron and patiently taught him the finer art of making love, when she could occasionally fit him into her busy nocturnal schedule.

Life in the kibbutz became routine. The days were filled with work, either above or underground, and the balmy Mediterranean nights were spent either making love or more often dancing with comrades whose dreams of building a new state consumed them. It was exhilarating to have a purpose, a reason to be alive. It was the only place in the world that wanted them. Now, they were caught up in the spirit of building something permanent, something bright and alive that could replace the horror of the life they left years ago and thousands of miles away. In this small piece of arid land it was almost impossible for Aaron and Zalman to recall that before coming here their entire focus was simply to survive one day at a time and kill as many of the enemy as they could before their inevitable demise.

In November of 1947, Wolf Posner had been languishing in a British prison for over a year for his "treasonous actions against the British authorities." He had became too much of a thorn in their side, and the British arrested and sentenced him to ten years in prison after a speedy mock trial that sent shock waves through the Jewish community. His incarceration only served to intensify Jewish resistance to British ruled Palestine. Jews numbered over 500,000 and over the past years had openly and brazenly fought with their British rulers.

On November 29, 1947, the United Nations, meeting at Lake Success, New York, accepted England's demand to relieve themselves of governing Palestine. The mandate they had received from the old League of Nations was terminated, and the territory was to be divided into a Jewish and Arab state with Jerusalem shared by Jews, Muslims and Christians. It seemed a logical plan but nothing in the Middle East related to logic, and without declaration war commenced in earnest between Arabs and Jews.

CHAPTER 35

In the distance a jeep containing three men approached the barbed wire fence surrounding Kibbutz Rachel just as the sun was setting into the calm Mediterranean Sea. Aaron had just finished his evening meal when he saw the vehicle racing down the dusty dirt road as it approached the fence bordering the kibbutz. The sight of the jeep gave him an ominous feeling, and the hair on the back of his neck seemed to rise. For Aaron this was a sure sign of some impending danger.

A shame, he thought, it was almost too peaceful here.

The jeep slammed to a stop in front of the communal mess hall, and Aaron heard the driver ask to see Aaron Garlovsky and Zalman Zacksman. Aaron approached the three men, one of whom he recognized as a high ranking Haganah officer. Zalman was summoned from the underground factory and an impromptu meeting took place in the large empty kibbutz mess hall.

"We've just been informed that the British intend

to hang Wolf Posner before they leave on May 15," the man called Ev Schwartz began. "They feel he has been responsible for the death of too many of their soldiers, and they intend to make sure he is killed before they leave." Aaron and Zalman waited silently for the man to continue. "We need someone to volunteer to lead a group to break him out of prison, and you two have been selected. We understand that some years ago you snatched a prisoner out of a German prison."

"That was an entirely different time and place, and the man we freed was dead within a short time after the escape," Zalman said in a restrained voice. This was clearly a suicide mission and the five men all knew it. Zalman continued, his voice now less restrained, "You're asking us to throw our lives away, you know that don't you?" His anger was rising, for he knew they could not force him to accept this assignment.

"We have ten hand-picked volunteers ready to go with you," Ev Schwartz continued.

"Zealots," Aaron thought, "this whole fucking country is filled with zealots ready to die for any cause. It's amazing that we have survived as a people for so long with so many zealots."

Aaron then spoke, "I know you want an immediate response, but Zalman and I need to talk about this before we give you an answer. By all rights we should have been dead years ago, so it's not a fear of death that prevents us from answering now. I just hate to throw away our lives and the lives of your ten volunteers unless there is some chance of success, no matter how slim." This seemed to satisfy the men and they agreed to meet again in two days. They deposited a file with Aaron and Zalman showing the location of the British jail in Tel Aviv, fortifications, statistics on defenses, and potential escape routes. At least they had done their homework.

Curfew time had come, and the men stayed the night leaving at dawn the following morning. By breakfast time everyone in the kibbutz knew what Aaron and Zalman had been asked to do, and the unanimous consensus was that the plan was ill-fated and doomed to failure. Mort Goldenberg, one of the kibbutz leaders, spoke for the kibbutz that morning.

"This plan is madness. The result will be the death of Wolf Posner, and the death of a dozen of our best young men at a time when we can ill afford to lose a single man." What was not said was that Aaron and Zalman were two of the most combat experienced and weapons knowledgeable men the Israelis had. Their premature loss could spell disaster in the battles certain to come. Better to let Wolf Posner be killed by the British than try a ridiculous suicide mission.

Two days later the Haganah officers returned to the kibbutz and the mess hall meeting reconvened. This time Aaron took the lead.

"We have decided not to volunteer for your scheme to break Wolf Posner out of what we see as an impregnable prison," Aaron paused to let his words sink in, as the men sat impassively before him. "We have, however, another idea that we think may have the same results. The difference is our plan may have some remote chance of success." He now had their full attention and in a conspiratorial tone began to outline his plan for the rescue operation.

CHAPTER 36

General Ian Campbell had commanded the British occupation forces in Palestine for the past two years, and he had dreaded every day of his command. The weather was generally too hot, the country a waste-land, inhabited by uncivilized Jewish and Arab radicals. He came from a long line of soldiers and like his father, grandfather, and great-grandfather, he knew that a soldier served where he was sent, not where he wanted to go. "Thank God this mandate is coming to an end. I'll be rid of this desert and the mad people who live in it," was his comment upon hearing that the United Nations had ended British rule in Palestine. Prior to coming to Palestine he had little contact either with Arabs or Jews, and after being in this command for two years felt they deserved each other. The Arab wanted no change and the Jew wanted to change everything. He was well rid of both of them.

It was known that General Campbell had ordered the arrest and incarceration of Wolf Posner and his aide-de-camp Desmond Stein. Before being posted to Palestine, General Campbell had met both Posner and Stein in England where they appeared to be decent chaps, especially Stein who was a much decorated British soldier during the war. However, their activities over the last two years, he felt, left him no choice. They had been directly or indirectly responsible for the death of too many of his men, and it would serve as a warning to others of their ilk who had challenged his authority if his last act as commander was to sign their death warrants. Besides, it would place him in good standing with his friends in Damascus when they discovered that he had been responsible for getting rid of the terrorist Wolf Posner.

Rumors had been flying for some time that the Haganah or the radical Irgun would try some rescue operation, and the General made certain that any such attempt would fail. Besides the extra guards posted at the prison and extraordinary security measures in place, orders had been given to kill both Stein and Posner immediately in the event of a rescue attempt. Blame would be shifted to the would-be rescuers and the matter would be ended.

General Campbell's daily routine generally differed only slightly each day. Breakfast at home from 7:00 to 8:00 AM, a twenty-minute escorted drive to British headquarters in Tel Aviv, lunch from noon to 2:00 PM at the officers club, then after another two hours at headquarters, he would be driven to his estate by the sea where he typically had cocktails on his veranda and relaxed before dinner, which was served promptly at 7:00 PM. He played bridge from 8:30 to 11:00 PM with friends Monday, Wednesday, and Friday evenings. He often was heard to remark that it was extraordinarily difficult to maintain a civilized lifestyle while living in an uncivilized society. Most people to whom he would utter these remarks had no idea of what he was saying since he never mixed with the local populace, but they would murmur their concurrence because that was what General Campbell expected them to do.

It was Friday evening and at 11:20 two of General Campbell's three bridge playing partners had just left. As was his bi-weekly habit the third partner, the dashing Major Kent Smythe, would share the general's bed that evening. Aside from the guards at the front entrance to the estate, only a skeletal household staff of a housekeeper and one servant remained to clean up. The rest of the staff always left early on Friday to get to their homes before sundown. That was another thing about these people that General Campbell despised, didn't they know that Sunday not Saturday was a holy day?

Two small rubber rafts with four men dressed in black tied up to the seawall behind the general's estate, and their leader, a lean, powerful man, quickly scaled a pre-positioned rope ladder hanging over the seawall leading into the compound grounds.

A terrorist attack on the General's impregnable estate from the sea side was always deemed out of the question, as the thirty-foot seawall faced the sea and scaling the wall, especially at night, without help from someone inside the compound would be suicidal. This fact, coupled with the three large Doberman pinschers that roamed the estate grounds at night, gave the General a feeling of complete safety. A small trip wire that sounded a silent alarm also bounded the grounds just inside the seawall. The alarm would summon the guards from the post in front of the estate as well as instantly flooding the entire compound with high-powered floodlights and triggering a high-pitched siren.

Mrs. Joan Hoffman had served as the General's housekeeper ever since he had taken command of the British forces in Palestine. He had inherited her from his predecessor and, finding her credentials in order, saw no reason to change. She spoke perfect English and treated the General with the utmost respect. Under her direction the household staff was well trained, and the General was pleased with his decision to keep her on. She was a slim woman in her mid-fifties, with tightly pulled back gray hair and always well kept. It was rumored that the General's predecessor had been romantically involved with her. General Campbell dismissed the rumor as being just that. Even though she was a handsome woman she was, after all, a domestic servant. The General, aside from preferring men to women, was a great believer in the class system.

Had the General been a bit more curious, he might have wondered why Mrs. Hoffman always wore a long sleeved blouse or jacket on even the hottest days. Had the General's intelligence officer done a more thorough background check on his loyal housekeeper, he may have discovered that she had been a headmistress in a Vienna girls school before the war and had survived Theresenstadt concentration camp. Mrs. Hoffman, whose real name was Bessie Madalia, was an agent for the Haganah and had been supplying information about the British high command and General Campbell from the day he arrived.

That evening, as the General and his lover Major Smythe fell into an exhausted sleep, Bessie Madalia quietly went to the back lawn area of the estate where she blew on a dog whistle whose sound was too high pitched for human ears. The three large Dobermans bounded to the whistle, for they knew dinner would be set out. The meal for the dogs this evening would be their last as they wolfed down the chopped raw horse meat abundantly laced with arsenic and sleeping powders. Bessie did not like killing these magnificent animals, but simply trying to put them to sleep would not do. There was a chance of sleeping powder not working and a dog awakening at the wrong time. Ten minutes later the three dogs were dead, and she pulled their inert bodies into the bushes.

She then scurried to the basement where she quickly removed the fuses that fed electricity to the trip wires surrounding the rear of the estate. Leaving the basement, she carried a thirty-foot rope ladder that had been carefully hidden. She secured it to a large tree near the sea wall and threw the ladder over the wall precisely to the spot where the two rubber rafts were silently being paddled. She then returned to her room, put on her night clothes, and waited.

Aaron, his powerful arms propelling him quickly over the wall, was the first to climb into the estate grounds. Climbing over the wall, he crouched and surveyed the area cradling his Sten gun. A half moon gave just enough light to see the manicured lawn of the estate and a light coming from a door purposely left ajar by Bessie Madalia signaled that she had done her job. Aaron dropped a stone over the wall, and the three waiting men raced up the ladder.

Once inside the mansion the four men found Bessie waiting. She silently directed them to the General's suite where they found the General and Major Smythe sleeping naked in the General's king-size bed.

Aaron roughly awoke both men who were startled to be staring into the blackened faces of the four dark-clothed invaders. General Campbell quickly recovered his composure and with obvious false bravado demanded to know what was going on.

It was Aaron who answered, "You're under arrest, General, and you will ask no questions. We are on a very tight time schedule, and you and your friend will either accompany us voluntarily or we will shoot the handsome major and drug you. Either way you will be coming with us. You have three seconds to make your decision." With that Zalman pressed his pistol against Major Smythe's right temple and one of the men dressed in black produced a syringe filled with a clear liquid. One look at the fear etched on the Major's face was enough for the General.

"We'll come with you. Can we get dressed?"

"Absolutely not," Aaron answered, "let's go." Within four minutes the group of six men, four dressed in black and two completely naked and handcuffed together, were paddling the two rafts away from the compound into the inky black Mediterranean Sea.

The abduction was not discovered until early Saturday morning when the upstairs maid found a letter addressed simply to "The British Commanding Officer in Palestine," on the General's pillow. Taking the letter to Mrs. Hoffman's bedroom, the maid, as she related to the authorities many times that morning, discovered Mrs. Hoffman in her bed, bound and gagged with a large bruise on her forehead where she claimed to have been struck by an unknown assailant.

The letter was delivered to Colonel Lawrence Albert, Chief of Intelligence and second in command to General Campbell. It was a typewritten one page letter that went directly to the point.

General Campbell is under arrest. He will be treated in the exact manner as your prisoner Wolf Posner. Any attempt to rescue him will result in his immediate death. If Wolf Posner is killed, General Campbell will be killed in exactly the same manner. If Wolf Posner is released from prison, General Campbell will be released as well. There will be no more communication from the General's captors except that a press release advising the public that the General and his lover Major Smythe have been taken prisoner will be delivered at noon in two days. Until then this incident will remain secret.

The General's staff was called to a rare Saturday afternoon meeting where, after an expected amount of damning, teeth gnashing, and finger pointing, Colonel Albert summed up the alternatives.

"Gentlemen, I see only two options. We release Wolf Posner at once before this matter is leaked to the press, or we keep him in custody, which will probably doom General Campbell and make us the laughingstock of the civilized world by allowing a pipsqueak band of terrorists to snatch our Chief of Staff and Major Smythe from their 'respective beds.'"

Colonel Albert emphasized the words "beds," but there was no one in the room who didn't know of the General's sexual preferences. What was unsaid was that they did not want the world to find out that this scion of the English military was a homosexual, and worse that British security was found lacking. In the end, the vote was unanimous to release Wolf Posner at once and the order was issued. An hour later the prison commandant excitedly telephoned Colonel Albert to advise him that there was a slight problem.

"The bloody little Jew bastard refuses to leave without the prisoner Desmond Stein and the terrorist Meyer Bishov," he spit into the telephone.

"Release them all at once," Colonel Albert ordered without hesitating.

"But, Colonel, they're terrorists."

"I know. You have your orders, release them all." Exactly two hours after Wolf Posner and his two associates were delivered to the Jewish authorities General Campbell and Major Smythe were found by a motorized British patrol on the road from Tel Aviv to Jerusalem. Major Smythe had a jaw broken in exactly the same manner as Meyer Bishov, who had been struck with a rifle butt by one of his guards as he was being released.

Three weeks later on Saturday, May 15, 1948, the hated British were gone and all hell broke out.

CHAPTER 37

For the second time in their relatively short lives Aaron and Zalman were in a declared war. The similarity between the two wars lay in the fact that to lose meant the virtual extermination of a people. It was this same fact that became their greatest weapon. Their leaders would say, "We have to fight to the last man, woman, and child for we have no place else to go," and as much as it sounded like propaganda, it was nonetheless true.

Outnumbered by forty to one, poorly armed, many of their soldiers speaking only a foreign language, with little or no military training, divided among themselves into Sephardic and Ashkenazem, orthodox and agnostic, Haganah, Palmach and Irgun, they held their ground.

Aaron and Zalman spent most of their days speedily training recruits in the use of the Sten guns manufactured in their underground factory. Small arms captured from dead or retreating Arab soldiers became another source of weapons for the two to examine and reconvert for use by the makeshift army.

The British, upon leaving, had turned over most strategic sites to the Arabs along with considerable military hardware. Aaron and Zalman were also charged with training specially selected recruits in the art of infiltrating these sites and killing the new inhabitants. In the entire country no two men had taken more lives than Aaron and Zalman, and their leaders reasoned, who better to train the next generation of terrorists for the tiny nation.

At least for now they were able to spend most of their time at the kibbutz and usually slept each night in their same bunk in the underground factory dormitory.

In his entire twenty-eight years Aaron had never received a personal letter, so in the middle of a war when the secretary of the kibbutz told him he had a letter from the United States, he was certain that it was an error. But it was no mistake and late that evening, totally exhausted and wanting nothing more than to fall into his bunk and sleep, he found the letter neatly placed on his bunk bed in the dormitory. It was postmarked "Chicago, Illinois, U.S.A." and addressed simply "Aaron Garlovsky, Tel Aviv, Israel." Carefully opening the envelope taking pains not to damage the stamps, Aaron found a one-page letter handwritten in Polish.

Dear Nephew:

If you receive this letter, I hope you are well. I have spent many hours trying to find members of our family but you seem to be the only one that survived the war. I was present at your Bar Mitzvah but left Poland shortly afterwards and now live in Chicago, Illinois, U.S.A. The news-papers carry articles of the war and I hope you will not be harmed.

I extend an invitation to you to come to Chica-go, Illinois, U.S.A. I will send any money that you need to get here. I remember that even as a young boy you were a good carpenter and made many things with your father.

It would be nice if you could write to me if you get this letter.

Fondly,
Your uncle
Samuel Polonsky
(I am your Mother's brother)

Aaron reread the letter several times that evening and then carefully placed it in the bottom of the card-board suitcase he kept tucked beneath his bunk. He tried not to think about the letter, for it had evoked shadows of a life that no longer existed. It was too painful to think about the past, and for years Aaron had forced himself to reject the memories. He decid-ed not to tell anyone about the letter, not even Zal-man. He couldn't remember what his uncle looked like but he did remember the adults in his family talking about "Samuel Polonsky" in hushed tones when they thought no children were around.

Exhausted as he was that night, sleep would not come. The letter had stirred images that Aaron had relegated to the far corners of his subconscious. As horrible as the memories were, the letter also cre-ated a thread of connection with his family, something that Aaron had never expected to occur. He had no rational basis for not telling Zalman about his uncle, but for some unknown reason felt that this had to remain his secret. He assumed that Zalman knew he had received correspondence from America, for getting a letter was an important event in the kibbutz and would be the subject of considerable gossip. He also knew that Zalman would never ask him about it, feeling that if Aaron wanted him to know something about his private life he would tell him.

The next morning, the letter deposited neatly in the bottom of his suitcase, Aaron went on with his life. There were guns to make, recruits to train, and a war to fight. There was no time to think of anything else.

Two days later Aaron had a late evening visit from one of his least favorite people. Desmond Stein was acting aide-de-camp to Wolf Posner, the recently elected Minister of Defense of the new state of Israel, and if anything, his new position of power served to reinforce his aggravating air of authority. Aaron enjoyed nothing more than antagonizing the man whenever they met.

Both men knew that Aaron and Zalman had been responsible for saving Stein from the gallows when they forced the British to free Wolf Posner. But true to his character, Stein could not bring himself to acknowledge a debt of gratitude. Neither man wasted any time on social amenities. Clearing his throat Stein declared, "The old man wants to see you, now."

"About what?" Aaron asked with perverse innocence knowing what would come next.

"I'm not at liberty to discuss that with you. I repeat, the minister wants to see you. I have a car waiting." Stein's voice was raised an octave, for he was not accustomed to being questioned, and Aaron always left him feeling exasperated.

"I'll be ready in about a half hour," Aaron stated simply and turned on his heels leaving Stein standing speechless.

Two hours later Aaron sat with Wolf Posner in the minister's well-guarded fortified bunker. Posner looked harried and had aged since they had last met. He had a hundred things to do and people kept coming into the underground windowless room with emergency situations. Seeing the old man at work Aaron felt a little foolish for having kept him waiting the extra half hour.

When they were alone Wolf put his arm on Aaron's shoulder and with a sly smile that Aaron knew well said, "You really enjoy terrorizing Desmond, don't you, my boy."

With a warm grin, Aaron looked at his host and answered, "Mr. Minister, it is one of the greatest pleasures this life allows me," and both men, exhausted to the bone in the middle of a war, roared with laughter.

Tea and sandwiches were brought in, and now Aaron was certain that the task he was to be assigned was perilous. Wolf Posner would waste little time and no food on an ordinary assignment. When they finished eating Aaron could only think, "Oh shit, I'm in real trouble now."

Posner rose from his chair and walked to a large wall map of Israel and the neighboring countries. Picking up a pointer he spent a few minutes showing Aaron on the map what was transpiring on the various war fronts and then he dropped the bombshell.

"Aaron, Arab armies are being guided and advised

by former Nazi officers who have been given refuge in their countries. These Nazis are experienced soldiers and are attempting to finish Hitler's work with their new hosts. The Germans operate openly with impunity and feel they cannot be reached in Cairo or Damascus. You, my boy, are going to change that and quickly. Professionally trained and battle-tested German tank commanders are designing the plan to lead Egyptian tanks across the Negev Desert to smash our tiny state. The new state of Israel has no tanks and few planes, so experienced tank commanders could speed ahead unabated across the wide open desert to destroy an enemy who had no way to stop them. Therefore, Aaron, if we can not stop the tanks, we will stop the German tank commanders."

For a full minute there was complete silence in the room. Even the constant interruptions stopped as the two men sat facing each other and pondering what had been said.

The old man and his staff had decided that Aaron was the logical choice for this mission. He spoke perfect German, was an experienced killer, and was the most adept man in the country at infiltrating German establishments.

As Posner described the mission Aaron's mind rolled ahead. He knew he was the right man for the job and the fact that it was assuredly a one-way mission didn't enter into the equation. If he could somehow substantially disrupt the enemy war machine with this type of bold stroke, he was ready to volunteer. Besides, killing Nazis was what he did best, and he had already lived far longer than he had ever expected. Clearing his throat, Posner told Aaron to take a few days to make his decision. Aaron rose from his chair and looked squarely at Wolf Posner.

"I'll be ready to leave in four hours."

The old man smiled knowingly at Aaron, "There is no rush. I knew you would volunteer, so take an extra hour."

Aaron was flown to Cypress where he was given forged documents identifying him as Wolfgang Wostl, a machinery salesman from Hamburg. Now, well fortified with German marks and dressed in a white linen suit, that following evening he boarded an Egyptian Airways plane bound for Cairo. The authorities in the Cairo Airport passed him through with only a perfunctory glance at his German passport. There were many Germans in the country, and airport officials had been instructed to make entry easy for them. After all, the Germans and Egyptians had a common enemy in the Jew.

As Aaron left the Cairo airport in a colorful Peugeot taxi for the hour ride to his reserved room at the Grand Hotel on Talaat Harb St., he was certain that Nazi Odessa agents were already busy checking him out. By the time they received information, or rather lack of information, about one Wolfgang Wostl, it wouldn't make a difference.

An hour after checking into the Grand Hotel and showering, he converted his marks to Egyptian pounds and left the hotel to take a long walk through the streets of the ancient city. He purposely remained away from his hotel for over three hours, knowing that his one suitcase would be thoroughly searched during his absence. In the lining of the suitcase, hidden but certain to be found by anyone carefully examining his things, documents identifying him as S.S. Captain Erich Friedler had been planted. Once again agents of Odessa would search their records. This time they would find records of one S.S. Captain Friedler. What they would not know was that he had been unceremoniously kidnapped and killed two days before by Israeli agents operating near Buenos Aires where he had hidden since the war's end.

Aaron leisurely toured the Citadel of Cairo and the Antiquities Museum. Upon returning to his hotel suite at dusk he quickly determined that his suitcase had in fact been searched. Attempts by someone to replace the clothing items exactly as they had been packed were flawed, and the documents hidden in the lining of the suitcase had been replaced out of order. Aaron wasn't sure if the searchers wanted him to know he was being checked or not. In either case the result would be the same. Old S.S. files on Erich Friedler were no doubt being examined at this moment, and by the time Odessa agents started to question sources in Buenos Aires, Aaron assumed he would either be dead or long gone from Cairo.

It was Friday evening, and the plan called for Aaron to frequent the Munich Inn, a Cairo beer hall located in the Garden City area that catered to the large German community. An Israeli spy had submitted reports indicating that on Friday and Saturday evenings most of the German army officers spent their weekends reveling there. The Inn had a small dining area on the second floor that was always reserved for about fifteen of the former German officer staff currently working for the Egyptian Army. Each Saturday evening they dined sharply at 9:00 PM. It was Aaron's goal to either be invited or force his way past the guards and into the dining area where he would attempt to kill as many of the diners as possible, then escaping through the rear kitchen area where, if he made it, he was to be guided by an agent working with the kitchen staff to a safehouse. Beyond that the plan was sketchy and arrangements to get him home had not been formalized. In truth, there were so many variables and things that could go wrong that it seemed to be a waste of effort and manpower to make the final arrangements until the first part of the plan was successful.

The success of the entire plan hinged upon the placing of a Sten gun and several hand grenades above the washroom ceiling tiles by the same kitchen staff person who was to guide Aaron to safety after the attack. Supposedly the package had already been deposited and Aaron's goal this evening was to survey the beer hall, attempt to ingratiate himself with the patrons, many of whom would already know his assumed identity, and most importantly verify that the weapons were in place.

At precisely 10 PM Aaron's taxi pulled up before the Munich Inn. The Inn had been designed as a replica of the beer hall frequented by Hitler and his gang of thugs in Munich in the early 1930s.

Architecturally the building was a success. Entering the hall Aaron felt as thought he had instantly stepped from the Middle East to Europe. The beer hall was crowded with celebrating patrons. Smoke and laughter filled the room, and buxom blond waitresses expertly dodged between the tables delivering trays filled with large foaming beer mugs. German was the only language spoken.

Aaron found a seat at one of the long wooden tables and ordered a beer and bratwurst. He knew that he had been observed from the moment he arrived, and rather than attempting to talk to anyone, he simply ate his food and waited.

He had been seated for about ten minutes when two men approached his table.

"Do you mind if we sit here?" the smaller man asked in German as they both took seats.

"No, of course not," Aaron answered trying not to be too friendly. He did not want to appear as though he was trying to make friends.

"Are you newly arrived?" the smaller man asked casually, "I've not seen you here before."

"Yes, I've just arrived. I was told the food and beer is good in this place."

The larger man did not speak and seemed to be sizing him up. Aaron could not help but think that the larger man might have known the real Erich Friedler, and the charade would be over.

"I'm Jakob Schwaben and my friend here is Otto Kruger," the smaller man continued, "we're from Dresden, and you?"

"Wolfgang Wostl from Hamburg," Aaron replied.

"I think not," it was the big man who now spoke. Aaron could feel himself tense. "Your accent says you are a Berliner, Captain Friedler." Aaron felt himself relax and let a smile cross his lips.

"No, you have me confused with someone else," Aaron protested, but not too convincingly.

"As you wish," the big man responded and started to leave the table. He was clearly the leader of the two, for as he started to rise, the smaller man jumped up.

Aaron returned to his beer and food, not bothering to watch the men leave.

Trying to figure out his next move he felt a hand on his shoulder. Turning quickly he smelled the beer breath of the large man who said, "If you return here tomorrow evening, perhaps you would join me and a few of my friends for dinner, say about 9:00 PM." It was phrased as a question but delivered as an order.

Not trying to be anxious Aaron said, "Yes, if I am able to return that would be nice."

"There is a small dining room upstairs. We will look forward to having you join us, Mr. Wostl." The man left and Aaron, trying to control his emotions, ordered another beer. No one else approached him and he engaged no one in conversation as he drank. He ordered a third beer and after finishing it, asked one of the barmaids for directions to the toilet. His kidneys were bursting but he wanted to have a legitimate reason before going to the washroom. Aaron was not accustomed to drinking beer and felt a little wobbly as he unsteadily strolled between the wooden tables to the toilet. Seeing that the single toilet stall was empty Aaron quickly entered it and latched the door. He saw no one else in the washroom and quickly stood on the commode pushing aside the ceiling tile and reaching up. His hand closed on a package wrapped in newspaper and tied with cord. The package was in place. Somehow, he thought, things are going too smoothly. Replacing the ceiling tile, he quickly jumped down and started to urinate as the next patron staggered noisily into the room to relieve himself.

Still a bit unsteady Aaron left the crowded beer hall and hailed a passing taxi to take him back to his hotel.

CHAPTER 38

Certain that he was constantly being followed, Aaron spent the entire next day sightseeing and remaining completely visible to anyone doing surveillance on him.

A strange way to spend one's last day, he mused as he attempted to maintain a facade of mild interest in the various curio shops, juice stands, and tourist attractions.

At sundown he returned to his hotel, showered, and left again at 8:30 PM for the Munich Inn dressed in a light linen suit. The cool night air from the open taxi window seemed to refresh him and sharpen his senses. Aaron never felt more alive. It was just before 9:00 PM when he handed the taxi driver the fare and entered the Inn.

If anything, the crowd was larger and noisier than the night before. Aaron found a seat at the same table he had sat at the previous night, and before he could order a beer he was approached by a large man with a crew cut and ill-fitting brown suit that did little to hide the shoulder holster under his jacket.

"Herr Wostl?" the man asked.

"Yes."

"You will follow me," and the man turned, never thinking Aaron would not be a step behind.

He led Aaron up a stairway to a doorway leading into a small second floor dining room. At the top of the stairs Aaron was searched for weapons by the man he was following as another man, also in a brown suit, watched carefully. When they were sure he was unarmed, he was admitted to the small dining room.

The dark-wood-paneled room was dimly lit. It took Aaron a few moments to survey the scene. A large dining table with about twelve to fourteen men filled the middle of the room. A rear exit for servants to bring food and drink from the kitchen was the only other doorway. There were no windows in the room and Aaron was relieved to see no washroom or toilet facilities, for his entire plan hinged on the plausibility of his having to use the toilet downstairs.

"Herr Wostl, so glad you could join us this evening," boomed the large man whom Aaron recognized from the night before. "Let me introduce you to your dinner companions." As introductions were made several of the diners rose and clicked their heels. Aaron could not help thinking that if the situation were not so dangerous, it could almost be comical. The last man to be introduced to Aaron did not rise nor did he smile.

"General Von Dorten, may I introduce Wolfgang Wostl," the large man said solicitously. General Karl Von Dorten was the leader of this group, and Aaron knew that he had commanded a Panzer Division in Rommel's Afrika Corps. He was a professional soldier who knew his trade well, and it was he who commanded the entire Egyptian Tank Corps. Aaron bowed slightly to the General and thought, "If I get no one else tonight, General, you are a dead man." They made room for Aaron at the table and filled his plate with sausage and dumplings. Aaron's interrogation would take place after dinner and by only a few of these men. It was imperative that he strike while they were all present. Aaron thirstily drank two large steins of beer and asked the man next to him if there was a toilet in the room. The man said, "No, you must go down the stairs."

As Aaron rose to find the toilet, he saw General Von Dorten nod to the brown-suited guard standing by the door who acknowledged the nod and followed Aaron down the stairs and into the toilet which thankfully was empty.

"Do you want to go first?" Aaron said to the man in German.

"No, you go, I wait," came the curt reply. Aaron entered the stall and latched the door. Quickly standing on the commode he stretched his arm into the ceiling and his fingers closed on the cord-wrapped package. Jumping down, he flushed the toilet and unlatched the door to the stall. The guard was washing his hands by the washbasin when Aaron, moving like a cat, wrapped the rope cord around the guard's neck and with his powerful arms and hands strangled him to death. It was over in seconds and Aaron dragged the limp body into the stall and seated him on the toilet. Now, moving quickly, he removed the dead man's pistol and placed it in his belt. Tearing the paper from the weapons package he put the four hand grenades in his coat jacket pockets and placed the Sten gun under his coat. Perspiration poured through his light linen jacket and down his face. Head down he walked quickly back to the stairwell leading up to the second floor dining room and his intended victims.

As he quickly climbed the stairs two at a time, the remaining brown-suited guard rose lazily to again search him.

"Where is Hans?" he asked as Aaron reached the top step.

"Dead, asshole, like you," and Aaron grabbed the man's arm and threw him down the staircase. As the man was tumbling down the stairs Aaron pulled the pin on one of the hand grenades and threw it after the guard. Bursting through the doorway, he proceeded in a fast walk towards General Von Dorten who half rose as he saw Aaron charge into the room. The machine pistol's first bullets tore the General's chest apart and Aaron then sprayed at the rest of the now confused and panicked diners. Chairs spilled over and men dove for the floor. Aaron never stopped moving. The Sten gun now empty, Aaron pulled the dead guard's pistol from his belt and fired at anything that moved.

He could hear screaming from the downstairs area where the first grenade had detonated. Aaron reached the back kitchen door, and as he slipped through it lobbed two more grenades into the middle of the dining room.

The entire attack lasted less than twenty seconds, and the dining room was filled with the smell of cordite. Blood and body parts covered the dining table and walls.

Aaron reasoned that no return fire had occurred because all present had been thoroughly searched for weapons before entering the dining room.

Once inside the second floor kitchen area he had been told he would be met by one of the kitchen help who would guide him to a safe house but the entire staff seemed to have fled.

Removing the last remaining grenade from his pocket Aaron surveyed the kitchen serving room and saw a rear stairwell that appeared to be his only means of exit. A white waiter's jacket lay in a heap on the floor, and almost as an afterthought Aaron pulled off his suit coat and donned the serving jacket. The pistol was empty, and he dropped it as he now raced down the rear stairwell hoping to mingle with the confusion that was surely taking place downstairs. The stairway led into the brightly lit main kitchen on the first floor, which was being used as a temporary haven for the grenade-wounded patrons. Screaming voices both in German and Arabic filled the room. It took a few seconds for Aaron's eyes to adjust to the bright kitchen lights, and as he surveyed the room and saw a door, which he hoped led to the outside, he felt a hand on his arm. Aaron turned and made eye contact with a slightly built kitchen aide. The girl could not have been more than fifteen or sixteen years of age, and although she did not speak, Aaron knew he had met his contact. She motioned for him to follow her and as they were slipping out the rear door, Aaron heard a commanding voice in German, "You there, stop!" Without turning and certain that a bullet would follow the shout, Aaron pulled the pin from the last grenade and lobbed it over his shoulder in the direction of the voice as he and the girl darted into the alley-way behind the Munich Inn. They raced down the alley while the grenade exploded creating a new round of death and mutilation. As they ran down the dark, narrow alley the girl tossed off her white jacket and motioned for Aaron to do the same. A small donkey cart was tethered approximately 100 yards from the Inn, which was now ablaze with red-yellow flames illuminating the Cairo night. The girl reached into the cart, pulling out a filthy torn abas and headdress for Aaron. She motioned for him to remove his shoes and socks and threw him a pair of rope sandals. His European-made shoes would be an immediate giveaway.

With Aaron now seated in the cart, the girl prodded and led the little donkey cart through a maze of narrow, crowded streets. Mobs of people were gravitating toward the fire, which was visible in the night sky for miles. The crowd paid no attention to the silent pair slowly making their way down side streets to some unknown destination. Aaron could not help thinking that he was not unlike a patient who puts his life in the hands of a surgeon whom he had never met and simply hopes that he wakes safely from the anesthesia. It was a feeling he did not like.

Cairo at night, at least the part they were traveling through, had an aroma all its own. The smell of dung and urine of man, donkey, dog, and camel melded with the odor of cook pots and unwashed flesh. At times the stench was so overwhelming Aaron was certain he would vomit. His abas had certainly never been washed, which was adding to Aaron's nausea. Yet his diminutive guide moved on, oblivious to the stench and the crowd of people about them. A shudder raced through Aaron as the smells suddenly reminded him of the concentration camp and its similar aroma of too many unwashed people crowded together. Aaron wished again that he had a weapon, vowing not to be captured, but to die first.

They had been traveling north through the narrow streets for almost two hours and were now on a sandy dirt road leading away from the city. She's smart, Aaron mused, staying off the main roads where there were certain to be police stopping anyone who looked suspicious. There were no lights on the road, yet now the little donkey needed no prodding as he picked up his pace anticipating his tether and feed.

They finally came to a stop in front of a ragged striped cloth tent that was one of several dozen formed in a loose cluster. The girl motioned for Aaron to go into the tent as she quickly unhitched the donkey from the cart and put an old leather feed bag on him. The night had turned cool, yet as Aaron entered the tent he was met by a blast of smoky warm stale air. The tent was dimly lit by a small kerosene lamp tended by a ragged-robed crippled old man who as he saw Aaron smiled weakly, exposing rotted and toothless gums.

Suddenly the girl was beside Aaron tugging his sleeve in an invitation to sit. For the first time Aaron really looked at her. He could not help but think, "My God, she's beautiful." A small oval face framed large, black, shining eyes. She had a small, straight nose, clear olive skin, and perfect lips. Knowing only a few words in Arabic Aaron said, "Ismi Aaron," pointing to himself. The girl put her head down and the old man said, "Anisa," as he pointed at the girl. Then the old man took out a curved dagger from his waistband and grabbing his tongue with his left thumb and forefinger made a motion with the knife as though he was cutting his tongue. He then pointed again to the girl. Aaron realized that the old man was telling him that someone had mutilated the girl's tongue and that was why she could not speak. Then the old man drew a small six-pointed star in the sand floor of the tent with his knife and then again pointed at the girl. Once Aaron saw the star, the old man quickly and fearfully erased it with his foot. The girl, it seemed, was an Egyptian Jew who for some reason had been mutilated. A small band of Jews had remained in Egypt since the time of Moses. Their forefathers, for whatever reason, had elected not to leave the land of the Pharaoh, and a tiny segment of their survivors had remained to modern times. This girl was apparently one of those survivors. The old man probably took her in needing someone to care for him. Somehow her background was discovered and she had become an agent for the Israelis. There was no doubt that a great deal of hate had built up in her small frame for her brother Arab.

The old man handed Aaron a piece of pita bread filled with fuul that was sand-covered, but rather than insult his host, Aaron thanked him and ate every morsel. As Aaron lay down for a few hours of sleep, he could not help but reflect on his predicament.

I'm probably the most sought-after man in Egypt, hiding in a tent where I speak almost no Arabic, my host speaks no language I understand, and the courageous little girl who saved my life does not speak at all. Ah well, I've been in worse places, I think.

CHAPTER 39

Aaron had fallen into a deep, dreamless sleep when he was roughly awakened by Anisa. For a few startled moments he was not sure of his surroundings. But the fear he saw etched into her small, perfect face brought him immediately awake. Looking around Aaron saw that she and the old man had gathered their meager belongings and were hastily preparing to flee. As Aaron stepped outside the tent he could see that everyone in the immediate vicinity was in a state of panic and abandoning the small tent village. A cloud of sand dust a few miles away seemed to be converging upon them. Squinting Aaron could see what appeared to be an armored motorized column of about ten vehicles racing in their direction. Somehow he was sure the authorities had tracked him to this place, and he was certain that he and the girl were the target of the column. He was just as certain that they would indiscriminately destroy the entire tent village and all its inhabitants in their frenzy to capture him. People carrying anything they could were fleeing in every direction except toward the oncoming vehicles. The attackers would be upon them in minutes, and Aaron made a split second decision. He grabbed Anisa's arm and started running toward the cloud of sand dust. He hated to leave the old man behind, but there was no way the lame old man could keep up with them, and speed was their only chance of survival

Aaron, unaccustomed to running in the rope sandals, stumbled and ran half carrying half dragging the slight girl, who was sure he had lost his mind. They ran directly at the oncoming vehicles for about 200 yards when the first armored personnel carrier came around a turn not more than twenty yards in front of them. Grabbing Anisa, Aaron dove to the side of the road into a small ravine where they lay completely still as the first vehicle passed them kicking up a blinding cloud of sand and dust, which covered their bodies, and as the remaining vehicles passed them they were virtually invisible. Aaron could hear the rapid explosions of automatic weapons already raking the small village and its terrified inhabitants. They lay perfectly still for a full thirty seconds after the vehicles had passed and then cautiously crouching low, rose and continued to run in the direction that the vehicles had come from. Again, Aaron wished he had a gun.

They walked most of the day without food or water and without any direction. Aaron assumed they were heading in a westerly path since the late afternoon sun was now shining in their faces. Somehow, he knew, he must go north to the Mediterranean and then east toward Israel. How to do this was a different problem. Right now their first priority was water, food, and a weapon, not necessarily in that order.

They came upon a small farming souk where Arab

vendors were hawking their wares. Anisa was prepared to steal whatever they needed, but Aaron still had a pocket filled with Egyptian pounds from the marks he had converted at his hotel. He did not want to bring attention to them by stealing a few morsels of food, especially in this country where one could have a hand chopped off for minor theft. Besides food and drink he had Anisa purchase a knife with a six-inch razor sharp blade that Aaron slipped into his trouser belt beneath his robe. The feel of the knife satisfied him as much as the food and drink.

Aaron and Anisa took their food to the edge of the souk and filled their stomachs with round unleavened bread made with coarse flour, gibna rumi cheese, and fuul. They drank Asab juice, rather than the water that was playing havoc with Aaron's bowels. Bellies filled, Aaron took time to try to figure out a plan. He had two basic choices. They could mingle with the millions of people in Cairo where he would pose as a mute and wait for some opportunity for escape to arise, or, still posing as a mute to hide his ignorance of the language, he could somehow now try to make his way to the Israeli border. Each option presented an equal amount of danger and, not one to procrastinate, he elected to try for the border. He had no way of explaining his plan to Anisa, yet he felt she would follow him in either event.

The most direct route would be to travel due east from Cairo, across the Suez Canal and the vast Sinai Desert to Israel's western borders. But if by some miracle the trip could be made, they would find themselves in the Negev. Going from one desert to another did not seem to give them much chance for success.

A better plan seemed to be to somehow get to Port Said on the Mediterranean coast where he would try to bribe their way on to one of the small ships traveling up the coast, perhaps to Gaza. It was about 150 kilometers from Cairo to Port Said as the crow flies. What they needed, Aaron reasoned, was a car with a full tank of petrol, and as his hand closed on the knife handle in his belt, a gun wouldn't be so bad either.

CHAPTER 40

Traveling as two mute beggars, Anisa and Aaron proceeded in a northwesterly direction. Once outside of the teeming, crowded streets of Cairo, the pair became uncomfortably visible to anyone traveling near them. The village of Ismailiya would be their first destination, and it would take them at least four days of difficult walking to reach it. They followed an old trade caravan route, and on the second day of their journey Aaron's stomach felt as though it was on fire. The strange food and contaminated water he had been consuming for the past few days were taking their toll. Try as he would, he was too weak to travel. He lay before a small fire that Anisa built and slept fitfully for twelve hours. He awoke feeling a little better but still too weak to travel. After two days their meager food and water rations had been consumed. Aaron knew he had to eat and drink to regain his strength. They had seen campfires a few miles ahead, and he gave Anisa some Egyptian pounds and pantomimed eating and drinking. She quickly understood and nodded as she took the money. "Be careful, little one," he weakly cautioned, knowing she did not understand the words but got the message.

I'm just like a Jewish mother, he thought as he watched her small frame, head erect, trudge off in the direction of the distant campfire. It was late afternoon, and Aaron calculated that it would take her two hours to reach the distant camp and return. She should be back before nightfall. He added more dried camel chips to the small fire and dozed off again.

When he awoke again a sliver of a moon shone overhead and he was still alone. Looking at his watch he saw it was 9:00 PM, and the girl had been gone for over six hours. Something was wrong. He felt a little stronger and forced himself to his feet. Having lived with danger, Aaron knew that weak as he was he had to push on if Anisa did not return. Staying in this spot without food and water meant certain death. It took Aaron almost two hours to arrive at the outskirts of the small camp Anisa had been sent to, and he dropped to his stomach as he laboriously crawled in the sand to the edge of the camp.

Four camels were tethered about twenty yards from the fire and he could hear men arguing and then laughing. He crawled closer and then he saw her. Anisa had been stripped naked; her frail arms and legs were tied to four wooden posts buried in the sand. Her face appeared to be swollen as though she had been beaten. Aaron watched helplessly as one of the men casually sauntered over to her and hiking up his robes dropped down, impaling her. Aaron could hear her moan and see her struggle against the rawhide that bound her tiny wrists and ankles to the posts.

As soon as the man finished, a second one fell

upon her, almost crushing her small frame. From the casual manner of the men it was painfully obvious that they had raped her earlier as well. Mercifully, as the second man finished his rape Anisa appeared to lose consciousness. A third man walked over and slapped her face a few times. Eliciting no response and not wishing to spill his seed into an unconscious body, he angrily delivered a kick to her groin and walked away. Anisa did not move and Aaron prayed that she had not died.

Grasping his knife, he waited silently, and after an hour of talking among themselves three of the men unrolled blankets and went to sleep as the fourth man went to check the camels. He would probably remain on lookout but knowing that there were no caravans in the area, Aaron felt the fourth man would probably doze off as well. An hour later with the fire dying down, Aaron's suspicion was confirmed. The desert night had turned cold, and Aaron knew he had to move soon if there was to be any hope of saving the girl. He watched as the guard, whose back faced Aaron, dropped off to sleep with his rifle across his lap. All thoughts of his illness out of his mind and acting on pure adrenaline, Aaron stealthily covered the twenty yards between himself and the sleeping guard. Coming up behind his target, Aaron's big left hand covered the man's mouth as the razor sharp knife slashed his exposed throat. Aaron had severed many throats in his short life, but none gave him any more satisfaction. The man struggled briefly and died silently as Aaron's hand covered his mouth and prevented any death scream.

Aaron continued to watch the other men, but none

had moved. Feeling rather than seeing eyes upon him, Aaron half turned to see Anisa, now wide awake, staring at him. Aaron picked up the dead man's rifle. It was an Enfield, undoubtedly stolen, he thought. Aaron walked over to the three sleeping men and placed the rifle barrel against the head of one of them and pulled the trigger. The man's body convulsed once as the back half of his skull disappeared into the sand. The two remaining sleeping men were jarred awake by the rifle volley and jumped to their feet as Aaron calmly fired two quick rounds hitting each man in the leg. Letting them lie where they fell, he struck each with the butt of the rifle, hard enough to knock them senseless but not enough to kill them. He then cut the rawhide rope binding Anisa's arms and legs, half expecting her to cry and reach to him for comfort.

Unsteadily she rose to her feet. For a moment he thought she would faint again but she was able to walk. Naked, blood covering her face and groin she motioned for Aaron's knife, which he handed her. Slowly walking to the rear of the two wounded rapists she grabbed the hair of one and just as she had seen Aaron do moments before, slashed the knife across his exposed throat from ear to ear. The last man was one of the two that Aaron had seen rape Anisa. Blood pouring from the wound in his leg he grabbed for her small, naked form. Standing directly in front of the man, completely fearless, she drove the dagger into his throat.

She then calmly turned to Aaron, who was standing at her side, handed back his knife, and proceeded to gather her scattered clothing. Watching her in action, Aaron could only marvel as he thought, "give me an army of men with her guts and I could conquer the entire Middle East."

It was dawn by the time Aaron and Anisa buried the four bodies in shallow sand-covered unmarked graves and finished taking inventory of the supplies in the camp. Whatever the four dead men were trading had apparently already been sold, for they had a significant amount of Egyptian pounds and food and water for a long journey.

Each man had an Enfield 10-round magazine rifle and two had British Webley Mark VI revolvers with ample ammunition for all the weapons.

Aaron was amazed at the resiliency of his diminutive traveling companion. Other than the swollen face, she seemed no worse for wear after her ordeal, and Aaron was certain that young as she was, she had been abused by men before.

They rested the entire next day and Aaron could feel his strength returning. He spent several hours teaching the girl how to clean, load, and fire a rifle and revolver. She was a quick study, and he could only imagine what faces she saw etched in her mind on the rock targets at which she fired round after round.

On the third day after the attack, with food and water supplies secured on two camels, they mounted the remaining beasts and headed east. Aaron's plans had changed with the captured camels and weapons, and he decided to head for Suez. From there he would restock his food supplies and try to navigate the 150 or so kilometers across the barren Sinai Desert to the Israeli border.

It was two weeks later when a motorized border patrol of Palmach soldiers intercepted the small caravan of four camels, a young girl, and what appeared to be a fierce-looking, dark, bearded Bedouin. One of the soldiers pointed his automatic weapon at them and in Arabic ordered them to halt and be searched. Aaron could see Anisa's hand reach under her robe for her revolver. He shouted at her, "Anisa, no," vigorously shaking his head. It would not do to travel so far only to be shot by one's own people. Leaving no room for error, Aaron threw his hands in the air and shouted in Hebrew, "I am Captain Aaron Garlovsky returning from a special assignment ordered by Minister of Defense Wolf Posner. Do not shoot."

"And I am David Ben-Gurion," came the snide reply from the Palmach leader who continued to point his weapon at Aaron. "Get down from that camel and be searched."

"I will, you pompous little prick, and then I will take that Sten Mark V submachine gun you're pointing at me and stick it right up your ass."

The Palmach leader stared at Aaron, then he and his companions started to laugh as he lowered his weapon, "Welcome home, Captain, you appear to be exactly the type of man Wolf Posner would send on some God-forsaken special assignment across this never ending desert."

CHAPTER 41

The vaunted Egyptian Tank Corps with its 250 combat-ready vehicles charged across the vast Sinai Desert to blast the Zionist Jew out of Palestine. Practice maneuvers, led by their German commanders under the direction of General Von Dorten, had previously exceeded even their expectations. They were the elite of the Egyptian Army, and knowing that the Haganah and Palmach had no tank force to challenge theirs, they were prepared to Blitzkrieg to the heart of Tel Aviv. The Sinai was no stranger to attacking armies as ancient Egyptian armies of the Pharaohs had used the same route to conquer Syria and Canaan. Similarly, Persians, Turks and Greeks had, in turn, used this same route to conquer the Nile Valley.

With the recent violent death of General Von Dorten and most of his staff, the new commander of the tank corps was one of their own. General Omar Ibn Aziz had bought his commission by paying a sizable fortune to the Minister of War and had further assured his quick rise through the Army by marrying the Minister's niece. He had graduated at the bottom of the class of the Egyptian officers training academy and then took a year of advanced training in Europe where he was unceremoniously dismissed from the French Military Academy for unspecified activities unbecoming to an officer of rank.

By the time his tanks rumbled to the outskirts of the southernmost Israeli outpost in the Sinai, their numbers had already been cut in half. Under General Aziz, a combination of suspected sabotage and mishaps had decimated their fuel and water supplies and perfectly conditioned, fully armed Egyptian tanks were now dotting the Sinai Desert where their crews had abandoned them.

Rumors had started to circulate through the Egyptian command that frontier perimeter kibbutzes had secretly received heavy artillery and were lying in wait for the tanks to attack.

General Aziz, rather than face a possible defeat in his first engagement with the enemy, ordered his tanks to halt a half mile from Kibbutz Sharon and commence a heavy shelling bombardment from that distance.

Inside the barbed wire-fenced frontier farming kibbutz the eighty-seven inhabitants, including thirty-three children under the age of ten, waited in underground bunkers armed only with a half dozen Sten guns, two light machine guns, and two 2-inch mortars with a total of thirty-five mortar shells. They had no armor, no artillery, and no way of defending themselves from any direct attack on the kibbutz by even one Egyptian tank.

Reports of the abandoned Egyptian tanks from nomadic Bedouin tribesmen living in the region had been speedily relayed to Wolf Posner at the Israeli War Command Center. Posner and his staff now faced a major decision. The opportunity to capture these tanks and turn them against their former owners had to be weighed against the chance for success and the removal of a number of fighting men from their current precarious positions. Posner could ill afford to divert a force of up to fifty trained soldiers with tank experience gained from serving in World War II in a mission that could fail.

In the end, the prize was too tempting not to go for. Aaron had done his job by cutting off the German head of the Egyptian tank corps. Now the opportunity to actually capture and use these tanks could turn the tide of the entire war. Jeremy Posner, Wolf's nephew, was ordered to organize and lead the raid into the Sinai Desert, and he was given a time table of thirty hours to plan and execute the attack. All he had to do was select the personnel, obtain supplies of fuel and water, transport all of them to the Egyptian Sinai Desert behind the enemy lines, find the abandoned tanks, refuel and start them, and then attack the remaining enemy tanks that were shelling Israeli outposts. It seemed an impossible task except for one factor: the mission was to take priority over every other operation.

Twenty-five hours later at approximately 3:00 AM one of the two overworked cargo airplanes owned by the Israelis and piloted by Eugene "Buddy" Rose, a former R.A.F. ace, took off from a secret runway north of Tel Aviv and headed west over the Mediterranean. Flying low, Rose turned south ten miles out to sea and flew toward the Egyptian coast. The plane had barely enough fuel for a round-trip and had been fitted with special balloon tires for a desert landing.

Its fuselage was crammed with forty-eight men, three jeeps, and enough fuel and water to operate twelve tanks with four-man crews. The plane was to be abandoned if no suitable area for a return take-off could be found. Radio silence was to be maintained at all times, and hopefully Egyptian radar would not pick up the low-flying airplane as it turned south toward the Sinai Desert and a destination forty miles from Al-Arish.

CHAPTER 42

The Sinai Desert, 24,000 square miles of little else than sand valleys and sandstone formations surrounding a west central region of limestone plateau. It was here that the ancient Israelites wandered during their forty-year desert sojourn.

God help these modern Israelis if the Bedouin information was not accurate. The plane had only enough fuel to return home with an empty fuselage. But those fears were quickly allayed, for as the eastern sun broke over a high-ridged sand dune, the desert appeared dotted with abandoned vehicles apparently in mint condition except for a lack of fuel.

The sturdy plane's balloon tires rolled to stop no more than fifty yards from a group of five abandoned tanks. Working quickly the men and material on the plane were unloaded, and within forty-five minutes Captain "Buddy" Rose was last seen flying low and heading north to the Mediterranean Sea and home.

Within three hours from the time the men landed, twelve "liberated" Egyptian tanks, now fully fueled, with extra cannon shells and machine gun ammunition cannibalized off tanks left behind, rumbled east. The cab of each tank left behind was doused with gasoline and set ablaze. The reports of exploding shells inside the abandoned blazing tanks reverberated through the desert. These burnt out vehicles would shell no villages. Small powder blue pennants had been stenciled on the front and rear of the twelve purloined tanks to distinguish them from Egyptian operated vehicles. It was mid afternoon when the group of twelve came upon the main force of enemy tanks. The midday heat in the tanks exceeded 100 degrees, and except for a group of a half dozen Egyptian tanks that were still systematically shelling the small kibbutz, most of the Egyptian tank crews were resting or sleeping in the shade afforded by their vehicles.

General Aziz's command tent had been erected behind the tanks, and the General, as was his habit, was in the middle of his mid afternoon nap.

Proceeding slowly, about twenty-five yards apart, the twelve captured tanks infiltrated the enemy ranks driving directly behind the tanks shelling the kibbutz. Upon radio command from Jeremy Posner they fired point blank, instantly destroying the shelling tanks. Turrets turning they randomly fired cannon shells at any vehicle without the powder blue pennant. Deadly machine gun fire raked the surprised and fleeing enemy tank crews.

Posner's tank rolled through the command tent, smashing it to the ground. The general's bodyguards tried to protect their commander but were no match for the 30 caliber machine guns that cut them down in seconds. The Israeli plan was to fire on the move, and as for those enemy tank crews who had the presence of mind to man their vehicles and return fire, they invariably destroyed tanks and crews of their own forces. Many of the tanks were not combat ready with machine guns broken down for cleaning and cannon shells stacked outside of the tanks.

General Aziz, bleeding from a minor leg wound, still in his underwear, threw his arms into the air and surrendered. His ignominious surrender was witnessed by his soldiers, who instantly threw down their weapons and followed his lead. The battle ended in less than a half hour.

The last thing Posner and his tank crews wanted was several hundred Egyptian prisoners. It was estimated that they were within a two day walk to the town of Al-Arish and the prisoners were ordered to leave, taking no weapons and as much food and water as they could carry.

Posner never let the prisoners get an accurate count of the number of tanks the Israelis had captured. He knew that the number would grow significantly as the defeated Egyptians made their reports. He kept his men out of sight and had instructed them to occupy additional abandoned tanks even if it was only one man to a tank. The captured Egyptian soldiers could readily see at least twenty-five tanks moving into formation with guns aimed at them, and any thought of a desperate counter attack was quickly smashed.

It was dusk as the Israelis watched the remnants of the German trained Egyptian Tank Corps trek over the sand dunes toward Al-Arish. As soon as they were out of sight of the Israelis, the defeated officers attacked and killed General Aziz, leaving his body to be eaten by buzzards circling in the open desert.

At Kibbutz Sharon the shelling had stopped for several hours when the first tank, now emblazoned with a large hand-painted Star of David entered the kibbutz compound. Warily the inhabitants approached the tank, knowing that this could be their Trojan Horse. But there was no doubt when Benny Alon poked his head out from the turret and shouted, "Please tell me if my sister Yael Alon is all right. Tell her it's her brother Benny and I've come for Shabbat dinner!"

CHAPTER 43

In May, 1948 the United Nations imposed a truce that
went into effect leaving a tenuous peace and divided
Jerusalem with the revered Western Wall of Solomon's
Temple in the hands of the Arabs. But the tiny nation,
grossly outnumbered, survived and captured the grudging respect of world opinion. Relief funds from the
United States and others started to trickle and then
pour in. Israel's leaders put out a cry to Jews worldwide to return to the homeland from the centuries old
Diaspora. Generally, the summons to return appealed
only to those whose current position was perilous, for
life in the new state was hard and dangerous.

Aaron returned to his kibbutz and continued in his
joint role of farmer and soldier. Anisa was transported to a settlement area where she was taught Hebrew
and indoctrinated into the ways of the twentieth
century.

The doctors told Aaron that there was a delicate and
costly operation that could possibly repair her mutilated tongue and allow her to talk, but it would be
many years before the procedure would be performed

in Israel. Here the medical efforts were geared toward saving lives and not cosmetics.

Zalman had discovered that he had a flair for politics. He was well liked in the kibbutz and outwardly maintained a genial disposition. Everyone, however, knew of his exploits with Aaron in Europe and the strength of his character. At twenty-eight years of age he was elected chairman of the kibbutz, and on June 30, 1948, during one of his visits to Tel Aviv at 85 Ben Yehudah Street, he was recruited into Shai, the newly formed government-sponsored information service agency. This was the founding group of Israeli intelligence.

While Zalman thrived in his new homeland, Aaron remained isolated. Other than Zalman, Wolf Posner, and Anisa he did not allow himself to establish any close relationships. He found himself questioning the meaning of his life, for he was certain that the war with the Arabs had just begun. It was not that he was afraid of another war; rather he feared living a life that did nothing except prepare one to die in some future battle. He only hoped that the bullet that surely had his name on it would kill him and not subject him to some living form of death.

During one of his early visits to see Anisa he was interviewed by a young overworked social worker who was assigned to her case. Other than having recruited Anisa as an agent out of the slums of Cairo, the Israelis knew little about her. Aaron could shed little additional information about her past life, but his insight into her character seemed useful, and the very blond social worker responsible for Anisa was attractive, so his visits were doubly pleasant.

Aaron was next assigned a new task that took him out of the country for several weeks at a time. The new State had a voracious appetite for weapons and Aaron, again because of his expertise with small arms and fluency in language, found himself shuttling between the Middle East and Europe to negotiate arms purchases.

His Israeli passport and documents identified him as Yitzhak Harry Rosenberg, a used machinery importer. Everyone knew the tiny nation needed machinery just as they knew his cover identity was a sham. Within six months of his first trip to Europe, Aaron Garlovsky at twenty-eight years of age had become one of the largest purchasers of black market armaments on the European continent. Aaron a/k/a Yitzhak Harry Rosenberg kept a small flat in Paris not far from the clandestine political department of the Israeli embassy, which he used as a base and from which he traveled the continent in search of guns. He grossly overpaid in most instances, but his orders were to buy the best weapons as quickly as he could. Hostile armies on Israel's borders could be unleashed at any moment. In thousands of Jewish homes in America and elsewhere people filled small blue and white tin boxes with coins collected to plant trees in Israel's arid soil. Some trees were planted, but the bulk of the donations went to purchase Aaron's guns.

Aaron hated his trips to Europe, for the memories the trips brought back were unbearably painful. On several occasions he thought he saw a familiar face in a railway or bus station, but in fact anyone he had known in his youth were long dead.

Mentally Aaron was in limbo. He found himself

dreading the tiring trips to Europe and conversely not looking forward to returning home. The secreted letter from his uncle in Chicago, Illinois, U.S.A., started to play a greater role as he contemplated his future. It was at the very least an option, an opportunity to start over in some place new without haunting memories or hostile neighbors. Aaron never really considered moving to the United States, but the mere fact that he had this chance to do so if life became too unbearable gave him a modicum of comfort.

Aaron found himself constantly depressed and physically and mentally drained, when fate once again intervened. Aaron had recently returned from one of his European "machinery" buying trips and decided to spend a night alone in Tel Aviv. It was a warm evening, and he was sitting at an outdoor cafe idly people-watching as he drank an iced coffee when she walked, or rather strolled, past him. They both saw each other at about the same time and after a fleeting hesitation she approached his table.

"Mr. Garlovsky? Aaron?"

"Yes, but I'm really embarrassed. I know you're Anisa's counselor, but I don't know your name."

"Abigail Friedlander, call me Abby," came the nervous, too quick reply.

Awkwardly Aaron asked, "How is Anisa?"

"Oh, she's doing very well. She is hopelessly in love with you, you know."

"No, I didn't, but I should get out to see her more often. She is a very special person."

"Well, she is extraordinarily bright and is already learning to read and write Hebrew and to use sign language. She still refuses to tell us anything of her past.

It seems her entire existence started when she met you."

Again, awkward as ever, Aaron asked, "Won't you sit down? Are you meeting someone?"

"No, I'm just spending a solitary evening, and I'd be delighted to join you."

They sat for most of the evening, this blond, lively sabra social worker and the dark, brooding, handsome soldier. They had so little in common in their backgrounds, yet that night they became friends. She was very attractive, yet strangely it was not a sexual attraction, but rather a relationship of two people who meet socially and instinctively like each other. Aaron found himself talking freely about himself, and Abby was genuinely interested in his story. Naturally he said nothing about his current duties. To Aaron this chance to talk about himself was a catharsis, and for the first time in as far back as he could remember he genuinely enjoyed the company of someone other than Zalman or Wolf Posner. Neither wanted the evening to end, but they had sat at the cafe for several hours and the fidgeting owner was closing for the evening.

For the next six months they met several times in between Aaron's trips. His demeanor changed and the depression that had been all consuming, seemed to slowly dissipate. They had still not slept together, although Aaron found himself becoming annoyed when Abby was the target of admiring stares from other men.

Could I be jealous? he would wonder and then dismiss the thought with a casual shrug.

They planned a picnic by the rocky shore near the lower Galilee and agreed to camp out that night. What was unsaid but tacitly understood was that they would for the first time make love that night.

It was an isolated spot by the water where they pitched their tent that afternoon. There had been a few recent incidents of rock throwing in the area by the local Palestinians but nothing considered serious. Both of them were a bit nervous and excited at the prospect of what the night would bring.

CHAPTER 44

The day began the same as a thousand other days for fourteen-year-old Ali Hammar. When he awoke at 5:00 AM his grandmother was already busy and had a small cooking fire blazing in their brick oven. Ali ate a quick breakfast of porridge with goat's milk and cheese wrapped with pita bread. He then went outside the small stone house that had been in his family for three generations and milked his grandmother's goats. She would barter some of the milk for flour and olive oil and make cheese with the rest.

Ali's formal schooling ended when the world allowed "the Jew" to establish their new state. Ali could not bring himself to utter the name of the Jewish state and its citizens would in his mind always be "the Jew." Before the war that had relegated him to third class citizenship in his own country, he had gone to school and had even played soccer with some Jewish children from a nearby kibbutz. But that had been a long time ago, and he had forgotten most of what the school taught him.

Although small for his age, he had recently been

invited to join a group of village boys a year or two older than he. They told him they were to be the vanguard of a new generation who would throw "the Jew" out of Palestine and return the country to its rightful people. Until the time for the great battle came, these boys were to inflict whatever damage they could upon the Jews. To date their actions resulted in some minor thievery and an occasional beating or stabbing of a Jewish settler or tourist who was unlucky enough to be caught traveling unarmed and alone.

Ali had not participated in any of these attacks, but as he listened to the stories of their brave exploits as told by the older boys, he became anxious to prove himself. Reprisals by the Israel Defense Force for these occasional acts of violence were swift and devastating, generally starting with them dynamiting the home of anyone deemed guilty of such action and the family either imprisoned or forced out of the country.

It was about 3:00 PM when Ali was summoned to a meeting with Nayef Jibril, the twenty-five-year-old leader of their group. His heart was pumping wildly as Nayef put his arm around him and Kamal Hilmi, another new recruit.

"You young soldiers are being given a great opportunity," Nayef began. "A man and woman have set up a tent by the shore about a mile from here and are apparently going to spend the night." Pausing for effect, with his arms still around the boys, he continued, "You will attack the camp and kill them with this." From under his robe he produced a large revolver and a dagger.

"When you are finished you will take any weapons

you find and return here, and may Allah be with you."
Finished speaking he handed the revolver to Ali and
the knife to Kamal. Exhilarated, Ali and Kamal immediately left the village to seek out their intended victims and to wait for nightfall. They found a spot on a
small hill about 150 yards from the couple's campsite
where they could spy on them. Aaron and Abby had
just emerged from swimming and Aaron was standing
by the campfire drying his large muscular torso. The
sight sent chills through the boys. Until this time they
had never thought that their intended victim would be
so powerful. In fact, up to this moment they had never
thought at all about the couple they were to attack.
The man's arms were huge, and if he even got close
enough to the boys to grab them, they would be dead.
Somehow, now the idea of attacking this man and
woman was now far less attractive than it had been
just hours ago. It was almost 10:00 PM when the couple almost reluctantly, it seemed, poured water over
the camp fire and retired into the small tent. The night
was moonless, but the clear, cold, star-filled sky
seemed bright as the stars reflected off the black
waters of the Galilee. There was movement inside the
tent for almost an hour after the couple had gone
inside. In a weak attempt at humor Ali whispered, "At
least they will be good and tired when they stop fucking and go to sleep." Kamal was too frightened to
laugh and had an overwhelming urge to urinate even
though he had done so just twenty minutes earlier.

It was almost midnight when the boys, bending low
and moving cautiously, approached the tent.

Had they started to watch the campsite a few hours
earlier when it was first set up, they would have seen

the large man set up a ground level trip wire around the perimeter of the camp.

They were about twenty yards from the tent when the flap was thrown back and a beam from a large flashlight caught them in its light. Screaming obscenities, Kamal raised the dagger and charged the light. He was about ten feet from the light when he was cut down by a short burst from Aaron's submachine gun. Confused and stumbling backward, Ali, holding the large revolver with both hands, fired two rounds. He saw the flashlight fall to the ground and he heard the man groan. Ali could see the man lying on the ground apparently trying to get up. Warily, he stepped forward and raised the revolver to fire again. Ali never saw the T-shirt-clad woman who had come out of the back of the tent point her automatic weapon and squeeze the trigger, instantly ending his short, troubled life.

CHAPTER 45

For Nayef Jibril, the attack by the two boys on Aaron and Abby was an unqualified success.

He and his staff never believed that the two young untrained boys would succeed in killing the Israeli couple. In fact, it was a greater victory for their cause if they failed. He referred to the dead boys as "cannon fodder" for the liberation of the Palestinian people.

Within twenty-four hours the two dead boys were being hailed as martyrs, killed by a heavily armed, crazed Israeli soldier who attacked them just outside their impoverished village. Three days of riots in Arab villages around the Galilee commenced when Israeli soldiers dynamited the homes of the families of the dead "martyrs." Nayef Jibril's group received fifty new recruits from the families of friends and relatives of the dead heroes.

Abby had placed a tourniquet around Aaron's thigh and drove the jeep like a woman possessed to Tiberias, which was the closest town. Aaron lost a lot of blood and had gone in and out of consciousness several times by the time he was rushed into the operating theater at the small hospital. Luckily for Aaron, few doctors in any country had more training in treating bullet wounds. He had taken a direct hit in the right knee, and the bullet had shattered, with the fragments damaging the major artery in his leg.

Aaron was in surgery for over seven hours with the surgeon's priorities to first save his life, then save his leg, and assuming they were successful in those efforts, to try and minimize the amount of residual damage and hope Aaron would be able to someday walk unaided. Aaron's last thoughts before the anesthesia took effect reflected on the fact that his luck had finally run out. He had survived two wars, a concentration camp, and a hundred battles only to be killed or at the very least crippled by a small frightened boy with a large revolver. "It seems that I have been waiting for this my entire life," was the last thought he had as the anesthesia rendered him unconscious.

Aaron remained in the hospital for three weeks after the operation. He refused to see anyone. The bullet that struck Aaron had irreparably damaged the patella. The bullet and the patella shattered, sending slivers of lead and cartilage into the patella tendon and into the anterior cruciate ligament. The surgeon tediously labored to remove them with a tweezer-like instrument. Stability and mobility of the knee normally achieved by its unique design were gone forever. Ruptured vessels had filled the knee joint with blood, and Aaron's knee and leg had swollen to grotesque proportions. The bullet fragments carried the additional chance for infection and the possibility of minute slivers of lead and bone escaping the surgeon's eye, necessitating subsequent surgery.

Aaron stoically accepted the constant pain and surgeon's frank discussion of his condition. He found little humor in the overworked young doctor's comments that the good news was that he would always know before anyone else when it was about to rain or turn cold.

Alone for weeks with only his memories, confined to a hospital bed, Aaron's mind raced with thoughts of a life wasted. He was almost thirty years old and during his entire adult life had never known peace. The image of hate in the screaming face of the young Arab boy he had killed became all-consuming. He too knew what it was to hate. He had hated the Nazis who had destroyed his family and his way of life. This was the same kind of hate he had seen in the face of the young boy with the raised knife whom he had so casually shot to death.

He knew he was not being rational, but his aura of immortality had been shattered and one of his worst fears realized. He was, at best, maimed for the rest of his life. Perhaps he would walk again, perhaps not. The next bullet or bomb could leave him alive and blind or alive and paralyzed. Dying would be easy compared to living without the ability to function freely. Perhaps this was just a warning—change your way of life now or you may not get off so lucky next time.

Aaron refused all visitors, and Zalman and Abby, who had themselves become close friends, respected his wishes figuring he needed some time to be alone. They were both certain Aaron would soon come to his senses and welcome their concern. But Aaron did not follow the expected path.

He had the hospital send an orderly to collect his personal belongings from the kibbutz, which were delivered to him packed in his old suitcase. When they were brought to his room he pulled out the wrinkled letter from his Uncle Samuel and reread it for the hundredth time. This time, however, was different, for he did not replace it but instead copied the return address onto a blank envelope and wrote a reply in Polish. It was the first personal letter he had ever written.

Dear Uncle Samuel,

I received your kind letter some time ago and truly never thought I would ever consider leaving this country. I must tell you that your letter was a source of great comfort to me in difficult times for it afforded me an option that few people here have.

I have been injured. I tell you this not for sympathy but to let you know that I may not be able to work as hard or as well as before my injury. If you do not want me to come I will understand.

I have no money of my own and cannot purchase tickets to travel to Chicago, Illinois, U.S.A. Also, I understand that I must be able to show your government that I have at least cash of $150 U.S. and a job.

If you can loan these funds to me I will make the necessary arrangements to leave for Chicago as soon as I am able to travel.

Also, I am telling no one here of my plans so if you write back to me I am told I will be at Tiberias Hospital for at least the next few weeks.

Respectfully,
Your Nephew,
Aaron Garlovsky

CHAPTER 46

They spent the entire afternoon and early evening together. Kevin had no doubt that the story Zalman had just finished telling him about his father was true, yet he could still not equate the father he knew with Zalman's courageous friend who climbed so often from the grasp of death. He could only imagine what those experiences had done to shape his father's personality. Almost every person Aaron had ever loved, other than Zalman and Abby, died violently. He started to realize that his father's failure to show overt affection to what he thought was his only son was probably his father's subconscious way of protecting him from the inevitable harm that came to all those to whom Aaron had shown his love. For the first time Kevin felt he started to understand the man who was his father.

They walked in silence back to the apartment, both deep in their own thoughts. When they were in front of the apartment building Zalman took Kevin's arm.

"I would like to see Aaron again before one of us dies. Tell him that when you go home. Tell him also about his other son and his grandchildren. It's time that he knew of them, and I know that after the shock wears off he will be filled with joy."

"I will, Zalman, I'll tell him about everything. Now what about you, would you be happy if your daughter ran off with a tennis player?"

"My daughter makes her own decisions, but I would be proud to have you as a son-in-law and the father of my grandchildren. Wouldn't that be a twist of fate after all these years, your father and I would be macha-tonum."

It was a somber Kevin Garland who lay next to Hannah that evening. She knew he had been told a shocking story and she felt she could best help him by just being there. Suddenly he turned to her.

"Come back with me, Hannah. You knew I'd ask." She didn't answer for a full minute and he thought she hadn't heard him.

"Hannah...," then she put a finger on his lips.

"Kevin, I think I love you, but we've only known each other for such a short time." He knew she would say this and he started to reply, but she continued, "I want you to go home to America and play your big tournament. When that's over I think you will need to make peace with your father. You certainly will have a great deal to discuss with him. Then, if we both feel the same and you still want me to come, I will." He knew she was right and how hard it would be for her to leave this place. Later as they lay wrapped in each other's arms, he had never been happier nor more at peace with himself.

They all spent the next day in Haifa relaxing at Barak and Danielle's home. There had been several recent border intrusions and in the middle of the day Barak was ordered to report immediately to a military base. He grabbed a duffel bag that was always packed and prepared to leave.

"It's the price we pay, Kevin, to have our own country."

"Good-bye, Barak, I'll see you soon." It's a strange country, Kevin thought after Barak left. I give a few dollars and people here treat me like a hero; my brother puts his life on the line when the telephone rings and no one even knows about it.

CHAPTER 47

The United Airlines stretch 727 banked sharply and
swooped down onto the runway. The newly remod-
eled McCarren Airport served the city of Las Vegas,
Nevada, which was growing by 5,000 people a month
and already had a population of over one million
inhabitants. Bugsy Siegel would never recognize the
sleepy little desert town that he had brought to worldwide notoriety.

A black limousine shuttled Kevin from the airport to his V.I.P. suite at the giant Miracle Hotel.
The tournament was a coup for the hotel, which
boasted a cage of leopards in the foyer and a giant
tank of tropical fish behind the reservation desk.
In a town where one could bet on almost anything,
the odds against Kevin Garland winning this event
were posted at 40 to 1. An international event of
this stature not only brought enormous media
hoopla and tourist revenues but also the high rollers
in their private jets who descended from all parts
of the globe.

The town fairly crackled with excitement about the tournament, and the promoters were gleefully estimating their profits. It was no accident that the players were treated like kings, for their talents were generating millions of dollars in revenue for the hotels, casinos, restaurants, and most importantly the promoters. It was like a narcotic for players like Bobby Stanik and Jaime Bell who were still very young. Even the seasoned veterans like Kevin, John Haas, and the number-one seeded Neil Kramer could not help but be caught up in the frenzy that was Las Vegas. Tennis had not captured this much attention since the first battle of the sexes between Billie Jean King and Bobby Riggs in the '70s.

The bell to his suite rang, and Kevin who had just stepped out of the shower, wrapped a towel around his waist and opened the door. Security on the V.I.P. floor prevented anyone without proper credentials from entering the floor, so Kevin had no fear of being accosted by fans or papparazzi.

"Welcome to Vegas, lover boy," Sy chimed as he breezed into the suite carrying his briefcase.

"I really expected you to bring Hannah. Any problems?"

"Nope, we agreed to give it a little time and space, but I'm hooked Sy."

"Great, she's terrific. Now, let's get down to business." For the next hour they reviewed the thirty-two-player draw sheet and practice schedule. Each player had agreed to give a one-hour taping session to network television before the event. Sy had arranged to have the interview done that afternoon to get it out of the way early.

When their business was concluded Sy nonchalantly asked, "Have you spoken to your father recently?"

Soberly Kevin answered, "No, but I plan to go to see him after this tournament. I'll tell you, Sy, I've learned things about him that are unbelievable. I believe I can truly forgive him for the times I thought he was shutting me out of his life." It was almost impossible for Sy to refrain from telling Kevin how wrong he was about Aaron shutting him out, but he held back.

"Well, you still may have some surprises when you see him," was as far as Sy would go.

In the television interview that afternoon Kevin gave the interviewer a scoop by telling him that he had met someone whom he hoped to marry, knowing that it would quickly be picked up by the gossip columnists who were sniffing for any bit of information about the players. It was especially tantalizing as he had always been considered a playboy. He hoped Hannah would be pleased, as it was his way of telling her that from his perspective he was going public with their relationship.

Kevin's first round match the following day was against Sy's former student, Bobby Stanik, and it was billed as age and experience verses youth and power.

Sy knew the young man's game intimately and devised a strategy to take advantage of his two weaknesses. Stanik had an inability to maintain concentration for a long period of time and a tentative net game in close matches. Kevin was to avoid playing to the youngster's powerful forehand as much as possible. The matches were scheduled for the mid to late afternoons to allow the fans to return to the gaming tables in the evening. The October weather, normally ideal for tennis, this year was still intensely hot. Kevin stayed true to the game plan and won the first set 7-5, breaking service by pounding deep backhand shots and then playing a well-disguised drop shot at set point that Stanik netted. Having lost the first set, the youngster started to wildly play low percentage shots which were great crowd pleasers on the infrequent occasion that they worked. Kevin's constant pressure on his opponent, who by the middle of the second set was down a service break, paid off, and he won the match by taking the second set 6-3. He was now in the round of sixteen and already fooled the oddsmakers who had favored his opponent by 3 to 1.

In the post-match interview, Kevin dropped another media bombshell and made his tennis playing plans official. He instantly became the crowd favorite.

"Bobby's a great player," he stated, "unfortunately for him he will not get a chance to avenge this loss as I will be hanging up my tennis racquet after this tournament."

With the first win under his belt and the anticipated moral support he would now get from the crowd in the next match, the bookies changed the odds against Kevin winning the tournament down to 20 to 1. The amount of money being wagered on this tournament was unprecedented and many bookmakers' efforts to balance the bets against each other went unaccomplished. Some gamblers were going to make a fortune and some bookmakers were going to be looking for a new profession, if they survived.

CHAPTER 48

A half of a continent away, an elated but tired Aaron Garland turned off his T.V. set. He had watched the entire match on ESPN and was emotionally drained. He had been feeling peculiar for the last few weeks with mild chest pains that he attributed to indigestion. He knew Doc would be calling any moment to congratulate him on Kevin's win. He wondered if he should mention the chest pains and fatigue to Doc, but decided that it was nothing. When the phone rang he picked it up and instead of saying "Hello," knowing it to be Doc, he said, "This is Aaron Garland speaking, father of the world's best-known tennis player."

Even though the match lasted only two sets, the intense heat and hard court surface had left Kevin fatigued, and his knees and left shoulder ached. A massage and an hour of ice had relieved most of the pain, but he knew he would still be stiff the next morning and each successive match would only serve to increase the aches and pain. Without Sy's intense exercise and strengthening drills there was no way he could have competed at this level. Two days later he again won, beating the highly touted young Mexican, Jaime Bell, in two sets, and the odds now dropped to 10 to 1 against Kevin winning the tournament. He was into the quarter finals.

It was early evening when Kevin returned to his suite. He ordered a steak from room service and placed an international call to Tel Aviv. When Hannah, who had been sound asleep, answered, Kevin started the conversation by stating, "Two down, three to go, and I still love you."

Now wide awake, she fairly shouted, "You won? That's wonderful! I miss you terribly." They spoke for a half hour and when they hung up, he was on an emotional high.

It was 9:00 PM in Las Vegas, and on the spur of the moment he decided to call Doc. It would be 11:00 PM in Chicago, a little late to call, but he decided to go ahead anyway. Doc answered on the second ring in a tone of voice that said this better be an emergency to call this late.

"How ya doin', Doc, it's Kevin."

"Jesus Christ, you scared the shit out of me. Kevin, are you OK?"

"Yep, it's me, the world famous tennis star. Is it too late, Doc, I'd really like to talk a while. A lot of things have happened recently. How's my father?" The question caught Doc by surprise, for he could not remember Kevin ever asking about his father in any of their conversations over the years.

"He's aged a lot, Kevin. But I think he's OK. He's got the normal aches and pains of an old man."

"I'm going to come back to Chicago after this tournament, Doc, to see if I can establish some sort of relationship with him. I want to tell you what's been happening in my life." For the next hour Kevin restated the events of the past few weeks. He told Doc what he had learned about Aaron and about his brother and especially about Hannah.

When he had finished his story, it was a pensive Doc who said, "Don't wait, Kevin, call him soon. You can't imagine how proud he is of you, and, Kevin, for what it's worth, so am I."

As he expected, getting out of bed the next morning was a chore. Kevin swallowed three aspirins and let an icy shower shock him fully awake. His quarter final match was scheduled for 3:00 PM that afternoon so he ordered a large breakfast. He would stretch out with Sy at 11:00 AM and they would limit their practice at noon to no more than thirty minutes due to the heat, just enough to work up a good sweat and get a good rhythm for his groundstrokes and serves. He desperately wanted to call Hannah again but resisted the urge.

There was a knock at the door and, assuming it was room service with his breakfast, with only a towel wrapped around his waist Kevin quickly opened the door. Three men stood in the doorway. Two very large men flanked a smaller thin man. They were all dressed in dark suits that seemed completely out of place for early morning in sweltering Las Vegas. The thin man grinned at Kevin, "May we come in, Mr. Garland? We represent some investors in your tournament and we would like to speak to you for a few minutes." Before Kevin could answer, they entered his room closing the door behind them.

The thin man sat down on the large couch and

motioned for Kevin to sit beside him. One of the large men stood blocking the door while the other stood beside Kevin. "These seem like great accommodations, Mr. Garland."

"Yes, they're fine. I didn't get your name," Kevin replied.

"Brown, John Brown. You played a fine match yesterday against the Mexican kid. We were quite surprised at how easily you won. How are you feeling today?" It was painfully obvious to Kevin that this was not a social call, and he wondered how these three had gotten through security.

"I'm fine. Listen, Mr. Brown, I really don't give interviews without my manager present. If you want to come back later I'll arrange to have him here and we can continue." Kevin started to get up from the couch and one of the large men moved forward and put his hand on Kevin's shoulder preventing him from standing.

"I'll get right to the point, Mr. Garland. From your marvelous play yesterday we believe that you could just possibly win this tournament. That is something we never expected nor would we want. We are simple businessmen who have wagered a lot of money on the outcome of this tournament. We think it would be much healthier for you to lose your next match. Should you just happen to win that match we would certainly not want to see you go any further." The thin man never raised his voice but his message was loud and clear. "We could prevent you from winning by a simple fracture of your left wrist, but we prefer not to use such archaic tactics. Also, it gives Vegas a bad image." He rose and motioned to the large man who jerked Kevin to his feet and then effortlessly threw him halfway across the room.

"This meeting never took place, Mr. Garland. For your continued good health, I wouldn't mention it to anyone. We control people in this hotel, some members of the police department, certain tournament officials, and others. You would never know if you're talking to our people or not. Good-bye, Mr. Garland," and they were gone.

Still sitting on the floor where he had landed, Kevin was stunned by the events of the past few minutes. For a few moments he felt as though it had been a dream, but he knew it wasn't. "These things happened only in the movies not in real life," he muttered half aloud. He was filled with mixed feelings of great anger and fear.

"Those rotten bastards are not going to intimidate me," he thought, and his inclination was to call the police and the tournament director. But then, how did they get past the tight security on this floor that was supposed to protect the players? They obviously had connections in the hotel and God only knows with who else. Paranoia gripped him and he resisted using the telephone for fear of it being tapped.

Still only wrapped in a bath towel, he picked himself up off the floor, grabbed a pair of tennis shorts, ran down the hall to Sy's room, and banged on the door. Sy opened the door, took one look at Kevin and knew there was a major problem.

"What's wrong?"

Kevin was bathed in sweat. "You won't believe what just happened," he panted, and he proceeded to tell Sy about the visit he just had from Mr. Brown and

269

his two henchmen. "They had absolutely no fear, Sy, and when he threatened me I believed every word. What do we do?" Thoughtfully Sy said, "We either tell the cops or the tournament officials, but now I'm not sure who we can trust. Let me handle this, you've got a match to play. Are you OK?"

"Yeah, now that I've told you I feel better, but I gotta tell you I'm scared shitless."

"I know, but the threat is for you not to win the tournament, that's several matches away if you're lucky. Leave it to me, Kevin."

Still obviously shaken Kevin returned to his room as Sy pondered his next move. He reached for the phone and called Doc in Chicago.

"Do you think it's a real threat?" Doc asked.

"I don't know but Kevin sure does."

"Strange as it sounds, Sy, I'd like to bounce this off Aaron. He's levelheaded, faced real danger, and it is his son. I'll call you back."

An hour later Doc and Aaron met in Aaron's apartment. A tired Aaron sat in an overstuffed chair silently listening to Doc's story about Sy's lengthy telephone call and the threat to Kevin's life. When Doc finished Aaron said, "We've got to get him some protection. I don't think the Las Vegas police are the answer." Aaron could never shake his deep-seated distrust of authorities and was always accustomed to handling his own problems. Had this been fifteen years earlier, he would have been on the next plane to Las Vegas and personally dealt with the situation, but now he was too old and knew he could not do what had to be done.

Whom could he trust to help him to protect his

son's life, the only thing in the world that he truly valued? Suddenly a thought came to him and he looked up at the pacing Doc.

"Kevin will be all right, Doc. I believe I know someone I can call to help him." Without another word Aaron reached for the telephone.

CHAPTER 49

From the moment the quarter final match started,
Kevin knew his opponent was hurt. Mirek Hoeschl
was one of the five best players in the world. Having
been bred on the clay courts of Europe, he had developed a strong, patient baseline game and generally
wore his opponents down with his superior strength,
conditioning, and heavy top spin shots that forced
opponents back beyond the base line. On the medi-
um fast hard courts of Las Vegas, playing in a temperature of well over 105 degrees Fahrenheit on the
court against an opponent eight years older, his strategy should have been to play his normal game and
make Kevin hit a lot of balls. By the third set superi-
or conditioning would have tipped the balance of the
match to him. But Hoeschl was trying to end each
point quickly by coming to the net or hitting low percentage shots for winners.

Intuitively Kevin knew his opponent was trying to
protect some injury, and Kevin changed his normal
game plan. He stayed on the baseline coming to the
net only on short returns. He tried to keep his oppo-

nent running by hitting to each side and patiently keeping the ball in play. By the end of the third game of the first set it became painfully obvious that Kevin's opponent was playing with an injured groin muscle and that it was only his competitive drive that kept him in the match.

With Kevin winning five games to two in the first set, Hoeschl fell running for a wide forehand and as he got up he could put no pressure on his groin and fell again. The trainer and Kevin rushed to his side and with an arm around each of their shoulders, they carried him off the court as the crowd clapped politely for the injured contestant.

"Ladies and gentlemen," the umpire announced, "Mr. Hoeschl cannot continue and has retired from this match. Mr. Garland wins the match and advances to the semifinals."

At exactly the same moment the chair umpire was announcing Kevin's tainted victory, a meeting was taking place thousands of miles away between two men who had never hit a tennis ball, yet had an unusual interest in the continued welfare of Kevin Garland. It was early morning in Tel Aviv, and Zalman Zacksman had hastily demanded a meeting with his former protege, Hershel Wolf, the current acting director of Mossad.

"Zalman, you and I both know this is none of our business," Wolf began. "The man is not Israeli and probably doesn't even want our help." What Wolf was really saying to his former mentor was "convince me."

"Hershel, you were always too practical. This man is a hero in our country. Didn't you read the papers a few weeks ago when he gave his tennis prize money back to us?" Zalman knew he would win this debate, but he wanted to give Wolf enough to justify the decision. "Besides that, he is probably going to be my son-in-law in the near future," he rested for a few moments to let that sink in and then played his first ace, "Also, he is the brother of your top agent."

"Half-brother," Wolf quickly threw back.

"All right, brother, half-brother, big deal. How would it look if Barak found out we had been asked to help his half-brother and refused?" Another pause and Zalman played his final card. "Consider also that he is the son of Aaron Garlovsky. The Juden Stern has asked us to help him. If nothing else, we both owe Aaron Garlovsky."

Hershel Wolf was married to the daughter of Meyer Bishov and there would be no peace in his family had he refused Aaron's request for help.

"Enough already, you old fox. We both know my decision, but God help both of us if any of our operatives are discovered or, much worse, killed."

"Shall I call Barak?" Zalman asked knowing the answer.

"Yes, you wake him up and tell him he and his team are leaving at once for vacation to Las Vegas, Nevada, U.S.A."

CHAPTER 50

Kevin slept fitfully that night. With every noise in the large suite he tensed, waiting for the lights to be snapped on and several large men in dark suits to appear in his bedroom. He had refused Sy's offer to share his room, assuring Sy in his most cavalier manner that he would be fine. He was not scheduled to play the following day as semifinal play started on Saturday so the finals could be televised Monday evening to gain the largest share of television viewers.

He desperately wanted to phone Hannah but felt she may discern some fear in his voice so he decided against calling. He lay in the large king-size bed knowing sleep would surely not come this night. Kevin had never thought of himself as either particularly brave or cowardly. Now with so much to live for, life became that much more precious. Conversely, the thought of dying at the hands of conscienceless criminals over a game of tennis bordered on the maniacal.

Perhaps I should get a gun, he thought, but decided that knowing nothing about guns he would probably have a greater chance of shooting himself in the foot as hitting a target. Could he take another man's life? His father could, first out of necessity and then solely for revenge. The more he thought about his situation the more he realized that for all his fame, money, and athletic talent he was not nearly the man his father was and a wave of nostalgia replaced the fear. For the first time since the death of his mother he truly agonized over all the years of estrangement and for the pain he must have caused the man who had suffered so much of his life in silence.

It was about 4:00 AM when he finally dozed off for a few hours of restless sleep.

The headlines in the morning newspaper fairly screamed with the latest "Mob Related Murders" that had occurred overnight in Las Vegas. The media and city officials tried to downplay this type of press for obvious reasons, but the latest rash of violence was not lost on Kevin as he read the morning papers in his hotel suite. The articles hinted that these were gambling debt-related killings, and a scowling picture of Kevin's recent visitor "Mr. John Brown," whose real name was Edwin Shappetti a/k/a Fast Eddie a/k/a Mr. Brown, was an integral part of the article. He and three others were the local suspected gambling kingpins with strong ties to organized crime families in Chicago and Detroit. Although the article did not directly tie anyone to the overnight murders, it was hard not to make the connection.

The telephone rang once and Kevin grabbed it.

"Hello," he answered quickly.

"Shalom, Kevin. It's Barak."

"Barak, how are you? This connection is so clear, you sound wonderful."

"It should be clear, I'm downstairs in your hotel. They tell me I can't get a room because everything is booked because of the tournament. Are you important enough to pull some strings for your brother?" Five minutes later Barak with two large suitcases, a bellman, and a security guard were all standing at the door to Kevin's suite. The brothers embraced and the sheer physical size of his older brother gave Kevin an instant feeling of confidence.

Within a half hour a second bed had been rolled in to the suite and Barak's clothes were deposited in the dresser in the living room of the suite.

"After I tell you what's going on you may not want to stay here," Kevin started to explain but suddenly stopped. He looked at Barak who had a slight smile on his face. "You already know what's going on and that's why you're here, isn't it?"

"Don't be ridiculous, I know nothing. I had some vacation time and I simply came to watch my brother play in the richest tennis tournament of all time, and by the way a few of my friends came as well. You may never see them but I will need four tickets for them for your matches, OK?"

"This could get messy, Barak, I think these guys play for keeps."

"Listen to me, Kevin, you're engaged to the daughter of the former head of Mossad, an organization not unlike your CIA, you're the son of Aaron Garlovsky, a pioneer hero of my country, you're my brother, and you're in a lot of trouble with the wrong people none of which is your fault. I play for keeps also."

They called Sy to come down to Kevin's suite and for the next hour Barak asked questions about their

277

training schedule and plans for the next few days. They reasoned that there was probably little danger until after Kevin's semifinal match, assuming he won. The gamblers would not wait until the finals to make their move, so the most dangerous period would probably start if Kevin won his semifinal match.

"You guys just stick to the schedule you've laid out, and my people will have you under surveillance at all times," Barak stated.

It was hard not to have complete trust in this assertive, large, powerful man. As he spoke slowly and confidently to Kevin and Sy they both had the impression that he had done this sort of thing before. Barak was 6'4" tall and weighed just over 230 pounds. Kevin could see no evidence of flab anywhere. Like his father, Kevin was certain his brother had killed several times before.

That night with Barak in the suite, Kevin slept a solid ten hours and awoke ravenous.

In the bathroom he found a note taped to the mirror:

Follow your schedule and you will be fine. Good luck in your match today. See you tonight.
Barak

It was reassuring to know he was not alone in this situation and for the first time in two days, he began to think about his semifinal match scheduled for that late afternoon.

In a small clean coffee shop three blocks from his hotel suite two men were also thinking about Kevin's match that afternoon. One man was a giant weighing over 300 pounds and standing 6'10" tall. Humphrey

"Fats" Blockstein was known as "the Messenger."
When he spoke to deliver a message for his employers, people listened.

"Let's face it, Eddie, your ass is on the line on this
one. The betting on this tournament got too big and
you were told to lay some of it off, but no, you wanted it all."

The air conditioning in the coffee shop worked
well, yet Fast Eddie Shappetti was sweating profuse-
ly. His giant breakfast companion represented the
notorious Cairo family whose tentacles reached out of
Chicago to control the major portion of the sports
gambling in Las Vegas. Fast Eddie had worked for
them for over twenty years and in turn they had made
him a very rich man. But it was strictly business and
by not laying off a major portion of the bets on Kevin
Garland, the Cairo family, as Fast Eddie's bank, stood
to lose over twenty million dollars if he won the tournament.

"Who woulda thought that a thirty-eight-year-old
over-the-hill sheeny could beat any of the best players
in the world? The odds at 40 to 1 were a steal. He
hadn't won a tournament in three years before that
thing in Tel Aviv," Shappetti was already pleading his
case. "Anyway he's only at the semifinals stage, and
if he wins today I'll take care of it so he doesn't go any
further."

The giant messenger continued to calmly shovel
large portions of food into his mouth.

"Remember, we want everything low-key, any hint
of our connection would be bad for future business and
real bad for you, Eddie."

The message had been delivered, and Eddie knew

full well that the Cairos would not lose twenty million dollars because of his greedy mistake and let him live. His death would be a message to others not to allow the same thing to happen. Shappetti had no appetite for breakfast and told his giant companion that he had to leave. "Fats" simply nodded and continued to eat. After all, it was nothing personal, it was not his life that was on the line, and he knew that breakfast was the most important meal of the day.

Kevin and Sy took the practice court at 10:00 AM and worked for thirty-five minutes, just enough time to work up a good sweat without tiring him out. Kevin's next opponent was to be George Maragos, a twenty-seven-year old Canadian who was the reigning U.S. Open Champion and currently ranked fourth in the world. They had met twice before with Kevin losing both matches in three hard fought sets. Maragos was a baseliner and Kevin felt that on the medium-fast hard court, with his serve and volley game he had a good chance of winning.

Kevin kept looking for Barak that morning, but he was nowhere to be seen. At 3:30 PM sharp the players entered the packed outdoor arena. Kevin looked to the V.I.P. box where he had wrangled five tickets for Barak and his "friends" and noticed that only one of the five seats was occupied and that one by a thin, young blond woman who looked to be in her early twenties. She was wearing a halter top and shorts and seemed to be more interested in the program she was reading than the players on the court.

Once the match started Kevin's competitive spirit took command, and any fear he had vanished. Like the professional he was, once the contest started, winning became all consuming. The aches and pains and outside pressures were pushed to the rear as the adrenaline flowed through his body. After a grueling two hours they had split sets and were on serve at 3-3 in the third and deciding set. This was another match destined to be decided by a momentary lapse in concentration or by a fleeting elevation to a higher plateau by one or the other. Kevin held serve and went ahead four games to three. As they rested between odd games, Kevin noticed that the blond girl was staring at him and smiling. For a brief moment she reminded him of Hannah. They looked nothing alike but each had that look of confidence that said to the world "I'm ready for whatever you have in store for me." She had to be one of Barak's team and her presence and attention to him gave him the slight extra incentive. "Strange," he thought, "there are 20,000 fans here and millions watching on television. I'm in love with a woman a world away and I'm playing to impress one young girl who hasn't taken her eyes off me since the match began. I must be nuts." George Maragos double-faulted his serve for the first time in the match and opened a door that Kevin stepped through. On the second serve of the second point Kevin anticipated Maragos going to his backhand, and he ran around the serve taking it with his forehand smashing a powerful return down the line for a clean winner. At love-30 the pressure was clearly on Maragos; he again netted his first serve and sensing that Kevin was going to attack his second serve he put extra pace on the serve, which hit the top of the net and landed in the alley. A second double fault in this crucial game destroyed his confidence, and five points later the match ended. Kevin had reached the finals, the blond girl had disappeared, and the real danger had now set in.

As he left the court carrying his racquets and equipment bag Sy caught up with him. "Great match, champ. Just one more to go and we're set for life, assuming we're both still alive."

"You shouldn't have said that Sy. Right now my life expectancy isn't that great."

"I've got instructions from Barak," Sy whispered as he and Kevin left the court, "No shower, no post game interviews with the media. We get back to your suite pronto." Ten minutes later they were in the suite where Barak and another man were waiting.

"Congratulations, I saw the end of your match on T.V. I am amazed at how much talent we have in our family." It was Barak's feeble attempt at humor in what was a humorless situation.

"Yeah, win a match, lose a life," Kevin retorted.

"Kevin, this is Shlomo Bulwa. He's been doing some legwork for us the past few days. This suite has been searched for bugs, so for now we can talk freely." Bulwa, who looked more like a dentist than a Mossad agent, got right to the point.

"The pressure is on Shappetti to make sure you don't win the tournament, but we feel with all the recent bad press he can't make it look like the mob is involved. He's scared out of his wits by the Cairo family. He figures he's dead if you win and they lose millions because of his greed in not laying off a large portion of the betting to other bookies. We assume that this is so important to him that he will be personally involved. We've got people watching his every move."

Barak spoke next, "We have two options. We can wait for them to make a move and hope we are ready or we can take the offensive. Either way we're going to bring this to a head before your match Monday evening, and we are going to hide you for the next forty-eight hours." Kevin started to say something but stopped. It was obvious that his brother was a professional at his job and he put himself completely in Barak's hands.

The telephone in the room rang and they all stared at it for a moment. Kevin picked it up and the voice on the other end asked, "Is this Mr. Garland?"

"Yes."

"We warned you, asshole, and now you're gonna pay. We're gonna take care of you and the people you're closest to." There was a click and the line went dead.

For a moment Kevin panicked and could only think of Hannah. Could these bastards reach her? He quietly relayed the threat to Barak who assured him that Hannah would be fine. They concluded that the phone call was made to establish his whereabouts and to wreak psychological havoc on him. To a limited degree, it was doing just that. They planned to move Kevin into Sy's room for the night and made the switch when the single security guard on the floor took one of his many washroom breaks.

CHAPTER 51

It was a little after 10 PM when Aaron snapped off the bright fluorescent lamp over his cluttered basement workbench. He hadn't been sleeping well for the past few weeks. Chronic indigestion and chest pains coupled with recurring nightmares would awaken him several times each night. The dreams started again shortly after he had seen Zalman on television. He felt like an alcoholic who had not had a drink for thirty years and one day walked unthinking into a bar for a beer. One reminder of the past that he had buried for so long opened the floodgates of memories as vivid as the day they occurred. The disease that he thought he had beaten had always been there, resting and waiting, just below the surface.

He was so tired, he thought as he trudged slowly up the basement stairs, maybe tonight he would sleep.

As Aaron approached his apartment he noticed that the hall light in front of his apartment was out. "That can wait until tomorrow to be replaced," he thought. Aaron put his key in the door and stepped inside reaching for the wall light switch as he closed the door behind him. He felt the switch and snapped it up but the room remained dark.

Suddenly, reacting like a wild animal, he sensed the danger and crouched low desperately trying to adjust his eyes to the dark. A blow from a hammer that would have crushed his skull had he been standing normally grazed the top of his head and he fell to the ground in a roll.

He couldn't see his attackers but sensed that there was more than one. Realizing that they were accustomed to the dark and could probably see him, Aaron started to scream for help. Windows in the apartment were partially open and the night was quiet, surely his neighbors would hear him. He felt he had to keep moving and rolled over again.

The next hammer blow came down, breaking his left shoulder and he screamed again, this time in pure agony. He kept rolling on the carpeted floor and got under the heavy wooden dining room table. He felt someone grab and pull his leg and he held onto the table leg with his right arm, continuing his screams for help. The blows were coming from all sides now and he tried to stay in a ball with his injured left arm over his head.

He screamed until he lost consciousness, which was about the same time that his neighbors broke open his front door sending his attackers fleeing by the rear doorway.

They found Aaron still rolled in a ball under the dining room table. He was unconscious and bleeding from several severe wounds. Minutes later an ambulance screeched to a stop in front of the apartment building and thirty-five minutes later he was in an operating room where his life depended on the skills of an overworked tired young surgeon.

One of Aaron's neighbors telephoned Doc, who raced to the hospital and was nervously pacing in the hospital waiting room when a large police detective approached him.

"You family?" the detective asked as he opened an unfiltered Camel cigarette package.

"No, just a friend."

"I'm Detective Al Afterman. Strange set of circumstances," the detective told Doc. "Ya know after twenty-five years on the police force ya start to trust your gut feelings as much as anything else. The apartment was a shambles so he could have come in while a burglary was in process, but I don't think so." The policeman paused to light his cigarette and then started again, "I think these guys wanted to make it look like a burglary, but their real motive was to beat up or kill the old man. Did he have any enemies?"

"None that I know of," Doc responded. "Why do you think it wasn't a burglary?"

"Well, first of all, all the neighbors say he didn't keep any cash around and he wasn't into jewelry. Also, the bulbs in the lamps in the apartment and the hallway were unscrewed. It was as though they wanted it dark in the apartment. It's hard to steal things if you can't see 'em, but if they were laying in wait for the old man they would be accustomed to the dark and he wouldn't. Also, the way the apartment looked is funny. Drawers were pulled out and contents thrown around, but they were quiet about it. The neighbors heard nothing until the screams for help.

I pegged these guys as pros, but a seasoned burglar

would hit and run, not hang around in the dark. The last thing a pro wants is to confront anyone. No, the more I think about it the stranger it gets."

Then as if to show he was not all hard-boiled cop, "He gonna make it?"

"I don't know. He was in bad shape and they think he suffered a heart attack."

"Too bad, his tenants all like him. Isn't his kid some kinda famous jock?" Doc was about to answer when the doctor came out.

Doc approached the sweat-covered doctor. "I'm a close friend of Mr. Garland's. How is he?"

Doctor Robert Stone was tired. He had been in surgery for over two hours with Aaron and was not entirely pleased with the results, nor was he pleased with the large detective smoking in his hospital.

"Well, we really don't know yet. We've stopped the bleeding and reset the broken bones in his shoulder, but his head injuries coupled with a suspected heart attack don't help his chances. He's a tough old bird and the next twenty-four to forty-eight hours will be critical."

"When will I be able to talk to him, Doctor?" Detective Afterman asked.

"Not for at least twenty-four hours. Mr. Garland is heavily sedated, and I don't think he'll be in any condition to talk to anyone for a while. And put out that cigarette!"

It was 1:00 AM in Chicago and Doc hesitated about calling Kevin. After all there wasn't anything Kevin could do, and he was involved in the richest tournament of his life. For a brief time Doc resisted calling, but he decided he must.

It was 11:00 PM in Las Vegas when the phone rang in Kevin's suite. Kevin was asleep in Sy's room and Barak let it ring a few times before answering with a curt "Yes."

"Kevin, it's Doc," the voice on the phone stated, "I've got some bad news about your father." It was a moment before Barak realized the voice was talking about his father as well. "He's been badly beaten and suffered a heart attack."

Slowly, so as not to lose contact with the caller, Barak said, "This is Kevin's brother, Barak Friedlander. I'm acting as security for Kevin. Please tell me what has happened."

Ten minutes later Barak was fully briefed on the events in Chicago that evening. He explained to Doc why he was in Kevin's room, and they both decided not to tell Kevin until after the final match and Doc would call Barak if there was any change in Aaron's condition. There was no doubt in Barak's mind that the attack on Aaron was directly related to the Las Vegas gamblers and Doc's relaying what Detective Afterman had said simply confirmed it.

The course of action was now clear. Barak was through waiting and the hunted now became the hunter. Anger filled him, and he could only think of the pleasure he was going to get in revenge for the vicious attack on a father he had never seen.

"He who lives by the sword, dies by the sword, Mr. Shappetti," Barak muttered to himself. A half hour later his team was assembled in Kevin's room.

CHAPTER 52

Sunday evening Fast Eddie Shappetti was eating a late supper in his booth in the huge coffee shop of the Miracle Hotel. The booth was always available for his use; it served as his office as well as his dining table. This was where he took his calls and received his business associates. From his elevated vantage point he could see the entire, room and with his back against the wall there was no chance of anyone surprising him from the rear.

His companions this evening were two of his trusted lieutenants, Ernie Giambra and Mel Voronoff. At a table just out of earshot and facing the entrance, Eddie's two bulky bodyguards sat lazily sipping coffee. It was a quiet evening and only about a half dozen tables in the large room were occupied, mainly by dealers on a break who could eat in the coffee shop at reduced prices. The high rollers were at the tables and the middle-aged ladies with blue hair were busy playing the slots. The balance of the tourists were at the late shows, which wouldn't break for another hour.

Eddie was feeling particularly annoyed this evening

and had drunk more than usual in an attempt to calm his nerves.

"I told those bastards to kill the old man and they fuck up a simple hit. I want that Garland kid to know I'm serious, damn it." In an attempt to mollify his employer, Voronoff offered, "But Eddie, our sources say the old man had a heart attack and will probably kick the bucket anyway."

Thoroughly annoyed now Eddie glared at his companions, "You dumb schmuck, everyone dies of a heart attack. I want his big shot son to know I killed his father. Don't you understand, my life is on the line on this one if he wins?" Then addressing Giambra he asked, "Who's the big guy that moved in with Garland?"

"From what we can find out he's a relative, a cousin or something. He's an Israeli and in the importing business. The maid heard him say he was on the West Coast on business and flew in for the tournament. He had trouble getting a room so Garland took him in."

"I don't like it," Eddie snarled, "it's too coincidental. If he's in the way he goes too, you hear me." They both quickly nodded at their boss.

"I want to move right away. Tell the guard on the floor to take a long break at 3:00 AM and make damn sure that Garland is unable to play when you leave his room. Take two soldiers with you. Four of you should be enough even if the big guy is in the room with Garland. He should be scared shitless by now with his old man in the hospital and the calls he's been getting." Then looking at his two companions with a stony glare, "You guys've been on a gravy train for a long time now. If you fuck this up don't let me see you, don't even think about going home. Because those two morons," pointing to his bodyguards, "are getting orders to snuff you out if Garland plays tomorrow."

Having made his point, Eddie dug into his food eating rapidly more out of nerves than appetite. As Giambra and Voronoff started to leave, Eddie stopped eating, "Call me here when it's over. I want to stay visible so there's no chance of my being involved. If I don't hear from you by 3:10 AM ....," and the rest was left unsaid.

They paid little attention to the thin, young blond girl seated alone at a table across the room. She was eating a fruit plate and reading a paperback book. She was wearing Walkman earphones obviously listening to a tape, for she would occasionally move her body and hands to some unheard beat of music. What they didn't know was that the Walkman was a high-powered audio receiver that had picked up and taped their entire conversation.

The thin blond girl finished her meal, marked the page in her book, removed her headphones and put everything in a large purse. She carefully examined her bill, left a $1.50 tip, and paid the cashier. Ten minutes later, she was meeting with Barak and the rest of the team in Kevin's suite. No one spoke as she played the tape, fast forwarding the pauses of silence.

When the tape was over there was a hush in the room. Finally, Barak spoke, "It serves no purpose for us to confront them in Kevin's room. When they burst in, the suite will be empty and when Shappetti does not receive his call by 3:10 AM he will start to panic. I don't want Renee wearing the listening device again. They may get suspicious. And I want Kevin and Sy out of the hotel. These guys will stop at nothing, and I don't want them to have a target." For the next half hour they made their plans and by 2:30 AM they were ready to move.

There was a soft knock on Sy's door at exactly 2:40 AM. Sy peered through the peephole and saw the blond girl whom he recognized as Renee Henri, Barak's second in command. He opened the door and she slipped inside. In a soft but firm voice that left no room for debate, she told them that they were about to leave instantly. She did not want to panic them but told Kevin and Sy just enough to convince them to move quickly.

"Leave everything. We are holding the freight elevator that will take you to the basement. You will put on these bellman's jackets and each carry a suitcase. A car is waiting at the basement exit and you will be taken to a safe house. Get moving."

CHAPTER 53

At 2:45 AM Max Solomon, carrying a *U.S.A. Today* newspaper under his arm, sauntered into the Miracle Coffee Shop. He looked around for a keno screen and spotting one, plopped himself at a table in front of the screen. He could peripherally see Fast Eddie's table about twenty-five feet away, and it was empty. He ordered coffee and motioned for the keno girl. When she came to his table he handed her a twenty dollar bill and a keno card.

"Play two dollars a game for the next ten games on the same card, and this is for you," he said as he handed her a dollar tip. She smiled and as she turned he heard her mutter, "A real big spender." He then ordered a roast chicken dinner, and being told it would take at least thirty minutes, assured the waitress that he was in no hurry. A few minutes later when Fast Eddie with two women, another man, and the ever present silent bodyguards came into the coffee shop Max was apparently preoccupied with his newspaper and keno card listening with earphones to his Walkman tape player.

At 2:58 AM a young couple came in and took a table across from Fast Eddie's two bodyguards. She was a thin, attractive brunette in a black leather miniskirt with a white blouse unbuttoned to the navel worn without a bra. The couple had obviously been drinking and her boyfriend couldn't keep his hands off her.

By 3:10 AM Fast Eddie was a basket case. He had twice called the maitre d' over to make sure his telephone was in working order and was again solicitously assured that there was no problem with the hotel phone lines. He spilled a drink on his date, and when she squealed, he slapped her hard across her face. By 3:15 AM there was no controlling him. Both women had been summarily dismissed and Eddie was ranting at Mitch Roth, who was the only one left at his table.

"Those fumbling bastards, they'd fuck up a two-car funeral," his voice could be heard by anyone within 100 feet. "I should have taken care of it myself instead of sending those idiots." Suddenly a large man who had just entered the coffee shop stood in front of his table.

"Mr. Shappetti?" he asked.

"Get the fuck outta here," Eddie lashed out.

Unperturbed the man continued, "I'd like to speak to you if I may."

Now fuming Fast Eddie snarled, "I told you to get the fuck away from me," and he looked over at his two bodyguards. Seated next to them was the young couple, now quite sober and each with a .38 caliber revolver pressed against the stomachs of the two body-guards.

Eddie's anger turned to panic, "The match ain't even played yet, tell the Cairos I'm taking care of it," he whined. The air conditioner in the coffee shop worked well but Eddie was again sweating. The large man sat down and told Mitch Roth to sit at the table with the bodyguards.

"Eddie and I want to talk privately," he said almost apologetically. Roth was only too happy to comply and scrambled out of the booth.

"They're not going to call you, Eddie, because they never found Garland."

Now Eddie was confused, "Whadda ya mean?" He was slurring his words and had soiled his pants.

"I mean, you pile of shit, that your plan to stop Garland from playing fell apart."

Still thinking that these were Cairo's people, Eddie whimpered, "But I'm still taking care of it. He won't win the match."

"Eddie, we're not who you think we are. I'm here to try to reason with you, but failing that, I have no reservations about killing you right now." Eddie looked over at his two bodyguards who were still immobile.

"Who are you?" Eddie started to realize that these were not the Cairos' people and felt that if he could stall long enough he'd figure something out. Ignoring the question, the big man continued.

"You've pissed off some people by what you did in Chicago to that old man and by your threats and attempt to stop Garland. I don't imagine you'd con-sider just allowing the match to be played."

"If Garland wins I'm dead," Eddie snarled like a trapped animal.

"I take that for a no then."

"Listen, maybe we can talk about this," Eddie was still stalling for time.

"No more talking, Eddie, unless you're convinced that I'm more dangerous than the Cairos. I suppose there's no way of persuading you to stop this madness." From under the table a shot from a small caliber hand gun with a silencer blew away Eddie Shappetti's left kneecap. He was momentarily shocked and surprised, and then as the pain traveled to his brain he screamed, clutching his mutilated knee. The big man grabbed him by the back of the head and in a soft voice said, "I'm giving you a gift of your other knee and your life, on two conditions. If you are going to persist in trying to injure Garland, I will take your other knee. If anything actually happens to Garland I will with great pain to you take your life. Do you understand me?" Eddie nodded. "Answer me, you sniveling putz."

"Yes."

The big man was gone as quickly as he had come, followed by the young couple who had disarmed the bodyguards. Roth and the two bodyguards rushed to their employer who was moaning and grasping his left knee, "Get me a fucking doctor," he groaned. They laid him bleeding on the floor as the maitre d' called for an ambulance.

In tremendous pain still screaming he grabbed Roth by the jacket, "Kill Garland. Stop the match." No one noticed Max Solomon who was passing the scene.

In the confusion he knelt by Shappetti as if to help and said, "You were warned to stop, you just lost your other knee," and he fired two quick rounds from a silencer-capped .38 revolver into Eddie's right knee. He rose and looked directly at Roth and the two unarmed bodyguards. "He was warned, next time he's dead," and he casually left the restaurant as Shappetti's screams of pain echoed in the background.

CHAPTER 54

The decision not to tell Kevin about his father's condition until after the final match was a unanimous one. Barak had called Zalman and Hannah to bring them up to date. He conferred almost hourly with Doc, who was keeping a vigil at the hospital. He also told Sy what had happened to Aaron.

Aaron was still in intensive care and under heavy sedation. So far his condition remained stable. Other than being physically present at the hospital, there was nothing Kevin or anyone else could do except wait. Aaron's life, once again, hung by a very thin thread. Kevin was preparing to play the final match of an illustrious career for a monetary prize that had never before been equaled in the sport. Purists argued that the money was too great and detracted from the sport. Kevin had no such illusions; this was to be his swan song, and if he won, the enormous prize money would be just fine.

During the past few days he had been under the type of pressure that would have broken a lesser man. The people closest to him agreed that the last thing he needed was to be told that his father was fighting for his life in a Chicago hospital because he had been severely beaten by thugs upon orders from a Las Vegas mobster who wanted nothing more than for Kevin to lose. Kevin's victory, if it were to occur, would be poetic justice.

Kevin and Sy had been taken from the hotel to the estate of Robert and Shirley Weinberg just outside Las Vegas in the exclusive suburb of Green Valley. The estate was actually a well-guarded compound, for the Weinbergs' jewelry collection was known worldwide. They had built a fortress to protect it. To the public the Weinbergs were the owners of a chemical plant that manufactured salt products. To a select few highly placed officials it was known that their real fortune had been made as international arms merchants, and their compound had been used many times by various governments to secretly shelter people in danger.

On Monday morning Kevin awoke at 9:30 AM. He pulled on a pair of shorts and found his way to the kitchen in search of coffee. He was surprised to find the kitchen filled with people devouring plates of pancakes, eggs, lox, and bagels. Other than Sy and the Weinbergs, who were busy acting as host and hostess, the people in the room were Barak and his "team." Kevin recognized the thin blond girl from the night before and the two other young men he knew as Max and Shlomo. Barak waved to him, "How do you feel this morning? Ready to go out tonight and win ten million dollars?"

"Jesus, I can't even open my eyes yet and you lay that on me. How'd it go last night?" Barak gave him a brief smile.

"I don't think Mr. Shappetti will be in any condition to bother you. Our intelligence indicates that he is in Sunrise Hospital with his two armed gorillas perched at his door with orders to search everyone who enters his room, including the doctors and nurses. We believe he has abandoned any thoughts of stopping your match and is focusing on trying to somehow convince his employers that everyone is entitled to make one mistake. In any event, today he's probably more frightened of us than he is of them. Now tell me, should I put a bet down on you?"

Kevin put his arm on the big man's shoulder and spoke softly, "I did a lot of thinking last night, Barak, call it mental masturbation, but I've decided that if I should win tonight, after I pay off the guy sitting next to you," motioning at Sy, "I'll be left with eight million bucks. I've got enough to live comfortably for the rest of my life right now, but another couple of million or so would make a great nest egg for any kids Hannah and I have. I'm giving my father a million dollars, a friend of mine in Chicago who taught me the game a million, and I'm giving you one million dollars."

Barak started to protest but Kevin stopped him.

"There's nothing you can say to change my mind. You came out of nowhere to put your life on the line for a half-brother you hardly know. My gift of money hardly seems adequate. The subject is closed. Will someone pass me some pancakes?"

For a fleeting moment Barak felt compelled to tell Kevin about his father but felt it would do no good and resisted the urge.

The match was scheduled for 5:00 PM that afternoon. The time was a compromise between the tournament promoters, casino owners and the T.V. sponsors. The sponsors wanted an evening match starting at 6:00 PM Las Vegas time to gain the massive East Coast audience and the highest commercial fees. The Las Vegas casino owners did not want the many high rollers in town for the match away from the gambling tables in the evening, so the 5:00 PM compromise was reached. The earlier time suited Kevin, who was a decade older than his opponent and was starting to have difficulty seeing the speeding yellow tennis ball clearly at night under outdoor lights.

In his most convincing manner Barak assured both Kevin and Sy that the Shappetti threat had been eradicated, but they all knew that if some maniac wanted to risk it, there could still be a real danger. Shappetti had been a cruel, brazen hoodlum, but at least he was a known enemy. Barak was reasonably certain that Shappetti was out of the picture, but the Cairos were another story. They stood to lose a fortune, and by now they knew that Shappetti was incapable of stopping Kevin. Barak felt that he and his team had to assume the worst and prepare as best they could.

Later that afternoon he could only marvel at the way Kevin handled himself as their white stretch limousine left the Weinberg compound for the stadium. They all knew that there was a high probability that some attempt would be made to prevent Kevin from winning, and yet he had put on his "game face" and seemed totally focused on the match. Barak could feel the danger in his bones.

"Maybe I've been in combat too long," he thought in silence as they drove to the stadium. "I see a terrorist behind every bush." But it was still too unlikely that the Cairos would take their huge losses without some last ditch effort to protect their investment. They did not have a lot of time to plan, so Barak felt that the effort to stop Kevin would be blunt and probably deadly. The time for psychological intimidation had long passed. He could have used a dozen more men, but he had supreme confidence in his team. Barak was also worried about the surprise waiting for Kevin at the stadium and prayed that Hannah had not come 5,000 miles only to witness her fiance's funeral.

Once at the stadium only Kevin and Sy were allowed in the locker room. Barak had given Sy a small caliber automatic which Sy slipped into his pocket.

"It's not much, but it's better than nothing," Barak whispered as Sy followed Kevin into the locker room.

"I'll probably shoot my dick off if I have to use it," Sy whispered back.

CHAPTER 55

Barak gave final instructions to his people and went to take his seat in the V.I.P. box at courtside. When he approached the box his spirits lifted as he saw Hannah standing and waving.

What a beauty, he mused, if I were Kevin I'd leave this place at once and live happily ever after with her. She threw her arms around him as he entered the box and kissed him full on the lips.

"Barak, I'm so nervous and excited I think I've wet my pants."

"That's my sister," he answered, "I haven't seen you in two weeks and you're talking dirty to me already." As Barak sat, he noticed that extra chairs had been crowded into the V.I.P. box and the tournament director was ushering four men down the aisle towards the box. As the director bowed and scraped before the quartet Barak heard him say, "I hope these are satisfactory, Mr. Cairo, we had such short notice…. If you need anything I'll be right there," and he pointed to a seat on the court just behind the umpire's chair. Geraldo Cairo at fifty was a dark, squat, powerful man.

He stood only 5'8" tall but weighed 230 pounds. He had a twenty-inch bull-like neck, and it was rumored that he had killed at least a dozen men with his bare hands. His brother Joseph was ten years younger. He was slim, blond, and a pretty boy, with a preference for young boys. Joseph Cairo was a product of Yale Law school and the London School of Economics. Geraldo doted on him and treated him more as a son than a brother. Joseph's special talent, besides law and high finance, was poison and he was as ruthless as his brother.

They had surely come to Las Vegas to see that their investment was protected. The two muscular men with them were bodyguards, who looked the part with their dark suits and sunglasses. It was still a half hour before the match would begin and Barak excused himself and went to find Max Solomon and his Walkman listening device.

"There's been a slight change, Max. You're sitting in the V.I.P. box with Hannah and me. I need your electronic ears there."

The noisy enthusiastic crowd stood clapping and cheering as the two contestants entered the packed stadium. On the screens of millions of television sets worldwide, commentators in a babel of languages, between commercials, were describing the scene and comparing the relative strengths and weaknesses of the players. The match, with its hype and enormous prize money, had taken on larger than life dimensions. Kevin Garland, the former bad boy of tennis, now an aging underdog in the last stages of his illustrious career, had become the darling of the fans and the media. His opponent was the reigning number-one ranked player in the world. At twenty-five years of age, Neil Kramer was a stoic German who possessed all the tools to be one of the all-time greats. Early in his career he had been given the nickname of "the Iceman" and the sportswriters had a field day calling the match the ultimate confrontation of "fire and ice." The matchup was a promoter's dream come true!

It took a few moments for the players to get their equipment organized. Sy gave Kevin some final words of encouragement before leaving for his seat in the V.I.P. box. Kevin told him he felt great. He knew the butterflies in his stomach would be gone as soon as the match started. Kevin turned to look for Barak, when he saw her standing and waving. He almost fell over a chair as he raced to Hannah and lifted her out of the stands in front of a half billion worldwide viewers. He had a hundred questions, but as he put her down she said, "Kevin just play your match, I'm here as long as you want me."

The tournament director gently tapped him on the shoulder, "Mr. Garland, please, we'd like the warm-up to start." Kevin gave her a last hug.

"Stick around. I'll be busy for the next few hours, but then I'd like to spend fifty or sixty years with you," and he reluctantly let her go.

The scene was not lost on Geraldo Cairo who mumbled to his brother, "Who's the broad? Looks like she's the one Shappetti should have asked us to ice instead of the old man. Have Rocco find out who she is."

Four seats away Max Solomon with his Walkman earphones on and the receiver pointed at the Cairos picked up and taped their quiet conversation.

The umpire tapped his microphones and the crowd became silent.

"Ladies and gentlemen, this will be a best three-out-of-five set tiebreak match. If the score is two sets each, there will be a twenty-minute break before starting the fifth and deciding set. On my left from Berlin, Germany, the current number-one ranked player in the world, Neil Kramer. On my right from Chicago, Illinois, Mr. Kevin Garland. Mr. Kramer has won the coin toss and has elected to serve."

So it began; the media, the hype, the crowd, all faded into the background. It now became a war between the bodies, minds, and talents of two finely tuned athletes, each of whom, on this late afternoon, was prepared to play the game at its highest level and a step beyond.

To the audience it seemed inconceivable that anyone would want to stop this magnificent event, but activity to that end was already taking place. Joseph Cairo spoke to his brother.

"Rocco says she's Garland's girlfriend, comes from Israel and just got in today. They're supposed to get married," he quietly told Geraldo. A minute later Geraldo said with a sinister smile, "I got an idea. If we can snatch the kid's girlfriend and get word to him that what we did to his old man is nothing like what we'll do to her, we may not need to use the hit. Get Rocco to tell the hitter to do nothing until I contact him again."

Max Solomon was relaying every word coming from the Cairo's seats to Barak.

"All right, this is it. Renee, Shlomo, follow that big guy, Rocco. Don't stop him but make sure he gets his message to 'the hitter,' then do what you have to."

Then whispering to Hannah he said, "You may have to do something dangerous to help Kevin."

"Anything," she answered.

"If Shlomo and Renee can't neutralize the hit man and Kevin wins two sets, we will need to use you as a decoy. Keep your fingers crossed that it's not needed but be prepared to leave your seat if necessary. I promise, you will never be out of my sight."

"I trust you, Barak, I'm not worried." She isn't worried, Barak thought, but I sure as hell am.

As the players changed sides at the end of the first game, Renee and Shlomo oblivious to the tennis match followed the broad back of the Cairo bodyguard, Rocco Greco, out of the stadium to a lower level supply area. Located just outside the stadium, this basement area was the supply room for the players. Extra towels, water, and soft drinks were brought up on court through an underground tunnel as they were needed. Shlomo and Renee watched from a distance as the massive Rocco spoke to a short, dark-complected man wearing a white jacket and red baseball hat, the uniform of a concessionaire.

Rocco, his message apparently relayed, abruptly turned and left the supply area, paying little attention to the young couple engaged in what appeared to be a lovers' quarrel. As he left the supply area, Shlomo followed him to make sure he was making no more stops, while Renee stationed herself just outside the supply area where she could see anyone going in or out. Two minutes later a perspiring Shlomo Bulwa returned.

"He went back to his seat and whispered to the Cairos. I'm sure this is our man."

CHAPTER 56

The match had been on for almost two hours and the fierce Las Vegas sun was no longer a factor. The temperature on the court was down to 105 degrees Fahrenheit, and the players had split sets and were on serve at four games all in the third set. They had each changed shirts three times and were consuming copious amounts of liquids on the game changeovers. The partisan crowd, initially certain that Kevin had little chance of winning, now screamed shouts of encouragement with each point he won and actually started to believe that he really had a chance at victory. In the V.I.P. box, the Cairos could feel it too, although their reaction to the possibility of Kevin's victory was evoking a far different emotion. The crowd's screams and cheers made it almost impossible for Max Solomon to pick up the whispered conversations between the brothers, and he was only getting bits and pieces. From small snatches he deduced that something would happen at the break if the sets were tied at two each.

Kramer won the third set tie breaker on a shot that hit the net and dribbled over for an impossible return and the crowd moaned. In the V.I.P. boxes there were mixed emotions. The Cairos were elated, and Barak felt a momentary relief. If Kevin lost the next set all their troubles would be over and no one would be the wiser.

In the fourth set Kevin seemed to get a second wind and broke the German's service to take a quick three-love lead.

It was dark in the supply room where Shlomo and Renee had broken in and were wasting little time on subtleties as they interrogated a whining and terrified supply room attendant. Their initial goal was to quickly convince him that he had more to fear from them than his mob employers, and they had to make sure that he was really the "hit man" and not just a cog in the wheel.

"Either way you're dead, you little shit," Renee screamed as she and Shlomo stood over him as he lay face up on the cold cement floor. Blood poured out of his nose where Bulwa had hit him. "How were you going to do it?" she continued. The attendant, terrified, lay shaking on the ground. Bulwa slowly screwed a silencer on the nuzzle of his .38, making sure that his intended victim watched his every move.

"If you don't answer me now, the first shot will destroy your right thumb, and we will then move to your left thumb," wasting no time Bulwa grabbed the man's hand and fired. A void appeared where the attendant's right thumb had formerly been. Blood spurted and covered his hand and he screamed in pain. Renee was afraid he would faint or go into shock and she decided to play her best card.

"We are going to let you live if you start to talk,

otherwise say good-bye to your left thumb." He was squeezing his hand trying to stop the flow of blood, and the words poured out in a torrent.

"Stop, no more, please. They paid me twenty G's to bring ice-cold mineral water to Garland if it looked like he was going to win, they put something in the water bottles, I don't know what, then the big guy came down and told me to wait until they gave me further orders. Help me, oh God, I'm bleeding to death."

"Which bottles?" Shlomo asked calmly lifting the attendant off the ground by his collar. He led them to a refrigerator filled with small ice-cold Evian Water and Gatorade bottles.

"They said Garland drinks mineral water. It's the six-pack with his name on it."

Bulwa grabbed the six-pack of the plastic bottles and by closely examining the caps saw that each had been opened and then tightly recapped. "What poison did they put in this? Don't lie to me or I'll kill you in the next three seconds," and he pressed the gun against the attendant's forehead.

"I don't know, I swear it. They said he would have some kind of attack about fifteen minutes after drinking it and would probably die, but I don't know what the stuff is, I swear." He then lost control of his bowels and collapsed in a faint to the floor. Someone was banging on the supply room door and trying to get in.

"Hey, Frankie, you there? It's Rocco, lemme in."

Bulwa motioned to Renee to open the door as he pulled the now unconscious Frankie behind several stacked boxes. Renee messed her hair, pulled her blouse out of her shorts and unbuttoned the top two buttons, "All right, hold your horses," she cooed as she unlocked the door. The massive Rocco filled the door-way.

"What's going on . . . " Rocco started to ask, but without looking at him Renee started to button her blouse.

"He's behind the boxes putting his pants on." She was now stuffing her blouse into her shorts.

"Get outta here, bitch," Rocco snarled at her as he strode past her. There was something familiar about the thin blond he thought. He heard the door slam and as he turned he knew it was too late. She was facing him with the .38 caliber revolver pointed at his chest. He lunged and she fired three times in rapid succession. Struck in the chest, his sheer size enabled him to continue forward and he grabbed her right arm and pinned her to the wall. He swung wildly with his free hand and broke her nose. Suddenly Shlomo was at her side and fired his weapon directly into Rocco's brain. Already dead, the big bodyguard slumped to the floor.

Kevin won the fourth set 6-3 and the players were preparing to leave the court for a well-earned twenty-minute break. Kevin turned to wave to Hannah who stood and waved back. Barak had not heard from Shlomo or Renee and he whispered to Hannah that shortly it would be time for her to leave the box, making sure the Cairos saw her leave. But just as the players disappeared into the locker room for their short break, Barak saw a smiling red capped white-coated Max Solomon approach the Cairo's seats with a tray of ice cold mineral water bottles.

"Compliments of the tournament director, gentle-men," he said to the Cairo brothers as they each grabbed a bottle. Geraldo Cairo peeled off a $100 bill and stuffed it into the attendant's jacket. "Thank you, sir, but I'm not supposed to accept a tip."

"Keep it, kid, it'll be a secret just between you and me," Geraldo said with a wink as he unscrewed the bottle cap and quickly guzzled the twelve ounces of clear ice-cold liquid.

The giant lights flooded the court as the Las Vegas sun had completely set and darkness fell. The stadium was bathed in a surreal golden glow that was a perfect setting for the final set of the match and a career. The contestants, so evenly matched, had all but forgotten the riches to be heaped upon the victor. This was a once in a lifetime event shared by the millions of viewers worldwide and the fortunate fans in the stadium. Each point had been played as in a chess game between masters. Kevin had been forcing play with his aggressive serve and volley style, while Kramer was counter punching with pinpoint passing shots and lobs. A mild commotion in one of the V.I.P. boxes temporarily halted the start of the fifth set. Two men had collapsed and were quickly taken out by stretcher. The players, fully focused on the match, did not even notice the episode.

An hour and a half later at six games apiece, the match would be decided by a tiebreaker. No one watching this match expected anything else. With Kevin leading the tiebreaker game six points to five, his return of a topspinning second serve hit the top of the net and limply fell over. Miraculously, Kramer got his racquet on the weak return and tried to go cross court with his shot. But Kevin's anticipation, honed by so many years of competition, were too quick and he volleyed the return past his lunging opponent for match point.

For a few moments the crowd sat stunned, not wanting the contest to be over. Slowly at first and then rising to a crescendo, the crowd rose as one cheering and clapping for the participants. The emotionally as well as physically exhausted players shook hands and then embraced at the net, and the crowd screamed its approval. The video tape of this match was to become a classic and would be replayed for years to come. Its rights and royalty fees would eventually exceed the giant first place prize money.

CHAPTER 57

It was an hour before the press and tournament officials finished their interviews and the award presentations. Kevin received a giant symbolic check at mid court while the real funds had been wire transferred to his bank in Miami and immediately invested in U.S. Treasury Bonds. His bank officer had been instructed to purchase the bonds in the names of Kevin's designated donees, which would serve to assure them a life of financial security. Kevin kept Hannah at his side throughout the press interviews and they jointly announced to the world that they were to be married.

"Life really can be sweet," Kevin thought as he stood in the shower with steamy hot water raining down on him. The minor aches and pains that had attacked his body during the match disappeared. "They never hurt as much when you win," he reflected.

As he stepped out of the shower, one look at Barak's and Sy's faces brought him back to reality. He stopped drying himself.

"What's wrong?" he asked, "Are we still a target?"

Without preamble Sy said, "It's your father. He's been hurt and suffered a heart attack. There's a non-stop to Chicago in an hour and we're all booked on it. I'll fill you in on what's happened as you dress."

Kevin was not prepared for the sight of Aaron in the Intensive Care Unit at Holy Mother Hospital. It had been many years since he had last seen Aaron, and it was an old man who lay in a semiconscious state with a confusion of tubes and wires connecting him to bottles and machines. It was hard for Kevin to feel anything but pity for this old man who appeared as a stranger in an antiseptic hospital room. His visit was limited to five minutes, and as he left the room, it was hard to believe that he had spent the greater part of his adult life trying to show this bedridden figure that he didn't need his help and could face the world alone.

After introducing Doc to Barak and Hannah he took Doc aside.

"Can I talk to you for a while, Doc?"

"You always could, Kevin. I think you know that," Doc answered softly.

"Doc, I look at that old sick man in there and I feel so sorry for him, but it's hard to feel any love for him. I understand so much more about him now, but it doesn't alter the fact that I feel you were more a father to me than he was. I know it's probably not the right time to say it, and I wish it weren't true."

Doc didn't answer for a while as they walked slowly down the early morning quiet hospital corridor. Finally he said, "Kevin, I've known your dad a long time now and I've become a close friend and admirer of his. There's nothing you can do here tonight, but I want you do to me one favor, O.K.?"

315

"Anything, Doc."

"I want you to spend what's left of this night, alone, in your father's apartment. Here's the key. Your father has an old suitcase under his bed. It's time you took it out and looked through it. I'll take care of Barak and Hannah," and then he pressed his car key and Aaron's apartment key into Kevin's hand.

As Kevin took the keys from Doc, he was surprised to see an entourage of several men in suits walking briskly towards him. It was after 2:00 AM and the men were obviously in a state of deep concern. The leader was a tall, gray-haired man of about sixty and it was he who spoke to Kevin, a bit too officiously, Kevin thought.

"Mr. Garland, I'm Dr. Frank Sturdevant, the hospital administrator. May I talk to you?" Kevin was exhausted and certain that there was probably something wrong with his father's insurance.

"Look, Doctor, I'm very tired, but I assure you that I will be fully responsible for my father's bill." Dr. Sturdevant looked confused for a moment and then recovered.

"No, no, there is no problem with your father's bill. I simply wanted you to know that we are doing everything humanly possible for your father. I am overseeing his treatment and I have personally brought in who I consider the finest cardiologist and neurosurgeon in the Midwest to treat your father." There was an uncomfortable silence for a few moments and the administrator then asked, "Your father is Jewish, isn't he?"

Now defensive, Kevin bitingly said, "Yes, why is there a problem treating Jews here?"

"Oh, my God, no," Dr. Sturdevant exclaimed obviously concerned that he had upset Kevin. "I just thought that he may have been Catholic."

"Why is that doctor?"

"Well, umm, I, uh, have been asked, no rather ordered to spare no expense in your father's treatment." Then almost to himself Dr. Sturdevant continued shaking his head, "It's very strange. I have been administrator of this hospital for over ten years and a doctor for over thirty years, and it's very strange indeed."

Now irritated and somewhat confused, Kevin snapped, "What's so strange, Doctor, and who is giving you orders concerning my father?"

"Well, umm, my orders are coming from, umm, the Vatican, Mr. Garland. I've been ordered by the Vatican to personally advise their representatives no less than every six hours on your father's condition." Small beads of perspiration were forming on the doctor's usually stiff upper lip. "Furthermore, I have been advised that if it is determined that this hospital staff has not done everything humanly possible in caring for your father that, um, I will not be retained in my present position. I must say this is extremely strange, Mr. Garland, and I'm here tonight to guarantee you that we have followed our orders to the letter. If your father were the Pope himself he could not receive any better care."

Now it was Kevin and Doc who were totally confused. Dr. Sturdevant and his group were about to leave when he said, "Mr. Garland, if there is anything you feel you would want of me please ask," then almost as an afterthought, "and by the way, Mr. Garland, I've further been instructed that no matter what the cost to treat your father, this hospital and its staff are to render no bill whatsoever." The doctor then shook Kevin's hand and looking directly at Kevin said, "Your father has some very powerful friends who obviously care a great deal about him, young man. He must be a very extraordinary person. I hope he makes it. We will do all we can for him," and they turned and left without further comment.

It was 2:45 AM when Kevin parked Doc's seven-year-old brown Pontiac sedan in front of the building his father had owned and called home for over forty years. Autumn was in the air, and Kevin, wearing only a light jacket, relished the coldness after spending so much of the past several months in desertlike climates. The night was clean and crisp, and he filled his lungs with cold, refreshing air. As Kevin got out of the car, he could see the lights in the park across the street illuminating the plywood backboard where so many years ago as a young boy he had hit countless tennis balls.

At the hospital he had been exhausted both physically and emotionally from the events of the past twenty-four hours, but returning to this place gave him an odd yet not unpleasant feeling of coming home. When his mother was alive this was where he had spent his happiest days. It was hard for him to visualize her in his mind, but he made a mental note to visit her grave. He could not ever remember having gone to the cemetery where she was buried.

As he entered the hallway of the building, old familiar aromas filled his nostrils. No matter how long we are away, he thought, we never forget the perfumed scents of our youth.

It was so late, and he tried not to make any noise as he walked down the Lysol-clean hallway to his father's apartment. He fumbled with the key for a few moments when the neighbor across the hall opened his door. Kevin, feeling like an intruder, mumbled, "It's all right, I'm Aaron's son." An old man looked at him for a few moments then said, "Yep, I seen your picture in the paper. Your father is real proud of you. How is he?"

"Not good, I just left the hospital and he's still in bad shape."

"Well, we're all praying for him, he's a good man. You're a lucky boy to have such a father," and he smiled and closed the door as an unspoken acceptance of Kevin's right to be there.

Kevin finally got the apartment door open and found the light switch. He hadn't really lived here since he was eleven years old, returning in his early teenage years only occasionally for visits during holidays. His father had moved out of the family's large third story apartment several years after Kevin left and moved back into his original unit. Kevin realized he had not been back at all for almost twenty years.

He felt as though he had stepped back in time. His mother's furniture, once bright and considered modern, was exactly as he had remembered, but it was now old and dull. Even the dull, faded curtains, once so colorful with flowered patterns, were the same.

Kevin could not remember, as a child, ever going into Aaron's bedroom after his mother's death. That room became his father's sanctuary and, although never expressed, it was off limits. Now, entering his father's bedroom Kevin had the uncomfortable feeling of violating his father's special place. The room contained a double bed, two dark brown dressers, and a night stand with a small reading lamp and a black rotary dial telephone.

On the dresser a small gold-bordered picture frame contained pictures of his mother and a picture of himself as an infant. Kevin could not remember ever seeing either of the old photographs.

Doc had asked him to look through the contents of an old suitcase that he would find under the bed. Kevin found and carried the dusty suitcase into the dining room and put it on the large dining table. The center lock had long been broken and the two side latches opened easily. As Kevin opened the top, he saw it was filled with envelopes and papers.

"Christ, it'll take me days to go through this," he thought and he went to the small kitchen. "Might as well eat something, it'll be a long night." Kevin made a salami sandwich, found a can of beer, and sat in front of the suitcase with his food. The first few envelopes contained canceled checks for his father's personal expenses. Each year's canceled checks were in a separate envelope and as he flipped through the checks, the patterns of his father's life became clear to him. Virtually no payments for any clothing, entertainment, or luxuries. Groceries, utilities, auto repairs, and taxes comprised almost all of Aaron's expenses. Each year it was the same and after going back ten years, Kevin was inclined to assume the other envelopes of checks would be no different. The envelopes marked 1975 and 1976 appeared to be a little thicker and Kevin opened them casually and flipped through the checks. When he saw the first check to Sy Rosen for $500 he was stunned. In all, he found checks totaling $30,000 paid to Sy for those two years.

What the hell was my father doing paying Sy in 1975 and 1976? I didn't even know they knew each other, Kevin thought. As he dug further into the suitcase he found a packet of letters postmarked from Miami to his father from Sy. There were at least fifty letters all neatly packaged, starting in 1975.

Now completely bewildered about this early relationship between his father and his coach, Kevin carefully removed and read the first letter.

Dear Aaron,

I'm pleased to report that our plans seem to be working out. Your son has agreed to have me coach him and has offered to compensate me with room and board and a small salary. Naturally, any money he gives me will be credited against the salary that you are paying me. I find Kevin to be a little standoffish and very stubborn, but I must tell you that in spite of it I really like him. He is the most talented tennis player I have ever coached and I feel that if he allows me, and if you can afford my fee, within a few months he will be back on the circuit and starting to win again.

His major fault lay in the fact that he believed he could do it all by himself. I would really like to tell him that you and Doc are the reason I'm here and that you are paying me. I will, however, respect your wishes and keep it our secret.

Please say hello to Doc for me, and I will write to you weekly as agreed.

Sincerely,

Sy Rosen

Now fully awake, Kevin hungrily read the remaining letters from Sy to his father. An hour later he replaced the last letter in its envelope visibly shaken he could only think, Christ, what a fool I've been. He thought about Doc and Sy who had probably wanted to tell him what a pompous ass he'd been a hundred times but in deference to Aaron's wishes had kept his secret. He felt no anger towards them, only grudging admiration for keeping the old man's secret as he had requested. He thought, Why couldn't he tell me he wanted to help me? But he knew that he would have refused his father's help out of youthful pride and in doing so, would never have reached the heights his career had taken.

Two yellow Indianapolis newspaper articles were the next items he removed from the suitcase. The first article brought back the crushing pain of the beating he had taken in an Indiana locker room so many years before. The article concluded that he was beaten by unidentified muggers who were probably surprised by Kevin while stealing articles from the locker room. The second article was dated a few days later and had made the front page. It described in detail how four local young men including Eric Fox, a young tennis star who had recently won his first professional tournament, had been savagely attacked and beaten by unknown assailants. The attacks had taken place at two different locations, and the only connection had been the statement from the victims that one of the attackers was a big man with unusually large hands who spoke to them in a whispered voice with a foreign accent and appeared to limp as he left the scene of the attack. The article further went on to say that Mr. Fox's tennis career was certainly finished as a result of the injuries he had suffered.

In spite of himself Kevin could not help but smile broadly. I wondered what ever happened to that prick, he thought, then aloud, trying to control his glee he fairly screamed, "A big man, foreign accent, big hands and a limp, that's my old man, you bastards, that's my old man," and he felt more refreshed and alive than if he had slept for hours.

Neatly stacked articles and pictures of Kevin chronicled by the years filled a large portion of the suitcase. Aaron had, throughout the past several years, followed Kevin's career in the newspapers and had subscribed to numerous tennis publications from which, it appeared to Kevin, he had reverently cut out and catalogued any reference to his son. Kevin had never seen most of the articles and was overwhelmed at the volume of articles and press releases his father had accumulated about him.

Near the bottom of the suitcase he found another packet of yellowed newspaper articles. The first article described the violent rape and assault upon his mother. The second was her obituary notice. Later articles described the vicious slaying of two small-time criminals by an unknown but obviously professional killer. These articles coupled with what he had learned about his father's youth from Zalman Zacksman painted a clear picture. He could almost feel the rage in his father as he had avenged the brutal assault of his wife and the mother of his ten-year old son.

It had been almost impossible for Kevin to picture his father as a cold-blooded killer, but the contents of this suitcase left no room for doubt. Aaron had been a young man when he had given up on God, the police, or any other authorities to exact justice or retribution on the guilty. Aaron exacted his own brand of justice on his enemies.

At the very bottom of the suitcase Kevin found two envelopes. One contained several snapshots of a smiling young Aaron, Zalman Zacksman, and a young very blond woman. They were all in shorts, and the men carried British Enfield rifles. The date on the back of the photos was 1950 and someone had scrawled the names Aaron, Zalman and Abby next to the date. The last photo was older still and had been creased several times as though someone had tried to make it as small as possible. It showed a family formally posing, and Kevin was certain the young boy in the photo who looked like Kevin as a child was his father at age nine or ten.

He sat staring at the brown photo and could only speculate at how his father had managed to conceal and save this memento of a life and family long disappeared in the Holocaust. What feelings must his father have felt as he would gaze at the faces in this photograph that, to him, represented real people.

Kevin carefully replaced the old photos and opened the last large envelope. It contained two letters. One was a two-page letter written in Hebrew on official letterhead with a medal clipped to it.

The second was a letter dated September 21, 1985 written in Polish on Vatican stationery. It appeared to be signed by someone named "Bruno." His father certainly did have powerful friends, and there was no doubt now about the Vatican connection.

Gently he closed the old suitcase and replaced it under his father's bed. It was past 5:00 AM when, fully clothed, he fell asleep on the old couch in the living room. He could not bring himself to sleep in his father's bed. He had invaded enough of Aaron's life that evening.

He was awakened by a knocking at the front door. Startled for a few moments by the noise, he glanced at his watch. It was 9:00 AM and he cursed himself, for he had set his father's old alarm clock for 7:00 AM but he must have slept through it. He stumbled to the front door. A young oriental boy with a tray containing a pot of coffee and warm muffins stood before him. He half expected the boy to speak pidgin English, and slowly said, "Is that for me?" Without a trace of an accent the boy replied, "Yes, it's from my parents. They heard that you had come in last night from Mr. Beskin," he motioned to the apartment across the hall. "Your dad's been great to my family. Years back when my parents first came to Chicago he literally gave them a roof over their heads, knowing they had no jobs and no way of paying rent. Without being patronizing he made them feel safe and welcome."

The boy placed the tray on the dining room table and turned to leave. "Everyone in the neighborhood is pulling for Mr. Garland. We're glad you're here. Your dad's a quiet man, but when he talks about you his eyes seem to light up." Then as he was leaving, almost as an afterthought, he turned, "Hey, when your dad gets better if you're going to stay for a while maybe we can hit some tennis balls together. I'm on the varsity tennis team at Northwestern and there's some courts right across the street in the park."

"Yeah, if my dad's OK I think I will stay a while, and I'd like to hit some tennis balls with you. I'm pretty familiar with those courts."

CHAPTER 58
Epilogue—Three Months Later

The giant silver El Al L10 11 slowly taxied to the airport terminal and the crew started busily preparing passengers for the disembarking. Inside the terminal of Ben-Gurion Airport, a quiet anticipation filled the many friends and relatives waiting for the passengers. Nowhere was the anxiety greater than among a small enclave of people waiting for the bittersweet return, after forty years, of Aaron Garlovsky.

In this small corner of the world where everyone was a soldier, he had fought with the best until he could do no more. Now he was coming back again.

Most of the passengers had come down the ramp when Barak called out, "There's Hannah and Kevin." Barak, Danielle, and the boys started to wave and Hannah seeing them poked Kevin and they waved back. Hannah was pointing to her ring finger and flashing her shining new wedding band. Right behind them, Doc exited carrying a camera and a small El Al duffel bag. Then slowly, almost reluctantly, Aaron came out, blinking in the bright sunlight. He limped down the stairway, politely refusing Kevin's and Doc's offers to carry his old suitcase. As Zalman Zacksman watched his old comrade, he smiled thinking, "He's still the same. I remember him carrying that same old suitcase when we came here a lifetime ago."

Zalman started to walk to the tarmac to greet his friend when a young soldier stood in front of him.

"Sorry, sir, all passengers must go through customs before...." then looking just behind Zalman, he smartly saluted and quickly stood aside. Several members of the Knesset including General Meyer Bishov, the recently retired Chief of Staff of the I.D.F. and his brother, Jacob, the current Minister of Defense, motioned him away as Zalman, never hesitating, proceeded forward. The two men met out on the tarmac about twenty-five yards from the terminal just outside of the hearing of all the others.

"You've put on some weight and aged a little, Zalman. It's good to see you."

"My God, Aaron, I can't believe it. It's only been forty years since I've seen you, and already you have developed a sense of humor."

Two old lions, once so young and strong, were both masking the deep emotions they felt with a thin veneer of humor. Aaron bent to put his suitcase down and embraced his oldest friend. With tears running unashamedly down his face Zalman whispered, "Can you believe it, Aaron, we fooled them all and lived to be old men. C'mon there's an official welcoming party of old warriors, including that putz Desmond Stein who insisted on being here to welcome you. But,

Aaron, the people I want you to meet first are your grandchildren." They turned toward the terminal and both reached for the old suitcase, but Zalman was quicker.

"I've got it, Aaron. Don't worry, I won't let anything happen to it. You can trust me."

"I always have, Zalman, I always will."

The End